THE CORSET GIRLS UNBOUND

ANNIE R MCEWEN

BLOODHOUND
BOOKS

www.bloodhoundbooks.com

Print ISBN: 978-1-917705-20-2

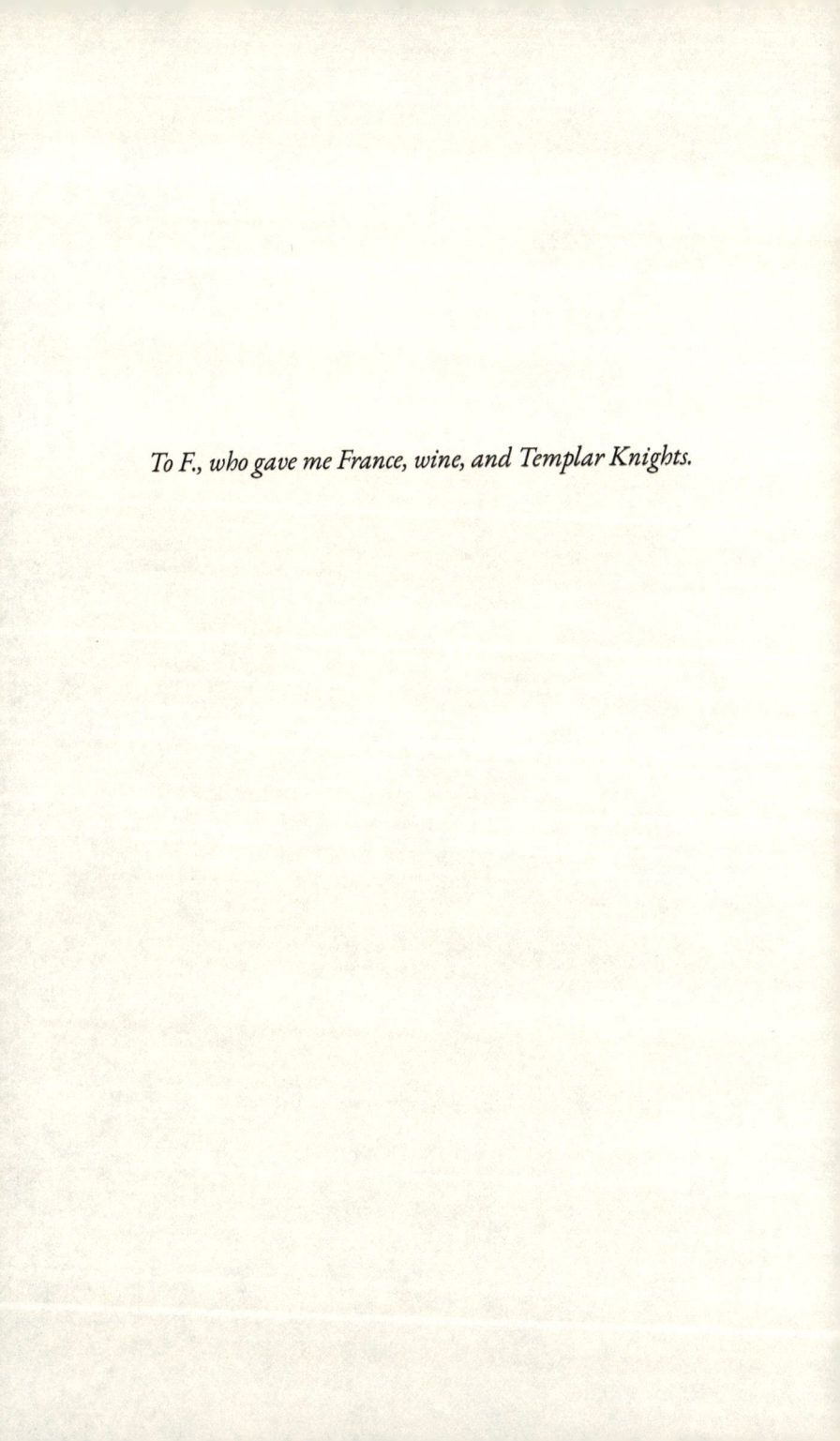

To F., who gave me France, wine, and Templar Knights.

CHAPTER ONE
BORDEAUX, FRANCE, 1894

The darkness was absolute. Blows came at her from all directions. She struggled and screamed. Tried to fight back but couldn't see the source. Only hear fists as they thudded around and into her body. A sharp jab to her shoulder, a glancing blow to her hip. All the while, an animalian roar from above. A huge, heavy form bore down upon her.

I can't get out. Billowing masses of cloth wrapped her head, her limbs. Shrouded and smothered, she thrashed and tore but could not escape. Even her screams were muffled in the folds.

Incontestable force lifted her off her feet, then slammed her down so hard that the impact stopped the bellows of her lungs. Gasping and flailing, she tried to rise, but the engulfing fabric was entangled with her skirts and she couldn't get purchase with either arms or legs. *Trapped. I'm trapped.* And still the snarling weight above pressed and pressed until she couldn't take in any air at all.

Wads of the damnable cloth were jammed between her assailant and her, but they could have been cobwebs for all the protection they afforded. Somehow, she got one of her hands free. The other was trapped in her sleeve, twisted when her bodice ripped open in the struggle.

She frantically clawed at the thing holding her down, raking her nails across what felt like a wrist and forearm. No reaction. She tried to wrench the limb away. Hopeless. The wrist was so thick her fingers could not encircle it. Red stars burst into fragments at the corners of her vision. Pain sawed at her chest. *Can't breathe, can't breathe...*

With a last desperate effort, she bucked upward into the crushing weight. Hot breath seared her face. The scrape of beard. A smell of sweat.

And almonds, painfully sweet amid despair and finality.

'Please... no...' The plea came out as thin as the air she could not draw into her lungs.

Light burst everywhere. The great weight left her all at once. Too late, it was too late. This house in France would be where she died.

The light telescoped into a single point, then blinked out altogether, taking her with it.

The nightmare peeled away like burned skin, one black strip at a time. The Lambeth Lads. Thirsting for blood one night in Seven Dials. Going for him and Kell. Six against two. Chains and clubs against his knives and Kell's fists. He had one of them down, his hand on the bastard's throat, when–

He jolted fully awake. He was on the floor on his hands and knees. A motionless body, swathed like a mummy, lay beneath him. Panic drove fire through his veins. What had he done? He got his fingers into the linen and rent it mercilessly from the body's head and face.

Sainte Marie-mère. His heart lurched into his throat. Never in his life had he so much as shoved a woman. Now, he had tried to kill one. A woman he *knew*. His roar made the walls ring.

'*Minerve, Minerve! Parle-moi!*'

The room's only window was adjacent to the bed. His wild convulsions had wrenched the heavy curtain from its rings. Bare glass admitted moonlight, merciless upon a scene of appalling savagery. Min's head was thrown back, her hair a wilderness of dark silk around a pale face, her eyes shut. A grey skirt was furled around her waist, white tides of petticoats washing up to her knees. Wound around, under, and across her like a shroud were his bed sheets. Her disloyal clothes had helped with the entombment.

Heart-stopping fear grabbed and shook him. '*Réveille-toi, Min. Je t'en pris, réveille-toi.*' He cupped her wan cheek, then slapped it lightly. Again. 'Wake up, Min. I beg you, wake up.'

A faint gurgle came from her bloodless lips – she lived! But her eyes remained closed, and she did not speak. Damn his worthless soul to hell! He might have somehow crushed her vocal cords.

Ah! Her eyelids quivered. Relief and anger surged from his feet to his scalp. Of the things he might have said, he chose the most irrelevant and shouted it into her face. 'What the *hell* are you doing in my bedroom?'

She gave a catlike, stifled yowl and her eyes popped open. Almost immediately, they widened to the size of shillings. The yowl might have been the effect of his stranglehold on her voice. The enlarged eyes from her spectacles, which were crookedly affixed to her face.

Or both might have been because a very large, very angry, very tattooed, and completely naked man was kneeling astride her.

He jumped off her and to his feet as though she were a bed of hot coals. Her eyes skittered up his body, then down, and widened still more. At which point, he realised something.

Despite the fighting and the panic and the shock of recognition, he had an erection like a tree limb.

What does one say?

If you would kindly avert your eyes while I put on my trousers?

Please excuse me while I step away to dash cold water on my privates.

Having wrestled her to the floor, he could not just leave her lying there. But if he helped her to stand, she would be up against his...

He fled the room.

CHAPTER TWO

Well, well. There was no dictionary in which the entry for 'awkward' defined what Minerva had just seen. Life was a banquet of novelty.

The moonlight was enough that she could see to scramble out of the bedding and began putting herself to rights. Her petticoats dropped into place easily enough, but her skirt was twisted entirely around, closure to the front and unhooked, the placket gaping. The buttons of her bodice had also taken leave of their senses. Six were unfastened, displaying the lace edge of her chemise and the ribbon tie at the top of her corset busk. The tie was undone, pink silk tails spiralling coquettishly down the front of her bodice. All very embarrassing, as though her clothing had been ready all along for the man with the–

She would try not to think about that, but when something was imprinted on one's retinas it tended to remain that way for a while, like the image of the flash after a photographer has fired the pan.

Thankfully, her eyeglasses had not broken in the scuffle. She removed them, straightened one earpiece that had gone slightly south, and replaced them. The disorder of her hair was less easily remedied. Hang her hairpins; she was not about to go rooting through the bed to find them. She'd had a hat, too, a small dove grey toque that her workmate and friend Evie had made. It was also apparently tucked in for the night.

'Sweet dreams, hat,' she said archly to the room. The bedcovers were partly on, mostly off the bed, an invariable consequence, she imagined, of boudoir wrestling matches. She straightened the linens and made the bed into some sort of order. Her hat did not make an appearance. If it was half as shocked as she was, it might never show its face again.

She'd had a hair ribbon, also missing. Perhaps it had run away with the hat, like the dish and the spoon in the nursery rhyme. She performed an exercise in futility, wrestling her hair into a single long plait. Without a ribbon to tie it off, her hair invariably worked itself out of a braid in minutes.

Her travelling handbag was on the floor; she retrieved it and stood with it in her hands, unsure of what to do next.

She would concentrate on feeling vexed. It seemed the safest place for her feelings to go. There was a toppled wooden chair next to the bed. She set it upright and sat in it, handbag in her lap. Folding her hands over the bag, she strove for composure. Her face, she felt, was a success. Her heart, less so. It continued to race like a rabbit who'd drunk a pail of strong tea.

He returned, clothed. She remained in the chair. He stood, hands behind him and expression truculent, an impenitent schoolboy called before the headmaster. They would now be forced to engage in convoluted and embarrassing speeches, but she couldn't see any way around it. They couldn't just pretend nothing had happened and start off with, *Lovely weather, don't you agree?*

Or perhaps they could. She couldn't make things any worse by establishing the civility she'd completely snubbed when she breached his bedroom and fell over him as he slept.

'Hello, Étienne.'

'*Minerve.*'

Now that he wasn't bellowing like a bull elephant, Min remembered how much she enjoyed the way he said her name. The way it reached deep, stroked deeper. The low rumble of it. The *French* of it, Meen-*airve*. It made her want to shut her eyes and bask, the way a cat does in the sun.

There would be no basking. Convoluted and embarrassing speeches commencing. Three, two one...

Étienne inquired as to her health. Was she damaged? Had he hurt her in any way? She was well, she told him, if a bit rattled. He was shattered by having fought with her. She insisted it was her fault. He'd been having the *cauchemar*, he said, and she sympathised, sharing her recurring dream in which she went round and round London in a hackney cab that never let her off.

He brought up (again) the inadvisability of entering a man's bedroom. She lied and said, yes, of course, she knew not to enter a man's bedroom at night or at any time. (In actuality, she'd never been warned. No one seemed to believe she was a woman to whom such a thing might happen.)

She mentioned that the door of the house was open. He countered by saying in the remote French countryside, doors were often left unlocked, the danger of housebreaking being somewhat less than the chances of volcanic eruption.

There was an absence of lights in the house, which she pointed out. He gave the point several swift kicks. It was the middle of the night, he lived alone, and he could find his way around his own house in the dark. Why leave a lamp burning?

Even though she knew she was pressing her luck, she claimed she was unaware she'd even entered a bedroom. Houses, she pointed out, did not usually have bedrooms on the ground floor. She'd *assumed* she'd gone into a sitting room.

Giving her the benefit of the doubt, he said he understood why she might make such a mistake. He then informed her (a bit patronisingly, she thought) that French farmhouses did not, as a rule, have parlours.

She sidled oh-so courteously up to the heart – or some body part – of the matter. 'While I am sorry for intruding, the truth is that I would not have expected to find you...' She hunted for the word and hoped she'd get it right. Her French was unreliable. '*Deshabillé*.' Needlessly, since he was French, she translated. 'Undressed. I was under the impression that gentlemen wore...' Another word she had to hunt for; she didn't think she'd ever said it aloud in any language. 'Nightshirts.'

He didn't quite smile, but a corner of his mouth lifted fractionally. 'You would know this, how, Minerva?'

He had her there.

She rushed on to assure him she would never have entered his house at all, except it was so very late and she was tired. She'd had the idea she could walk from the train stop in the village, but wasn't entirely sure how far it was since the train had pulled in so late. There wasn't really anyone to ask except one very old person. The old person was asleep on a bench and she didn't like to wake him. Did Étienne know the stop wasn't a station, really? Just a sort of shed – well, he probably knew that.

But, with the walking and the night and being alone and not entirely sure where she was, she was unnerved. So, when she discovered that (she was repeating herself but thought it was a strong point in her favour), the front door was unlocked...

'I let myself in.'

'*Boucle d'or et les trois ours.*'

'I beg your pardon?'

'Goldilocks and the Three Bears. Not important.'

He apologised again for the buffeting. Very nicely, she thought, for a man who'd tried to press her to death.

Walking ahead, he brought her to the kitchen – she thought she'd passed through it on her way to the bedroom, so it was by way of a return trip – and put her in a chair at a broad wood table.

Then, he went around lighting lamps until the room took on a golden glow. She exercised rare prudence and kept her mouth shut, watching.

Five lamps, four minutes. After two years apart, that's all it took to drop her right back in the same stunned emotional state as the last time she'd seen him. His height. The broad span of his shoulders. The leonine grace in his movements.

In a Mayfair shop or a French farmhouse, he made her newt-stupid with desire.

She knew he would ask The Question sooner or later. Once he stirred the embers of the fire in the kitchen hearth to life, he did.

'What are you doing here?'

'Here, in France?'

'In France, in the Entre-deux-Mers. In my house.'

Yes, indeed, that's where she was. And what a long journey to get here. When he wasn't so irritated with her, he'd appreciate that. North Devon to Plymouth by rail, with multiple changes. A ferry from Plymouth to Dover. Then, across the Channel to Calais, which she'd studied and determined was the best place to board a train running more or less directly to Bordeaux. At last, travelling right down the length of France to the river-striped southwest. She had everything to lose by turning and running away. Everything to gain by saying what she'd come to say.

'I'm here to ask for a service. Please be assured, I would never presume to ask without offering compensation. I have funds. If they are not enough, I am prepared to offer you...'

She'd rehearsed the speech a hundred times, but that didn't stop ferocious heat from rising from her chest to her face. An unnecessary display of maidenly shyness, considering what had happened in the bedroom.

She put her hand to her mouth and discreetly cleared her throat. 'I am prepared, if the money is not enough, to offer you my body.'

It gave her no little pride to see that she was in what was surely a very small number of people who had shocked Étienne 'Le Dague' Sansecours – lawbreaker, bladesman, former member of London's most notorious gang. His jaw didn't quite drop, but his brooding dark eyebrows drew together and the whisky-coloured eyes beneath them seemed to wobble for a split second.

He spoke with the caution of someone stepping over broken glass. '*Eh, bien*. And this service you ask of me? What is it?'

'Oh, silly me! Of course, yes, you'll need to know that. I'd like you to kill a man. Please.'

———

'I have been begged for death, but never with such *politesse*.'

He looked away as he spoke, and began doing something with an iron kettle hanging in the hearth. She wasn't sure he'd given her a compliment. Whether he had or hadn't, she couldn't think of a rejoinder, so she took a few minutes to look around the kitchen. It was everything she always conjectured a French country kitchen would be, large and warm and rustic. A whole spitted pig would fit in the hearth with room left over for a few chickens. Enough copper pans hung above the mantel to plate a battleship. Garlic bulbs and onions dangled in braided ropes from the blackened timbers of the ceiling. It smelled comfortably of woodsmoke, herbs, and country air.

She finally thought of something to say. Scrubbing at a stain on the table with her thumbnail, she observed, 'My grandmother believed that politeness, when extended, would always be returned.'

'I dislike to contradict *la bonne grandmère*, but in this case, she is wrong. No matter how polite you are, Minerva, I will not kill a man for you.'

'But I–'

'How did you find me?'

'Find you... here?'

'No, on the top floor of the Louvre.'

'No need to be sarcastic.' She scrubbed the stain more vigorously. 'Eileen Kelly let it drop some time ago, and I wrote it down. She'd overheard it from her sister Ada. Ada and Eileen are–'

'I know who Ada and Eileen Kelly are.'

He knew because they were Michael Kelly's sisters. And Michael – Kell – had been in a gang called the Jacks, with Étienne. The head of the gang had been Ewan Exeter, now the most improbable detective inspector at Scotland Yard.

For the moment, Étienne didn't say any more. He just stood in front of the hearth, taking up a great deal of space, and looked at her. Assessing much, revealing nothing: something his eyes did extraordinarily well.

It was ridiculous to imagine a man his size as something so small as a falcon or a goshawk. But in the lamplight, his brown eyes were rayed with gold and sharp, sharp as any predatory bird's. If she were less desperate, she might cower under those eyes, but she couldn't afford weakness. Correction. She couldn't *show* weakness. His scrutiny turned her spine into wilted celery.

She lifted her chin, using up the inch of courage that remained from getting to the kitchen from England. 'I can explain.'

'You will. Just now, you are *trop fatigué*.' He turned his back and returned to faffing about the hearth.

She was fatigued, yes. Not so much she could be diverted from her mission by a chair and a kettle. 'About my offer. Perhaps I was wrong to assume the addition of my, er, *person* to the compensation is attractive, but...'

Doubt siphoned away the rest of her argument. It was laughable to think a man like him would feel desire for a bespectacled corsetmaker from Devonshire via London. At the same time, instinct urged her to think he might. She wasn't quite the wide-eyed ninny the other *corsetières* in Salon Sirena's workroom thought she was. It was true that before she'd gone to London, her life in Little Farnleigh had been sheltered. But on her grandparents' smallholding, she'd seen the way animals behaved in the field and barnyard. The stages of attraction males and females exhibited. Ignoring each other, noticing, touching, until the male got on top and...

'I was reared on a farm.' *Oh, Min.* She'd blurted it completely out of context. She might be a ninny, after all.

Étienne stopped what he was doing and regarded her solemnly. 'Ah, I solve the dark mystery of your request.' He brought a teapot, brown with a chipped lid, to the table and lowered it to a faience tile. 'You seek a farmer and that, I am.'

What she sought was a man named The Dagger, not an ironic Sherlock Holmes with a teapot. There was a long interval, empty of speech. A nightingale filled it with arpeggios from beyond the open windows.

She finally ventured a question in a voice as high and small as the bird's. 'What do you grow?'

'Grapes.' He walked to a neatly organised dresser against one wall and removed cups and saucers from a rack. One pair went to her place at the table, one opposite. 'I am a *vigneron.* If you wish to split hairs, I am a *proprietaire viticulteur,* one who owns the land, grows the grapes, and makes the wine. Although, if you ask Remy Bertaud, my foreman, he will tell you I am the brawn and he is the brains. Les Pinsons is a vineyard.'

Étienne Sansecours owned a vineyard. Clearly, crime paid better than corset making. She haltingly assembled a sentence. '*Les pinsons sont... des petits oiseaux avec... avec de belles voix.*'

'Chaffinches are small birds with pretty voices. Now that we have established we both speak French, we will be attentive to tea.'

Yes, she wanted tea. Not enough, perhaps, to justify the thirsty flicking back and forth of her eyes, teapot to man. The pot was ordinary, but the man had figured in her dreams so often he seemed half mythical, like King Arthur or Ulysses. Now the real man was walking, standing, and speaking a yard away.

Before tonight, she'd met him just twice. He was the largest man she'd ever seen up close, but the details of his body had been hidden under a suit. Here, in his kitchen, there was no concealing wool cloth, no stylishly tailored coat, high collar, polished shoes. Just loose trousers, a haphazardly tucked linen shirt, and slippered feet that made no noise as he moved across the stone floor. Under his worn, much-laundered clothing, muscles rippled as under the skin of a lion.

He brought a plate of runny cheese and a loaf of bread to the table. A knife stuck upright from the centre of the loaf, reminding her, for an uneasy second, that she was breaking bread with an assassin.

He plucked the knife from the bread and began slicing it. She hadn't noticed before, but on the smallest finger of his left hand, he was wearing a gold ring, a signet ring. It appeared to have some sort of engraving but, with her eyes, she'd need it at the end of her nose to discern what it was. He hadn't been wearing it two years ago, she was sure. She didn't think farmers wore that sort of thing. The ones around Little Farnleigh certainly didn't. But on Étienne, it seemed right. Carelessly elegant.

The scent of the fresh-cut bread gave a tacit order to her stomach, and it made a noise. Min blushed again to the roots of her hair.

'You are fatigued and hungry.' He said it *'ungry*, which would have charmed her if she hadn't been so keyed up. 'English tea,' he lightly tapped the lid of the teapot with the knife, 'which you will prefer to coffee at this time of night. Let us eat. After, you may tell me more of your very wrong grandmother.'

He took the chair across from her. His broad hands, surprisingly artful in both shape and motion, slathered cheese on a slice of bread and handed it to her.

Hands weren't the only artful aspects of Étienne Sansecours. His nose was like a ship's prow, large and proud. Some people might say a face with a nose like his couldn't be called handsome, but she liked it. It suited him. It was straight, except for a slight lean to the left. Something Ada would call a lucky punt had gotten through the Great Wall of Muscle at some point and broken it.

From what she'd just seen in the bedroom, another part of him was large and proud and straight. It didn't appear to lean to the–

'*Le thé?*'

Startled out of a thought that was headed somewhere shockingly inappropriate, she directed her eyes to her cup and nodded. He poured for them both. There was no sugar or milk on the table. For some reason, that comforted her. He took his tea the way she did, black as the things that had brought her to his door. Black as the future, if he didn't help her.

They ate silently.

CHAPTER THREE

After eating with the guileless greed of a baby goat and drinking three cups of tea, she fell asleep without word or warning. One second, she put her teacup precisely back in its saucer. The next, her head drooped, a spent flower on a stalk. He was out of his chair as she tilted to one side and caught her before she slid off the seat.

He knew that sleep. It came when long periods – days, perhaps weeks – of punishing tension were released, followed by death-like torpor.

He gathered her carefully in his arms. Notwithstanding recent events in his bedroom, she was nearly a stranger. It might be wrong to hold her so intimately, but it felt in every way natural and right. Her head, with its silky mass of chestnut hair, all unpinned and half unplaited, was heavy against his chest. Her body was small and perfectly formed. She filled his arms but weighed no more than a sack of the grain he gave the chickens who scratched in the yard.

Carrying her, his fingers said pleasant hellos to every curve and line of her body: the roundness of her arse, the tautness of her waist. His forearm supported the small of her back and he felt steel splints through her dress. She wore a corset, very likely one she had made with her clever, small hands. But if ever there was a woman who did not need stays, it was Minerva Hawkins. From the first time he saw her, he had instinctively known his hands could encircle her slender waist as he would a bunch of lily stems.

Because there was nowhere else, and because he wanted to, he carried her back to his bedroom. He walked carefully, to not wake her, though that seemed unlikely. She was so deeply unconscious she had not even murmured when he lifted her. She sighed once, now, as he lowered her onto his bed, and her eyelids fluttered but did not open.

He sat in the chair beside the bed and took his time, not jostling her, removing her boots. They were scuffed, the soles almost worn through and caked with the red clay of the road. She had been walking too much. Where? For what?

Here. For me.

That could not be, and so he stamped on the thought as one might a glowing ember flown from a fire. She had cajoled, annoyed, or otherwise prised his direction out of Eileen Kelly. Why, then, had she not posted a letter? Rather than do that most logical thing, she had travelled, unwisely and alone, across land and sea. Carrying no equipage beyond one preposterously large handbag, left on the kitchen table. An exhausting journey, to deliver a request as preposterous as the handbag. It was a gesture wholly and dramatically French, despite her being so very English.

And she had not once said she was frightened. 'Tired,' she had said. 'Unnerved. Alone.' Never *afraid*, though he sensed it in every part of her. She could have given up, given in, become a shivering jelly of surrender. She had not. 'Unnerved' was the most extravagant word she used for some bone-deep fear that had gotten its teeth into her and gnawed away for weeks, perhaps months.

Having got her boots off, he applied himself to her spectacles, delicately unhooking the earpieces to remove them. They were fragile things. Glass lenses with a gold bridge, gold staples at the top corners to hold the earpieces, also gold. Barely visible when she wore them, they did not stand in the way of appreciating her eyes, green-brown and large. Hazel, the English said. In French, *noisette*.

The eyeglass case would be in her handbag. He could put the spectacles in the case and, while he was at it, go through the bag's contents. Years ago, he would have done such a thing without hesitation. Now, the notion was – distasteful. Some extremity had driven her in this strange manner to his door. It was hers to explain.

Not that any extremity and any explanation would alter what he had told her. He inwardly cringed to admit no impression Minerva Hawkins had of him could match the truth for horror, but he would never practise the black arts of death again. Not for her, not for anyone.

He folded the eyeglasses and placed them on the bedside table, atop his copy of Verne's *Le Château des Carpathes*. He had purchased the book more than a year ago, but never seemed to get more than a few pages in before he fell asleep. Gothic fantasy was no competition for a day of hard farm labour.

He should return to the kitchen. There, he would display great wisdom by doing the washing up.

Or he could embrace folly.

He sat back in the chair to watch the slow rise and fall of the bodice of Min's tidy grey travelling dress. As inadvisable as the watching was, he compounded it by indulging himself in a fantasy. He had not had one of any sort since he had last seen her, two years ago in London. Then, he had taken himself in hand so often he had felt shame, like a boy unable to master the first stirrings of lust in his groin. Now, the soft sound of her breathing was a fakir's flute, and the snake of desire rose in his body again.

He could shed his clothes and ease into the bed beside her. Light kisses at first, on her smooth forehead, her pink, slack mouth. She would wake at the touch and smile, with a murmur. His name, or just inarticulate sounds of longing. By then, he would be rampant as a stallion. He would take her hand, put it to his cock, haul up her skirts...

Cursing softly, he shifted the swelling mass in his trousers. To even have thoughts like those was proof he was a sinner beyond redemption. Who was he to foul a sleeping woman with his erotic imaginings? Before the insanity of an hour ago, he had barely touched her.

Twice. He remembered each with perfect vividness. The first was in the alley at the back of Salon Sirena, the Mayfair shop where she was employed. He had stood behind her, his hands on her dainty shoulders, and breathed in the chamomile scent of her hair as he taught her how to juggle sugared almonds from a bag he had brought.

His second touch had been the fraught morning he, Ewan Exeter, and Michael Kelly charged into the shop after Jillian Morehouse – now Jillian Kelly – was abducted. He had asked Min a question about events preceding the crime and held her hand to calm and encourage her. It was how he knew the weight and softness of that hand in his.

Two touches, followed by an absence of two years. Tonight, some cloth-wrapped wrestling half on the bed, half off. Now this, the touching necessary to carry her to bed and remove her shoes and spectacles. Not enough to warrant the waking of the carnal beast in him. There was something else at work in him, something restless and waiting. Hungering.

He had known from the start it was not only lust he felt around Minerva Hawkins. It was a drive to hold, to keep. Tonight, having her an arm's-length away, the force of the returning drive discomposed him to the point that his hands shook. He, *Le Dague*, the killing arm of the Jacks, quaking like a frightened hare.

It is a formidably excellent idea to leave the side of the bed. He padded to the window and looked beyond the front drive, at his vines. They were there, always there, whether sunlight blazed upon them or they hid Les Pinsons' horrors – which the vines surely remembered, for they were very old and forgot nothing – in the night. No one knew quite so well as the vines that Les Pinsons was the mother of horrors, the womb from which his every nightmare had been born.

He glanced at Min again. Even in the dark, he could see she had not stirred. She might sleep for ten or twelve hours. He had done so after long, wakeful periods of trouble. She would be more comfortable if her corset were loosened, but he dared not lay hands on her even one more time tonight.

He passed silently into the hall, then to the front door, opening it with stealth that suggested he was breaking in, not out.

His *sabots* were on the floor, just inside the threshold. Kicking off his slippers, he picked up the wooden clogs and leaned against the door frame. In a minute or two, duty would grow strong enough to push him out of the house and into the vines. Away from the houseguest whose arrival had startled him no less than if the queen of England had driven up to his door in a royal coach.

After a few slow, deep breaths, he stepped outside and sniffed the air.

Somewhere a bird sang a few notes and then recalled it was asleep and fell silent. The sky was watered ink, more light than dark. Two or three hours, still, until dawn. A good time to walk among the vines, hearing them whisper as the breeze gave them mouths. *Sémillon*, promising sweetness. *Sauvignon blanc*, the wild white. *Trebbiano*, itself undistinguished, but he had a trick for turning it into memorable brandy.

He would listen only to the grapes in their reassuringly regular rows, stopping his ears to that other voice. The one that could so effortlessly carry him, and her, to calamity.

If the money is not enough, I am prepared to offer you my body.

Clogs still in his hand, he shut the door noiselessly behind him and walked away.

Chapter Four

'At least read the letter and the note.'

Was Étienne even listening? Pottering away at the hearth, he didn't answer Min's question or so much as peep at the folded papers she'd put on the kitchen table. She couldn't guess the time and she'd forgotten to wind her watch. Mid-afternoon, probably, since a brazen sun poured warmth and light into the room.

Étienne appeared, if possible, larger and more muscular than he had last night. Would she ever get used to seeing him without the camouflage of a suit? He was in the same loose linen shirt as the day before, sleeves pushed up. The same trousers and slippered feet. At least he'd neatly tucked his shirt and pulled braces over his shoulders. Concessions to a guest in the house.

Yesterday, though, the shirt had been closed to the neck. Today, both top and second buttons were loosened, and a triangle of tawny flesh, flecked with brown curls, showed in the gap. The chest hair was nowise as shocking as his uncovered forearms, tattooed from wrists up to where the skin disappeared under his turned sleeves. The mannerly presentation of shirt and braces was shot to smithereens by the coiling, coloured serpents on each muscular forearm.

Sheer, hypnotic, barbaric, masculinity. She tried but couldn't drag her eyes from the view.

Don't be a child, Min. You saw a lot more than his forearms last night. And she'd seen tattoos, before, on Kell. He and Jillian, her former workmate, operated the East London Pugilists Academy in Poplar. When Min, Evie, Ada, and Eileen visited for Jillian's classes in women's self-defence, they often saw Kell at work, teaching men how to box. Once, she and Evie had been stopped in their tracks by the sight of him stripped to the waist in the ground-floor ring, sparring with a member.

Later, Evie had whispered that Eileen, Kell's youngest sister, said her brother was inked *all over*, and that it was a custom of the Jacks. She'd be lying through her teeth if she said Evie's disclosure hadn't led her to feverishly envision what Étienne's illustrated body looked like.

I certainly know now. Remembering, her mouth turned into a dry well.

At the same time, she was uncomfortably aware of her own looks. By comparison to the man in the kitchen with her, she was a bedraggled, colourless waif. She doubted she looked any better than when she'd retired the night before, an action she frankly didn't remember. She must have done it. She woke in full daylight, in bed. His bed, Étienne's.

She'd found the washstand and poured water from the pitcher into the bowl. Her longing for a bath was unsated by splashing her face. A neat array of shaving tools lay on a cloth next to the bowl. A clean linen towel, china mug and boar-bristle brush, folding razor with ivory handle. All his.

She'd sniffed at the concave lump in the bottom of the mug. Windsor soap, smelling of almonds. It was the scent that had wafted to her just before she'd blacked out the night before.

Where had he slept? His bedroom was on the ground floor, but the house was broad and had an upper storey. Surely, there were ample beds, and he'd found one. Best not to speculate too much on that.

From the hearth, he glanced over his shoulder and spoke without replying to her comment about the letter and note. 'You look like you slept in your clothes.'

'You know I did. You spied on me.'

Touché. Her wild surmise was worth it for his priceless expression when he whirled toward her. She'd stunned him, the second time in twenty-four hours, and his glower suggested he didn't like it. The beard on his clenched, unshaven jaw contributed to the glower. Something else she should apologise for. How could he shave when his tools were in the bedroom he'd given to her?

He tucked his glower away, returned to whatever he was doing – she hoped it was making tea – and addressed his hands.

'*Le café avant tout*,' he said, and brought a tray to the table. The aroma from the spout of the stacked, two-compartment china pot swept Min off her feet and into the same chair she'd occupied the day before. French coffee, strong enough, she knew from her limited exposure to it, to wake the dead.

Too grateful to disturb the ritual with words, she watched him half fill a bowl with steaming dark liquid and top it with milk from a long-handled copper warmer. He slid the bowl over to her. She put the folded papers she'd brought to the table to one side and wrapped her hands around the bowl, sighing. He stood, drinking from his own bowl, neither sighing nor talking.

A few restorative swallows later, she began anew. Holding her coffee in one hand, she used the other to push the papers forward a few inches. 'Read them, Étienne. A man is threatening me.'

That got his attention. His bowl stopped midway to his lips and he narrowed his eyes. For a few seconds, Min was elated. She'd like to see those knife-sharp eyes directed toward her enemy.

'Threatening you, in what way?'

The five words came forth in a chesty snarl, a sound she

imagined a mastiff would make before it attacked. That was elating, too. And exactly what she'd come for.

'I am being *blackmailed*.'

Extortion clearly didn't carry as potent a charge for him as for her. His steely gaze and guard dog growl subsided, and his bowl continued its progress toward his lips. 'Blackmail is a matter for the police,' he said calmly, after a swallow. 'Go to them. Go home, Minerva.'

Well, that wouldn't do, wouldn't do at all. At the very least, he could've asked her what she'd done to get the attention of a blackmailer. For all he knew, she'd plotted against Whitehall. Stolen state secrets. Sold them to the Boers or the Fenians or the Cossack Brigade.

'Can you please not loom over me, Étienne? There are two chairs.'

He sat, somehow bringing the looming with him. And a wary readiness to react, as though she might jump into the air like a mongoose and fly at his throat. *Oh, for heaven's sake.*

She'd go at the problem sideways. 'I know you may have difficulties if you return to England.'

His laugh was short and caustic. 'It would indeed be difficult for me to miss the *vendange*, the harvest. To miss the next forty *vendanges*, as that is the term of imprisonment I risk, if I am lucky enough to evade the noose, upon my return to England.'

Her brain scrabbled for grounds on which she could dispute the danger she was asking him to walk into. Were there any? No. She might as well agree and try to find a way round it.

'You face an arrest warrant.'

'Warrants. The sons and daughters of warrants, their grandchildren.'

'Can't Detective Inspector Exeter–'

His hand came up, stopping her. 'Ewan Exeter has bent, and continues to bend, the law into knots as complicated as the lace of Breton. But one must never forget that self-interest inspires him to such dexterity. Watching his old criminal *confrère* hang might provoke a twinge of dismay in his stony heart, but afterward, he would smoke a cigar and forget about it and me.'

Settling his bowl on the table, he slowly and deliberately pushed the papers in her direction. Then, he crossed his arms and watched her, impassively.

The tattooed serpents were now lying one atop the other. A stray thought reminded her that snakes mated that way. She'd ask Ada to confirm it in her *Wilmott's Encyclopedia and Unabridged Dictionary*.

She tapped the papers with two fingers. 'These are the originals.' She slid them back in his direction. 'I made copies.'

Not the slightest tincture of curiosity coloured his voice. 'You are wise to make copies. The police will wish to retain the originals.'

'I also have this.' She put down her own bowl and used both hands to work a thin black ribbon necklace from under her collar and lift it over her head and off. A round silver pendant hung from the ribbon. Étienne watched her with an intensity that belied his disinterest. When she pulled at it from each side, the pendant opened into two parts, revealing its secret. What appeared to be a single disc was a pair of interlocking halves, each with its own loop at the top for the ribbon to pass through. Each half glittered with a gemstone. She lay the pendant on the table, midway between him and her.

'It's the sun and moon.' He gave them the barest glance, returning to her face. 'The sun, with the topaz, came with the letter. The moon,' she tapped the half-circle bearing a single diamond, 'was on a string around my neck twenty-four years ago. That's when I was left as an infant with people I came to know, wrongly, as it turns out, as my grandparents.'

Again, she pushed the papers toward him. 'Please, Étienne.'

At first, he didn't move, didn't even twitch. Then he took a dark, flat case from a basket of apples on the table and opened it.

The case nearly disappeared in his big hands. And it was familiar. When they weren't on her face, her spectacles rested in a case just like it. The eagle-eyed, knife-throwing marksman of the Jacks wore *glasses*?

'Only for the reading,' he grumbled as he hooked them over his ears. With a sigh Parisians probably heard, he unfolded the papers and began to read them.

While he read, Min drank *café au lait* and let her gaze sneak around the room. If she got a good look at it, the room might give her bits of knowledge about the man sitting across from her, as a cat brings mice to its master.

A few minutes later, she decided to sack the cat. The kitchen was pleasant; the house, what she'd seen of it, equally so. It certainly wasn't a lair. Not the place she would have guessed a former gang member lived. Not like the place where Kell had lived before he met Jillian. That was a shabby room at the back of a brothel.

But there were no mice of memory in this pleasant kitchen in this pleasant house. Nothing said, *This is me, my life. My mementos, my family. My past.* Where were the framed portraits on the wall? Maman in her crocheted collar and lace cap, Papa with a long beard? Tante Louise and Oncle René, their four children arranged in front of them like nested dolls, baby Marie-Rose to Felix-almost-thirteen?

She played her fingers across the scarred, honey-hued wood of the table. It was as bare as the walls. No cutwork cloth lay upon it. No cleverly embroidered napkins, a red-thread 'S' in a corner of each. The cups and saucers in which they'd had yesterday's tea and the bowls for today's coffee were common stuff. One bought them everywhere, at *Le Bon Marché* in Paris and stalls on Portobello Road. Where were the heirloom plates and wine goblets? The Deuxième Empire demitasse cups? The Sèvres vase from great-grandmother's wedding goods? The glass-front cabinet to guard and display them?

What had happened to make Étienne erase his family past so thoroughly?

She knew something about erasure. Her grandparents' cottage in Little Farnleigh was comfortable enough. But it had a purposeful anonymity. The windows were few and small. Grandmother had always kept them heavily curtained, since she had a deep fear of drafts. Grandfather forbade any art other than a few framed homilies. No summer views of the Cotswolds, no sailing ships a-toss on the waves. The furniture was dark and undistinguished. Even the front door, painted the sad colour of a rain cloud, seemed to cringe into the stone walls, lest it commit the sin of being noticed.

'If you must be proud,' Grandmother told her more than once, 'pride yourself on your modesty.' Grandfather frequently droned, 'God resisteth the proud, and giveth grace to the humble.' First Peter, chapter five, verse five. A reminder to dim whatever unruly light struggled to gleam from her person.

'*Eh, bien.*' Étienne laid the papers in front of him, half sheet below, letter on top. Removing his unexpected eyeglasses, he replaced them in their case, the case to the fruit basket.

'First, the letter. Let me repeat to you what I read, and you will tell me if I have understood it. It originated three weeks ago, at a place called Raeburn House.'

'In Devonshire, yes. I received it two weeks ago.'

'In London.'

'No. It had been posted to my grandparents' cottage in Little Farnleigh. That's also in Devonshire.'

'How is it the sender knew your direction?'

She shook her head. She still hadn't found anything to tie off her braid and loose strands of hair tickled her cheeks. 'No idea at all. I was only there because I had to resolve the estate. My grandfather died very recently.'

'*Mes plus sincères condoléances–*'

She waved the sentiment aside. 'Raeburn House is near a village called Meeth.'

'It is a madhouse.'

She hated that word. 'It's an asylum. A shelter for those suffering... mental derangement.'

'*Bon*. An asylum. The person who writes is the superintendent, a doctor.'

'So he says. He's an alienist. That's a–'

'I know the meaning of the word. A physician of the mind.' He splayed his hand on the letter, nearly covering it. 'He signs himself Charles Augustus Raeburn, Superintendent, along with a great many initials.'

'The initials are his supposed degree. I looked out Raeburn House and the superintendent in The Lunacy Commission's records. They do exist, but it wouldn't surprise me if his name is a criminal alias. You know, like Sharp Stubbins or Bag Man Bart.' Too late, she remembered the man across from her had a criminal alias.

'The superintendent names a firm of solicitors in Glasgow. Have you received any communication from them?'

'Yes. Their letter arrived in Little Farnleigh by the same post as the other. But–'

'Raeburn's letter also mentions two persons. Mary and–'

'Asa. Mary and Asa Hawkins were the ones who took me in as a foundling. I was a newborn. Grandmother – Mary Hawkins – said the blood was still fresh on my...' She waved vaguely toward her abdomen, confused by why it was embarrassing to say 'umbilicus' to the man across the table. She'd seen a lot more than his navel.

He said it for her. '*Le cordon ombilical.*'

'Gran said it was tied with a bit of thread. Blue,' she added irrelevantly.

'The woman in the asylum, the one named in the letter. What do you know of her?'

'The Commission keeps a register of inmates. Her name is on it.'

'*Eh, bien*. Is there any reason to believe she is, as Raeburn claims, your mother?'

It took her a half minute to compose herself in order not to shout it. 'A birth to that inmate is also in the register. 'Stillborn female'; that's the entry. But the date, Étienne, the *date*! February first, 1870. It's my birthdate!'

Blast. She'd let herself get upset, even though she'd told herself to stay calm. She plucked off her eyeglasses. Removing them might blur the dozen objections she could otherwise see behind his tawny eyes. She'd raised those objections herself, all the way to France. And she was acutely aware that her story, recited aloud, sounded like lines in a play. But it wasn't theatre. It was her *life*. She just wasn't sure how to make him believe it.

Trying to fend off a headache, she pinched her nose, then replaced her glasses. 'Don't you see? You have to *see*, Étienne!'

'*Minerve*.' Briefly, the steel left Étienne's eyes and was replaced by something softer. 'When one enters a fight, one first relaxes all the muscles of the body and empties the mind, focusing only on one's objective. Energy misdirected is energy wasted. You comprehend?'

She shifted uneasily. 'I suppose so. You're the assassin.'

'I am not an assassin. I have never killed for hire.'

'But you have killed. You killed those men who kidnapped Jillian.'

His eyes closed and something like a spasm crossed his face. She was affected but couldn't take back what she'd said. She wasn't sure she should try. The abduction and attempted murder of Jillian Morehouse was two years since, her rescue carried out by Kell, Étienne, and Ewan Exeter. Done in darkest night, in the catacombs beneath Old London Bridge, it yielded Jillian's release and seven dead criminals. No one made any attempt to deny that at least some of them were the work of the man who'd just given her coffee.

And which work had also sent him back to France, back into exile.

He opened his eyes. The cold steel was back. 'Did Jillian Kelly tell you that?'

Min shook her head.

'Ada Kelly?'

'No. Well, not entirely. Evie and I worked it out.' She fidgeted in her seat, uncomfortable with the conversation and her clothes. She'd never worn the same clothing for three days straight and she itched all over. 'Did you give up killing because the Jacks aren't a gang anymore?'

'What do you know of the Jacks, Min?'

'I know what Ada told me. And Jillian, too, once Ada's mother told her everything and she let Kell know she knew. It's too late to pretend the Jacks didn't exist, if that's what you're thinking of doing. *La chatton est au dessous du seau.*'

'You have just told me the kitten is on top of the bucket.'

She flicked her hand dismissively. 'You know what I mean. The cat's out of the bag.'

What he did next was what all men did when cornered by a clever female: changed the subject. 'How is the corset shop faring?'

Oh, for the love of... She huffed out the answer in a rapid-fire volley. 'It was trying, at first, without Jillian, but her time is taken up by the boxing academy and the offspring, Andy. He's two years old, now, I think. Toddling and babbling and all that. Ada and Evie are where they've always been and there's Eileen, now, who's learning the ropes. Madame's the same as always. I guess owning the shop doesn't give her much time for character development.

'Why are we not discussing my blackmail letters, Étienne?'

He folded them as they had been, the letter inside, the half sheet of paper – which he'd not even mentioned – wrapped around it. Then, he flanked them with both hands, palms down, as though daring them to try an escape. He pushed to his feet. Because she was seated and he liked to loom, she had to tilt her head back and look up and up to detect a motive in his face for the sudden change of elevation. His words supplied what his face didn't.

'While you were sleeping, I made a soup with potatoes and parsnips in cream. We will have one of my own wines with it, a dry white from Sauvignon Blanc and Sémillon grapes. Together, they will restore your equanimity.'

'There's nothing wrong with my– equan.' Was that the Latin for balance? It might mean horse. She was terrible with languages. Fussily, she scooped up her pendant, fitted the halves together, and worked the ribbon over her head. She didn't hear a thing from him while she was doing all that, but when she looked up again, he was gone.

Oh, figs to him and his sneaky cat feet.

CHAPTER FIVE

She had once again fallen asleep after the meal, as he knew she would, but he had not needed to rescue her before she tumbled out of her chair. Soup and a full glass of the reserve *blanc sec* had easily persuaded her to a nap. He watched her walk, a trifle unsteadily, in the direction of his bedroom. It was a warm evening, and she was what the English called tiddly. She began to unbutton the front of her dress before she even left the kitchen.

The talk between them before he had diverted it to soup probably had done nothing to ease her frustration. Nonetheless, it was she who had brought the impossible to his table. Had come to him with a belief that she could order up the death of a man like a dish in a restaurant.

She had listened not at all to his objections; determined people never did. Instead, she had examined his tattoos, her hazel eyes even bigger than usual behind her eyeglasses, and her pink mouth slightly ajar, like a scallop on the beach. Apparently, her eyes had no trouble doing one thing while her mouth did another, because she kept proposing and he kept refusing.

His refusals did not reflect disinterest in her problem, only the need to separate her from the *idée fixe* that murder was the solution. And, as well, his very strong desire to detach her from whatever solving would be done. To accomplish either required him pushing her away from Les Pinsons with dispatch. The longer she stayed, the more chance there was he would become ensorcelled by her presence, a spell that could only produce pain for them both.

He did not like to think of her so troubled that she had not slept, truly slept, in days, perhaps weeks. He liked still less to think of her travelling alone, unprotected, too dazed with fatigue to see trouble heading her way until it was upon her. It would require much thinking to determine if he could do anything about her trouble, but at least he could give her this second night of rest and safety.

Tu mens, débauché. Lying to himself, perhaps. He did not think he was a lecher. And yet, he had given her wine so she would remain under his roof another night. So he could have her in his sight a little longer.

He strained his ears for the sound of her snoring. She did snore, a faint, whiffling noise he had heard when he watched her sleep. The interior walls of the house were too thick to hear it from the kitchen. He counselled himself, wisely. *Stay away, stay away.* But, as the night before had proved, he was a fool. He rose from the kitchen table and went to his bedchamber. If she had closed and latched the door, he would turn away.

She had not, so he could not. The door was half open; he opened it further and stepped in.

Sitting in the bedside chair again was his plan, but it was thwarted by a disorderly pile of Min's clothes on the seat. The woman who'd discarded them was on her back in the bed. Eyes closed, arms flung overhead, mouth slack, deeply asleep. Bedcovers pushed down to her waist.

Naked above.

He collapsed against the door frame for a minute, while his heart sprang like a racehorse from the starting post and galloped in his chest. He went so hard, so fast, he nearly fainted from the blood leaving his head.

Breasts – he had seen quite a few. He did not consider himself a man who had a 'type'. Nor did he expect women to compare with art. Flesh was always preferable to painted canvas or cold stone. Even so, having seen Manet's *Olympia* in the Musée d'Orsay, he considered the model's breasts lovely. High, full but not too large, pert nipples the precise shade of the pink orchid in her hair.

Min's breasts shot past *Olympia*'s to a standard for which he had no words. *Perfection* was the closest he could get.

Still with closed eyes, Min sighed and said, very clearly, 'Smaller stitches.'

He froze. If she woke now, how would he explain himself and his tented trousers? Perhaps he would not need to. She might smile at him and crook her finger in invitation. He could drop his clothing, climb atop her and...

Breathe, breathe. A minute or two of struggle and his horseracing heart slowed to a canter. By then, enough oxygen had returned to his brain to consider, in blindingly rapid succession, five reasons why he should crawl into bed with Min. Only one, why he should not.

Ironically, the one was attached to a fantasy. Not the sort in which he had indulged the night before. A far more dangerous one.

My house, my bed, my woman, my life. If she was his, they would work contentedly all day, he in the vines, her in the house and garden. Or in her corset shop, if she wanted one. She would visit him at noon, carrying a basket with a folded cloth on top. Sitting together on the cloth on the ground, they would eat. Bread and cheese and herbs and salt. Wine, passing the bottle back and forth. Sharing an orange. Her eyes and mouth laughing. A drop of wine on her lip; he would kiss it off.

At end of day, he would return to this house and the bed they shared. A bed where they would make love and sleep and wake again for all the days and nights of their lives. A bed where, if the Fates were kind, they would one night lie down, hands joined, to endless rest. To sleep, when they were old and had passed thousands and thousands of days and nights like those.

If he lay beside her now, he would be tempted to believe the fantasy could be real.

But no, you madman. No, no, no. Belief – or worse, acting on belief – would carve a new circle in hell for them both. *Remember who you are. Remember what you have done.*

She stirred again in her sleep, then flopped over onto her stomach, taking her perfect breasts with her. Out of his sight. Into safety.

This must stop. With quiet learned from years of housebreaking, he eased from the room and returned to the kitchen. If only for the hours of pleasure he had felt with her in his house for the past day and a half, he owed her a careful second reading of her distressing post. If nothing else, he could advise her on the best way to respond.

Nearly every instinct for self-preservation told him not to get more deeply involved than that. One rebellious instinct persuaded him otherwise.

If he did not deal directly with her problem, she might find some other man who would. That man would be happy to take his fee from the body she had offered Étienne. That man would wrap his foul hands around those perfect breasts and... He ground his teeth.

A strong cup of coffee should get him through the papers. If not, there was brandy.

———

The letter infuriated him exponentially, each reading by a factor of ten. By the third time through, he was envisioning the dismemberment of the writer while he still breathed.

> Raeburn House
> Meeth, Devonshire
> Dear Miss Hawkins,
> This shall be the first and last occasion to address you by that name, since, as the contents of this missive will reveal, it is not yours.
> Asa and Mary Hawkins are not your grandparents. Your parents are well known to me. Your father was Edgar Sterling Halpern Langworth, Earl Dunmara. Your mother is Lady Amica Joan Langworth, the earl's first and only legal wife. After four stillborn infants, you were her last and sole surviving child. By then, alas, she had lost her wits, and the Earl was forced to place her in my care. He and his lady remained wedded – a fact unknown to all save the earl and myself – until his death in March of this year.
> You had a half-brother, James Halpern Langworth, heir presumptive to Dunmara and the only child of the earl's putative second wife, who died in childbed. I regret to say James Halpern died in the same carriage wreck that took your father's life three months ago.
> In Scotland, where Dunmara lies and the title originated, female succession is perfectly legal, provided there is no living male heir. You must now arrive at the happy conclusion that you are the Countess of Dunmara. If not already, you will at some point soon gain confirmation from the late earl's men of business,

Gordon and Blackford, Solicitors, Glasgow (with whom I took the liberty of sharing your direction). You may trust that I have additional proofs.

Étienne looked up from the page, gauging the time from the slanting light through the kitchen windows. Six in the morning, a bright and peaceful hour in what promised to be a bright and peaceful day.

Apart, that is, from the barbed caltrop he held in his hands. That was designed to put life-threatening holes in the life of the woman in whose path it was placed.

His Minerva was a *comtesse*, the sender claimed. Had she any inkling, before the letter? If not, did she now believe the claim? There were other proofs, Raeburn stated, and Min admitted to receiving something from the late earl's solicitors. Even so, she seemed reluctant to accept it, when many women would have crowed. Nor had she taken pains to look any different, while another woman might have straight away followed the news with a trip to London's most fashionable *modiste*. Min had not even a change of clothing in that absurd handbag she had brought.

Continuing with the letter was as disagreeable as toothache, but it had to be done.

Your mother has long been resident at Raeburn House. It is an asylum. I am the Superintendent, as well an alienist who treats the inmates, one of whom is your mother. Now that you are so fortuitously heir to the lands and title and income of Dunmara, it remains only for you to take up your mother's maintenance. She has long resided in comfortable private quarters, graciously provided for by your late father.

Raeburn House has a separate facility to house

*indigent inmates. Your mother would not like it. I am
sure you would not like to see her placed there. Her
Ladyship will remain in her current rooms until the end
of the month instant. You may expect particulars soon.*

    Respectfully yours,

    Charles Augustus Raeburn, L.R.C.S.

He put aside the letter and resisted the desire to scrub his
hands in the sink. He removed his eyeglasses and wiped them
on the tail of his shirt, sparing, as he did, a moment of
grudging admiration for Raeburn's vile efficiency. The letter
was so patently above board and irreproachable. The content,
if somewhat soulless, was what most people would expect.
*Mother's a lunatic, very sad, but it's the daughter's burden of
care, now, and surely she can assume it. She's an heiress,
isn't she?*

No one would expect an asylum manager to retain an inmate
in private rooms indefinitely once financial support was
withdrawn. Not a single line or word of the screed suggested the
superintendent was doing anything untoward. Some might even
call him kind, for allowing the dowager countess to remain where
she was for months after her husband's death, with no apparent
plan in place for her future.

As to hinting at the woman's move to a pauper's ward... Just a
fact of life, most people would opine.

Instead of following his impulse to take the letter outside and
piss on it, he set it aside. Then, he unfolded the second, smaller
sheet of paper Min had brought. Adjusting his eyeglasses, he read it
for the third time.

```
15,000 Pounds Sterling per annum. No
police, for the health of our mutual
friend.
```

A masterpiece of anonymity, the note. Posted, like the letter, to the Little Farnleigh cottage, arriving a day later. The note was produced on a typewriting machine, on paper sold in any village shop, common as grass. The envelope was equally common, and the direction printed in block letters. Not even a postmark linked it to Raeburn or the asylum; it was franked at Barnstaple, a distance, he would guess, of thirty miles.

The demand was, as Raeburn had promised, particular. It was also exorbitant and extortionate. Worst of all, it threatened harm.

He diverted his gaze to the open kitchen windows. Hours had passed while he examined the vile instruments before him, and the lightening sky made the lamp over the table unnecessary. One of the chaffinches for which Les Pinsons was named had alighted in the branches of the laurel tree that brushed against the house. The bird's song was achingly sweet and cheerful.

He had never lost his wonder at the way ugliness and beauty so often appeared side by side, and how little anyone seemed to notice. In Seven Dials, he had watched an opalescently perfect moon rise over a lane where a corpse had lain all the day, grinning in rictus. A dead carthorse, covered with flies, rotted six feet from a pair of young women, laughing and comparing bonnets in a shop window. If he now suggested to the chaffinch in the tree that it take its pretty little song somewhere else while ugliness was being dealt with in the kitchen, it would not understand any better than he did.

He folded the two papers together as Min had brought them, the half sheet wrapped around the full one. In the old days, the Jacks days, he would not have touched this business with a barge pole. The alienist, the mad dowager countess, the abandoned infant, the juggling of titles, the extortionate demand. It was a profitless game between nobles and their entourages.

But in those days, he would not have touched Minerva Hawkins. Touching Min, wanting her, had dragged him into a different game, one that offered none of the gains that had lured him into the first game. And yet the risk to him was the same. The scaffold.

He would not deny the lure of a straightforward solution. The kind the Jacks might have applied to the problem. He could simply travel to Raeburn House, wait for an opportune moment, and break the neck of the blackmailing leech. A few tempting minutes went to visualising that solution until he rejected it. With reluctance, but firmly.

A trickle of sweat worked its slow way down the middle of his chest, tickling. The sun was rising higher, hotter. Time to wake Min. Time to launch her back to England and hope she stayed there. He had not wanted to immerse himself in this or any criminal enterprise ever again, but it was more important that she be plucked out of it. She was, above all, innocent. Raeburn was a nothing compared to some of the operatives he had faced, but the man's evil was of a magnitude Min could not even imagine, much less defeat. She had rightfully brought the fight to him after the *salaud* of an alienist brought it to her.

And while it chafed him, he must admit he was wrong when he told her that blackmail was a matter for the police. Ewan Exeter was a model of how a policeman could turn the law. A few thousand pounds a year could make such a turning desirable, especially in remote Devonshire where such opportunity was rare. Raeburn would surely have taken pains to promote just such desirability in the local constabulary.

There were other complications. Min seemed not to have considered that her mother might not be alive anywhere. Or that the woman in the asylum was or had ever been a countess. Or, for that matter, Min's mother.

There was also the pendant. Sun and moon. One left to Min at birth, the other sent by Raeburn with his letter. Proof? Proof of something. But what?

He twisted the gold signet ring on the small finger of his left hand. He had never worn it in the Jacks, where it was nothing but an incitement to theft. Like Min's pendant, it was highly problematic proof of descent. In his case, from Robert de Lille, Knight Templar, Grand Master. Burned at the stake in the thirteenth century. He had never quite believed in his lineage, despite his mother's insistence.

'Someday, you will have need of this.' She had said it when she gave him the ring. Aged ten at the time, he had run his thumbnail over the escutcheon incised in the signet. *What do I need with jewellery?* he had thought. *At least it is gold.*

That was a year before his swine of a father punched Maman one too many times in the head. Apoplexy, the doctor reported, as frightened of the master of Les Pinsons as everyone else.

Étienne had begun wearing the ring when he returned to Les Pinsons from London, after Jillian Morehouse's rescue. After the things he had done that, if discovered and added to his outstanding warrants, would have landed him in gaol for the rest of his accursed life.

Perhaps the ring was an amulet, a charm to ward off the ghosts of his father and his two brutish half-brothers. And the ghosts of his years in the Jacks; those came as a herd.

If the ring was a charm against phantoms, it was a weak one. The hauntings continued.

He rose from the table. Time to boil the kettle. Min would want fresh coffee, and he had settled his thoughts on her problem.

Whether or not the woman in Raeburn's custody was a dowager countess was immaterial. Whether or not she was Min's mother, and if or if not Min was an earl's heir and a countess herself... They meant nothing to him. But to her?

Raeburn's assertions, a letter from the late earl's solicitors, a coincidence of birthdates, a broken pendant restored. To Min, those were reasons enough to hope.

And hope was making her vulnerable to a human scavenger, the extortionist Raeburn. His task would be to locate the threat and, one way or another, remove it from the life of Minerva Hawkins.

If executed properly, the correction of her problem would be simple. He steadfastly turned his mind away from simple corrections in the past that had ended in blood, his own or someone else's.

In any case, and as reluctant as he was to accept it, the time had come for him to emerge from retirement.

Chapter Six

Go home, Minerva.

Easy enough for him to say. Étienne had planted himself at his door, watching her drive off in a donkey cart with his stocky, grizzled man of all work, Rafael or Raoul or Remy, at the reins. Judging by the pin dot of emotion he'd displayed at her departure, she could have been setting off for the village shops. The moment she was out of sight, he'd probably gone back to his grapes and forgotten all about her.

She sagged back into the tufted train seat, frowning. In her compartment in the *wagon-lit* section, wood panelling and an etched half-glass door kept out the noise and smells of the rest of the train. There were even well-appointed dining and lounge cars, everything a far cry from the uncomfortable second-class carriage in which she'd made the long and broken journey to Bordeaux.

But what was it in service of, the first-class rail ticket Étienne had forced on her? Had he been displaying gratitude for her offer to prostitute herself? Or an apology for his disinclination to take her up on it? Either way, it was too late for her to blush in shame. She'd thrust herself at him as blatantly as any Covent Garden nightwalker.

At least, thanks mostly to him, nothing had come of it. Other than a momentary lofting of his eyebrows, he'd been utterly unaffected. She was relieved. Somewhat. As to the other thing she'd brought to his door...

Go home, Minerva. As though she could! Was he truly asking her to paint over the cracks that Raeburn's repellent letter had opened in her life?

Unthinkable. But if Étienne was not inclined to deal with Raeburn, what was she supposed to do? Ignore him and his letter? Go back to London, blinkered like a carthorse, and take up her needle at Salon Sirena? Find something to do in Little Farnleigh? It was the place to which Raeburn had posted the letter and there was some security in that. He presumably had not known about Salon Sirena and the life she'd made after leaving Asa Hawkins' hell-and-brimstone zealotry in her dust.

Oh, bamfoozle. Some French person was tapping on the glass of her compartment door, holding up a flat basket of buns. Between the coffee and toast Étienne had pushed at her before bundling her out his door, and the twisting of her stomach now, the last thing she needed was buns.

She sat upright and gave her head a forceful shake. The French person didn't budge, just tapped on the glass again. '*Non, merci!*' she shouted. '*Je ne veux pas–*' What the fuzzy piglets was the word for buns? '*Un petit peon!*' That couldn't be right. She made a shooing away motion with both hands.

Alarmingly, the bun vendor slid open the door, which Min had foolishly left unlocked. 'Good morning,' the woman said in French-accented English. Calmly, but with a bite. 'Since you do not want one, you will not be dismayed to learn I am not, today, selling the small peasants. If you later wish to buy one, I suggest you leave the train and walk in the fields. Perhaps a farmer's wife will sell you one of her children.'

It wasn't that easy to slam a train compartment door, but the bun seller did it.

With a sigh, Min put her palms on her skirt and dragged them from centre to side, trying to smooth the travel-wrinkled cloth. Flashes from the compartment window painted the skirt and her hands with sunlight as the train rumbled on and on through the Centre-Val. The view – tile-and-slate roofs, the bunched canopies of trees, and the intermittent flickers of silver she knew to be the River Loire – gave her something like homesickness. The land wasn't at all like Devonshire, but it had the same ancient, unchanging beauty. The Loire reminded her of the Torridge, the river that skirted both Little Farnleigh and Meeth. Perhaps it touched the grounds of Raeburn House.

Go home, Minerva. He might just as well have said, 'Go be a countess in Scotland and stop bothering me.' Hah! Even had she wanted to go to Scot-blinking-land and claim her earl-blinking-dom, there were things to be done as soon as she was back in England. For one, she'd have to dispose of her grandparents'... No, she must stop calling them that. The cottage in Little Farnleigh was Asa Hawkins' and his will had left it to her, along with his modest savings. Concluding the sale of the cottage was the last visit to Little Farnleigh she planned to make. After that, she never wanted to see it again.

Asa, the old misery-guts, had been so certain that she would simply take over where Mary Hawkins had left off when she died. Fetching his slippers like a loyal hound, doing the cooking, the cleaning, the shopping, the pressing of clothes, the trimming of wicks.

'If you go,' he'd told her when she packed her things and paused, ill-advisedly, on the doorstep to tell him goodbye, 'do not think to come back. Ever.'

She hadn't bothered with a reply.

She certainly knew now what she hadn't known then: neither Asa nor Mary Hawkins had ever had the right to give her ultimatums. They hadn't even been her kin, though, in fairness, they'd never said they were. When she'd grown old enough to ask,

Mary had said they were distant relations and discouraged further questions. She'd encouraged Min to call her Grandmother and Asa Grandfather, and Min was content with it. It made her feel less like what she'd always known she was, a foundling.

In Asa's case, Raeburn's confirmation that he was no relation was cause for rejoicing, but she still missed her connection to Mary. It might be some time before she accepted that the kind-faced woman with faded ginger hair wasn't and had never been her grandmother.

She'd certainly been everything a grannie should be. A baker of scones and knitter of tea cosies. A soother of skinned knees and finder of lost mittens. Her only flaw, really, was her inability to stand up to her husband. Min imagined Mary was just grateful to remain a wife after she didn't give Asa a child. That she was so much younger than he – Gran said they married when she was sixteen, Asa forty-five – argued for his expectation of offspring. In that, he was disappointed. Perhaps Gran was, as well.

She knew Gran was grateful that, years later, she was allowed to take in a motherless babe, in spite of the way it set tongues to wagging in Little Farnleigh.

'*Tiz one o' they Scotch bantlings, I yers.*' The worst gossip in the village had said it. It was roundly repeated, but she'd never understood what it meant, other than that Gran had always been suspect for no reason more compelling than her Scottishness.

At least, she'd finally learned who her parents were. An earl and a countess. A mad countess, admittedly, but what was one more titled lunatic in Britain? What a stir that would make in Little Farnleigh when it got out! Which it would. Everything got out sooner or later in Little Farnleigh.

Not due to hunger but just to have something to do, she lifted the lid of the wicker hamper Étienne's man had given her when she boarded. A quick rummage uncovered bread wrapped in a cloth, apples, figs, a small wheel of cheese. And a wine bottle, half full. She pried off the cork and sniffed. Blast, it was only water. A disaster-prevention measure, no doubt, since one glass last night had felled her like a shot grouse.

Tucked at the bottom was a roll of banknotes. She laughed wryly. Insofar as she understood the transaction, there was normally vigorous activity between a woman offering her body and a man giving her money. It was both gentlemanly and insulting of him that Étienne had skipped over the activity and gone directly to the payment. She examined the notes. French francs, which was convenient. She'd brought only English currency, making even the purchase of refreshment at railway stops a struggle.

She closed the hamper and sank back in the seat, considering what to do with the money Asa Hawkins had left her. The sum was more than tidy, safely tucked away in a London bank – Asa's choice, since he'd trusted nothing in North Devonshire. His end coming as no surprise to him, he'd arranged beforehand for her to draw on the funds.

She thought wryly that Asa would be gratified at her reticence to touch the money. She hadn't rushed out to buy furs or transatlantic voyages. She'd booked only one trip to France and there wouldn't be another, since it was painfully clear that she could have offered Étienne the Hope Diamond and he'd have still refused her. All he'd handed her was rejection, a few meals, and some dizzyingly good wine.

And the bed, of course, his. Without him in it, though no one could say she hadn't issued an invitation.

Brooding over the humiliation of that occupied her until the scream of the locomotive's whistle jarred her alert. The train slowed. She peered out the window to read the signboard above the station. *TOURS*. Even so late in the day, the place was thronging. She'd wait for a quieter stop to step down, stretch her legs, maybe find a hot drink to go with the food in the hamper. A cup of tea would be excellent. No chance of that; she'd have to take coffee. She was still in France and would be for many miles more. It was a long way to the coast, then across the Channel, only to undertake that tiresome, broken rail journey back to Little Farnleigh. Frustratingly, it was more difficult and took longer to get to the village from Dover than from London.

The expedition would have been so much easier if she'd been able to set out for France from London, but she didn't dare risk being found out by one of her Salon Sirena workmates. Maidenly Minerva, the Devonshire Dainty: that's how they'd always viewed her. The reality was that she had gone to the Continent, to the very door – and into the bedroom – of one of the most dangerous men in France or Britain. And she'd done it alone.

The locomotive whistle shrilled again, and the train left Tours with a long hiss and a shudder. Steam billowed outside her compartment window. When the train gained a little speed and the smoke and cinders blew away, she'd open the window. The compartment was uncomfortably warm.

Perhaps she'd go from the coast to London, even stop there a while. She'd be hard pressed to say she missed Salon Sirena, but such friends as she had, Evie and Ada and Eileen, were in London. Jillian, too, if she could tear herself away from the East London Pugilists Academy and the demands of motherhood. But even if she had her friends about her, she couldn't really share what she'd done on this trip. Not just the soliciting of her own prostitution. The rest of it.

She had asked Étienne Sansecours to kill for her. Not the sort of thing a woman should ask any man to do. Not, 'Oh, sir, could you kindly direct me to Paddington Station?' Or 'Would you mind helping me with this heavy parcel?'

And she'd asked without a single forethought of what the question implied. Of what it said about her opinion of him. That must have seemed no higher than the one the British police held. Dangerous. Gangster. Lawbreaker. Deserving of gaol or the gallows, whichever came first.

Nor had her question shown any respect for what his

compliance might do to his soul. She'd asked as though he hadn't had one, as though he was defined by the years he'd spent in the Jacks. As though he'd *wanted* those years and all they entailed. Min didn't know what had driven any of the gang members she knew – Étienne, Kell, Ewan Exeter – into the Jacks, but if a career in crime seemed like an improvement, it must've been awful. She had no right to judge his past – and yet she had.

She and her mood sank lower into the seat. While she was totting up harms, she should add what her ill-considered plan had done to any chance she might have had for a future with the man in whom she saw so much.

Because she had dreamed of that future from the start. How she'd hoarded the scraps and threads of him she'd salvaged from the twice they'd met! The French way he rumbled her name (once), the touches (two, a touch on her shoulder, a clasp of her hand), his smiles (three), his scent (almond soap). From less than the twigs a robin used to make its nest, she'd built a bridge between desire and fulfilment. She'd crossed it a thousand times in her mind, long after he left London.

In her imagination, the crossings went both ways. He came to the alley behind Salon Sirena when Madame was out and tapped on the back door of the workroom. Min opened it to see him as she'd seen him the first time, offering a grin and a paper bag of sugared almonds. Or she came across him in the street, in a park. *'What a small world!'* she said. *'Are you in London for long? Have you been well?'*

'Minerve,' he replied, smiling the broad, warm smile so at odds with what other people thought of him. *'Do you go well?'* And his eyes, the colour of sun-warmed honey, travelled across her body, touching every part of her and setting it afire.

But now, what a fool he must think her! A fool and a goose and a callous female thinking only of herself. A countess, her? Countess of Nitwittery, perhaps.

Tears started up, hot and blinding. She turned her face toward the window. French fields rushed by in a green blur.

Go home, Minerva.

After a while, she sniffed into her handkerchief and pulled herself together. She couldn't afford to lose her head over missteps and humiliations. At least, she had seen him a third time, not in London but in France. If she never saw him again, she could rebuild her imaginary bridge with the two whole days and nights she'd had with him, the sound and scent and sight of him.

She wouldn't dwell on exactly how *much* of him she'd seen. Maybe at night. In private.

For now, she still had the problem of the blackmail. Since Étienne wouldn't help her, she'd have to implement her alternate plan. Honesty compelled her to admit she'd only formulated it in the last ten miles of track. Regardless, it was a plan she could execute by herself, entirely without the aid of a large French criminal.

Devonshire and the disposal of the Little Farnleigh cottage could wait, though that would be a private, not the public, story. She would stop a few nights in London, restore the 'equanimity' Étienne rightly said was deserting her, and prepare.

Her first task would be to write a letter to the alienist, agreeing to his demands and including earnest money. Fifty pounds, say, which she could extract from her inherited funds. She would make any further payments dependent on seeing her mother – a reasonable request. Even annuities required proof of life and Raeburn was demanding she support him for the rest of his days. In her letter, she would set a reasonable date to visit the asylum. She would go there. Once she affirmed that her mother lived and was well enough to travel...

At that point, the plan was a little fuzzy, but her resolve was clear. Mad or sane, she and her mother would leave Raeburn House together.

CHAPTER SEVEN

He did not linger to watch the donkey cart disappear up the drive to the village road. Seething with unspent urges, he went straight to his bedroom, reached to the top of the wardrobe, and took down the leather-bound case of his *poignards*, his throwing knives. Rebuking his eyes when they strayed to the rumpled bed where Min had spent two nights, he carried the case to the kitchen and opened it on the table.

'*Je suis de retour,*' he told the black-handled blades ironically, removing them one by one. *Yes, you're back*, a darkly amused voice in his head told him, *as you will always come back.*

Four knives in each hand, he made for the long-disused throwing lane in the fallow field between the house and the winery. He had not launched a *poignard* with deadly intent since the rescue of Jillian Morehouse, and that had been the first and only time since the dissolution of the Jacks years earlier. But reputations and skills like his were long-lived, forged in violence and hardened in hot blood.

Or so he hoped, since he might need both, now. As he walked through the unscythed weeds in the throwing lane, he worked to efface Étienne Sansecours and bring forth The

Dagger, the most-feared member of London's most-feared street gang.

The transition used to be easy, even magical. The knives had always seemed extensions of his hands, his eyes, his brain, needing no effort, just intention, to fly to their targets. *Tu pense?* the dark voice mocked him. *You think?*

It was not magic, but repetition made it easy. All those fights, all those targets.

Brushing leaf fall from the man-shaped wood and straw figure he had constructed years ago, then largely ignored, at the far edge of the field, he admitted, however much it galled him, that the mocking voice was right. In the Jacks, killing skills had no chance to rust. Life in the gang was just one battle after another. The great trouble with being at the summit of the game was that rivals and foes never stopped trying to force the Jacks off it. Returning force with force was the order of the day, posted by Scraper – their leader, Ewan Exeter – and carried out by every soldier from the latest wayward youth plucked from a rookery to founding members like Étienne and Michael Kelly.

It had taken years for the bitter taste of that life to leave him. Had the skills that enabled him to survive it left him, too? He plodded twenty paces from the target and turned to face it. Pulled back a mighty arm and threw the first knife. The second. The third and the fourth.

'*Putain!*' He was disgusted with himself. Four throws, two misses. The blades had kept their edge, but he was losing his. Too much enjoyment of his own cooking, too much good wine. That would cease. Now, today.

Thunk. Another useless throw, unless he hoped to disable an opponent by nicking their elbow. As unnerving as it was, he should perhaps consider the effects of age on his skill. In a month, he would be thirty-one. He brushed aside the thought. Perhaps he was merely preoccupied.

Assuredly, he must stop thinking about Min. She was a

distraction as much as she was the reason he was here, hurling knives into a straw man. He had told her he was not going to do what she asked, but her worried eyes and trembling mouth made him want to destroy whatever – whomever – put that look on her face. Made him take up his *poignards* and remember what he did best with them.

Thunk. Better. Square in the chest. It was not a warm day, but he was sweating from the tension and exercise. Another thing he must correct, and quickly. He had always been able to stay calm, cool, and focused, not sweaty and swearing like a teamster. It was not that he had been idle in recent years. He worked, all day and every day. Six days a week with Remy and alone the seventh. But work in the vines, however hard, was not the same as *lancer de poignard.*

Knife throwing was no circus trick for him. His daggers were never intended to land in pretty circles of paper or outline the scantily clad body of a female assistant. He had learned the art in Dieppe, where survival of the fittest was not, to him and his smuggler brethren, a Darwinian concept to be discussed over sherry. It was a way not to die like a dog in the street. When he unleashed a knife, it went with the power of his whole body behind it. At the top of his career, he had sent a blade into a three-inch-thick oak door and out the other side.

Thunk. Another chest hit. One blade left, and then he would retrieve the ones he had thrown and start over. He wiped his dripping face on his sleeve. Growling, he pulled down his braces and stripped off his shirt. The sun was rising strongly now, but there was a breeze. It felt good on his naked back, his shoulders, his chest. He rarely wore underclothing. He kept his body clean and could never find undergarments in a size to fit. His shirts and trousers were tailored, but when he had asked the old Rumanian who sewed them if he could make him underclothing, even a singlet and drawers, the man looked at him as though he had asked for a bespoke sling for his balls.

Thunk. A shoulder hit. '*Fils de putain!*' Adequate to slow a man but no prize, and it left his opponent with a free arm to throw something back. Like a knife. Or a bullet.

Sounds reached him from the drive where it skirted the front of the house and curved toward the outbuildings. Remy, back from the railway station in the cart, amiably cursing the donkey Balthasar, who gave an amiable bray now and then in response. The two had an odd relationship.

He gave his foreman time to unhitch the beast and stable him, then waited a half hour beyond that. The interval was useful to make two more rounds of throws, wipe his knives, and bundle them in his shirt. And to discuss with himself the various ways he might, without having to employ the *poignard*, persuade an extortionist to leave England for a mission in Buganda.

Finally, he went to where he knew he could find Remy, where he could always be found at Les Pinsons when he was not in the vines. The *cuvier*, the fermentation shed, brooding like a hen over his vats and casks.

Once they were face to face, Étienne was unable, at first, to form a question about how it had gone, the putting of Min on a train headed for England. Because he was too slow to organise words into something detached and colourless, Remy got there first.

'She was not singing with joy, but she went. By now, she is halfway to Tours. I am filled with admiration that you kept her here for two days. Two days with a woman, 'Tien. There is hope for you.'

'Remind me, Remy. When did I ask for your opinion?'

'If you had a woman here more often, you might be less of a crustacean.'

'If you insulted me less, you might keep your job.'

'I quake in my shoes.' Remy shivered all over and grimaced.

Étienne only grimaced. 'Did you give her the money?'

'*Oui*, Monsieur Moneybags. She could go to Morocco if the

fancy seizes her, though she was too busy being irritated with you to notice me stuffing francs into the food basket you sent.'

People showing irritation with him was becoming a common malady. After his foreman was through expressing his, Étienne could return to knife throwing and be irritated at himself without a chorus.

'Ah! The bundle of francs was consolation!' Remy said it brightly, as though comprehension had just popped into his mind, when Étienne was sure he'd worked out his jibes an hour ago on the donkey cart. 'The pretty, bespectacled one left in a state of vexation because you did not satisfy her, *hein*?'

'Nail your beak, Remy. There are innumerable winemakers in France looking for employment.'

'And yet, despite performance from you that tarnishes the honour of Frenchmen everywhere, she was reluctant to leave. It is a mystery, that.'

'She is not for me.'

'*Comme tu dis.* Still, one has to wonder why, of all the men in all the world – none of whom would hesitate for one second to give a woman like that mindless pleasure – she came to *you.*'

'*Ça suffit*, Remy. Enough.'

For some minutes, they worked in silence at the repetitive and endless job of cleaning the vats. Not a single atom of dirt must be allowed to find a hiding place from which it could spoil the fermentation. Finally, hoping to give the impression his mind had refocused entirely on wine, Étienne posed a question about the grapes.

'What do you think, is the harvest close?'

A noncommittal up-down-up flip of Remy's meaty hand. 'The Trebbiano will be the slow coach, as always. The grapes do not fall easily when I give them a tug and the colour is still too fresh. I test every day.' Not at all taken in by his *patron*'s attempts to squelch the topic of Minerva Hawkins, Remy added, 'You have plenty of time to chase after the woman, *mon brave*. Find her, marry her, have a quick honeymoon on the Côte d'Azur to start a baby, and be back in time to pick the grapes.'

He would ignore Remy's unsolicited marital advice. He would also be careful not to look him in the eye. 'I am as aware of the ripening grapes as you, old man. I ask only to determine if you know as much about their condition. Some... pressing business calls me away. I cannot say how long I may be at it.'

'But, 'Tien, you dislike to miss—'

'The *vendange*. Thank you for the reminder.' He gave a final swipe at the rim of his vat. To be absent for the months-long, harvest-to-bottling process was no small thing. 'I will miss the *sauvignon blanc*, perhaps. But I will surely return for the sweet grapes. Even if I do not, you have managed the *vendange* without me before. You can manage it again.'

He could almost hear the click and whirr of Remy's brain, that reliable, organised brain that had kept the vines healthy even after Étienne's cruel sot of a father was dead, his sons not long after. Even after many of the other farms in the region had lost their vines to the twin plagues of blight and mildew. Even while Étienne was still carving a path through London's underworld with his knives. Steadfast and efficient as a waterwheel, Remy had kept the wine of Les Pinsons flowing until the Jacks fell and Étienne crawled back to France.

Le bon Dieu knew he had been useless when he first arrived. He was eaten up with bitterness and rage against his father, the Jacks, himself. The very day he alighted from the train, he bought three bottles of wine and proceeded to drink them as he walked the six miles from the village to the vineyard. He fully intended to lie in a heap of straw in the stable and drink himself to death like his father.

A few weeks of that, and the workman he barely remembered from his young years at Les Pinsons came to the stable at dawn, carrying a pail of icy water from the spring house. Without a word, he poured it over Étienne's head, then followed it with a picking basket, jamming it on his victim's head like a wicker hat.

'Get to work!' he yelled.

Sputtering, furious, and sober, Étienne had fought his way out of the basket and watched his tormenter walk away. It was the beginning of a fractious and essential friendship for them both.

A friendship Remy never hesitated to presume upon, as now. 'This oh-so pressing business to which you must attend. I hope it will not take you to England.'

Étienne ignored the hint. 'Wherever I am, Remy, I will rest easily, knowing I may trust my old friend completely.'

'And in the case of pressing business at Les Pinsons, where might this trusted old friend reach you?'

'I will send word.'

Remy shrugged. To be French was to shrug, but no one did it as well as his foreman, whose shoulders rose to a summit of insouciance, then climbed another inch for arrogance.

'*Tu n'en fais qu'à ta tête.* May it be on your head, since you will do what you want, foolish or not.' Remy jerked his chin toward the stable. 'Compared to you, Balthasar could lecture at the Sorbonne.'

He briefly cherished an image of Remy, boiled down and bottled, but said nothing.

His foreman, naturally, filled the gap. 'And the woman? Will she be back?'

'I hope not.'

Remy spoke to Justine the farm cat, lounging atop a barrel a few feet away. 'She will be back.'

CHAPTER EIGHT

She didn't think of herself as indispensable, but after an absence of under a month from Salon Sirena, it was unsettling to see how well everyone had coped. 'Everyone' being Madame, Ada, Evie, and Eileen.

From the terminus of the train, she'd gone directly to her room and donned a dull black gown of cotton and silk. She was, after all, bereaved by the passing of a grandparent.

The ensemble was respectable and reasonably smart, though by no means new. Also, a bit chewed along the hem, thanks to a mouse she'd never been able to trap. The bodice was pretty, festooned with silk rosettes, and she'd pinned a matching bonnet to her gathered-up hair.

As she stepped away from a hackney cab at Shepherd Street, she paused for a few moments to compose her face into what Mary Hawkins would have called 'a brow of woe'. Then, since she wasn't ready to think herself a countess, but didn't quite think herself a *corsetière*, anymore, she entered the shop by the front door, just as a patron might.

At the sound of the bell, Madame looked up from a catalogue she was perusing at the counter. Her face trotted through astonishment, pleasure, and confusion, finally pulling up solemnly at sympathy. It was the face most people assumed when presented with mourning black. Min, the reason for the face, felt a stab of remorse. When Mary Hawkins had died, her sorrow had been genuine, but Asa?

Bustling from behind the counter, Madame offered conventional condolences. *So terribly sorry. Our loss is Heaven's gain. Your grandfather is with the angels.* Min responded with conventional murmurs and thanks, wondering how the angels felt about having Asa Hawkins to boss them around.

Having met etiquette's demands, Madame returned to her brisk self and waved toward the drape separating showroom from workroom. She clearly assumed her fourth corset girl, front door or not, bereaved or not, could barely wait to get back to her needle. Min nodded and went where she was directed. Revelations to Madame about the future could wait.

When she entered the workroom, Eileen – who looked so much like Ada they might have been twins – was sitting at Evie's right side, in Min's place. Eileen must have noted her twitch of surprise, since she immediately and unnecessarily blurted that the corsets Min had been sewing when she left for Little Farnleigh had been parcelled out to her. Finished, they'd all been boxed and delivered.

'I hope you don't mind,' she finished, 'but I took off that white lace you'd tacked onto the Number Seven Starlight.' Madame's latest brainstorm had been to give the styles whimsical names: Starlight, Moonglow, Night in Spain. 'I replaced it with ivory. Me and Ada, we thought it'd look, well, better.'

Oh, by all means. Min shot a glance at Ada, who was vigorously punching stitches into a casing. For a few giddy seconds, she wanted to intone, loftily, *'You dare contradict the taste of a countess?'* just to see the uproar it would cause. Suppressing the urge, she smiled, unpinned her hat, and hung it from one of the wire hooks on the wall, aware that everyone was staring at her. Or at the mourning attire. Both.

For pity's sake, it's only me. Minerva Hawkins. Not one of the Tower ravens day tripping in Mayfair.

She slid into the only empty chair at the worktable. In front of her, a peach satin Number Ten looked abashed to be showing its half-stitched seams.

Ada pointed with her needle. 'I'd just got stuck in that one when an order for a dozen fancies dropped on us like a load of bricks. All for the Duke of York's ascension ball and we had to drop everything else to do 'em in time. You can finish the Ten, if you like.'

'Why, thank you,' Min chirped. Absolutely no one noticed the irony. Her threading a needle, though... That prompted everyone to speak at once, and they ladled out the same tired condolences as Madame. With a bit more feeling, perhaps. Apart from the initial small contretemps over lace and the fobbing off of the peach stays, her workmates were all pity and kindness.

As, of course, they would be. They thought she'd used her absence to grieve and settle her inheritance in Devon. The condolences went on uncomfortably long, considering she'd spent a third of her leave in France, some of it eating, drinking wine, and lolling in Étienne Sansecours' bed.

Thankfully, the talk wandered from death into London news. Mountains of manure in the streets were provoking calls for fewer horses and more motorcars, and everyone bewailed the flies. *The Shop Girl* was packing the stalls at The Gaiety and all the corset girls wanted to see it. Ada said she'd heard the songs were fast as a cat with its tail on fire. The mention of fire led to Madame's interest in installing electric, rather than gas, lighting in the salon. They'd all heard rumours about how the odd wired streetlamp here and there would soon be a flood of electrical illumination in houses and shops. And telephones! Madame also mentioned getting one of those. A map purveyor just three doors along Shepherd Street had one.

'It ain't practical,' Ada grumbled. 'Can't measure for stays over the wire, can we?'

Eileen said no, but it might be useful for taking appointments. The shop might even offer a slight mark down for interested parties who rang up and then visited.

'Madame could give them a code. A number or a password.'

'Harebrained, there's your password, El.'

'No different than if they got a circular somewhere. "Bring this in and get ten per cent off your purchase."'

'Don't even *think* of puttin' that idea in Madame's head. Unless you're volunteerin' to plod around Mayfair with an armload of paper.'

'I was talkin' about telephones!'

The argy-bargy went on until Min reached over and tapped the Number Eight Moonglow Eileen was sewing.

'That's the wrong colour thread,' she said. 'You'll have to pick out the edge binding and do it again, with this.' She reached for the correct bobbin and set it smartly on the table in front of Eileen.

'Told you so,' Ada sniped at her sister.

Eileen took up her seam ripper with an angry cluck. 'It's cos I got distracted. I was just gettin' started on Muckglow here when Evie opened one of them passionate letters from–'

'*Philll*-ip!' The sisters squealed it together.

'You are both very rude.' Evie spoke levelly, but her eyes flashed and her tea-with-milk skin flushed darkly. 'I am sorry to have brought my correspondence to this nest of sticky noses.'

'Sticky beaks,' Min corrected.

'*Exactement*. My letter is not their affair.'

'It's an affair, all right,' Ada persisted. 'He's courtin' her.'

The workroom had clearly advanced a few pages in *Seamstress Scandals* while Min was gone. 'Philip?' She looked the question at

Evie, who didn't look an answer back, so she redirected it toward Ada. 'Do you mean Jillian's brother, Philip Morehouse?'

'Only Philip we know,' Ada smirked.

'There's Phil the grocer's boy.' Eileen was incandescently wicked. 'Evie might like 'em young.'

Her sister snorted. 'He's thirteen, El.'

'Big for his age, though.' And the two were off, laughing like drains.

'Philip and I have a friendly correspondence only,' Evie said stiffly. 'He is in every way proper.'

'On paper.' Ada's smirk widened into a grin. 'Let's see how proper he is when he gets you in a hotel in Bristol.'

'*Ada!*' Min and Evie hissed it at the same time.

Perhaps because Ada noted that Evie had possession of the only pair of scissors at the table, she changed the subject. 'All right, Min?' At Min's nod, she went on. 'How'd it go in Little Foggy?'

'It's Little Farnleigh, and there's a lot still to do. I found an estate agent for my grandparents' cottage.'

'You don't want to move back there?'

'No.' Min hoped her revulsion wasn't visible. 'I must finish some estate business, a week's worth, maybe. Then I'm done with Little Farnleigh for good.'

'That's fine, then. Keepin' your room in the Court, are you?' Barrett's Court was now St Christopher's Place, but everyone Min knew still used the old name. Since she'd first come to London, she'd let a bed-sitting room in a teetering ruin of a house there.

'I was thinking I'd get something larger.' Because she'd have her mother with her, and they'd need the space. And a better location, if she could manage it. Kensington, maybe.

The screech of brakes in Ada's head as she stopped herself from asking *Left you well-fixed, your granddad?* was nearly audible. Min could forgive her for wanting to know. When Jillian married, she'd moved out of the cramped Soho room Michael Kelly gave her when she was still Jillian Morehouse, fugitive from the law. Jillian and Ada had shared the mousehole, which didn't get any roomier when Jillian left and Eileen moved in. Ada hadn't gotten any more broadminded in two years, either, and still refused to take money from her brother. A free-of-rent room would continue to serve for herself and her younger sister. Indefinitely, if Ada had her way.

The few words about housing seemed to drain the conversational pond of the topic. Ada paddled into other waters. For the next hour, she and Eileen, with occasional comments from Evie, nattered about leg o' mutton sleeves (Ada suggested they could be filled with gas to transport the wearer like a hot air balloon), curly fringes (Ada against, Evie and Eileen for), and men who dyed their beards (general agreement: disgusting).

Min sewed with her head down, present with offhand remarks but mentally absent. The chatter both tired and fascinated her, like listening to a cageful of birds speaking in bird language. Finch talk, maybe, and that thought sent her back to Les Pinsons, where birdsong drifted from open windows and a big man moved through sunlit rooms with the quiet strength of a panther.

Her dress seemed to tighten and chafe. The rustle of her taffeta underskirt as she shifted on her chair put her in Étienne's bed, the crisp sheets rustling as she crawled into them. The second morning she'd awakened there, she'd been mortified to find herself naked under the blanket. To be sure, she'd been sozzled on French wine the night before and didn't remember undressing. She was almost certain that was the only thing she didn't remember. She had mixed feelings about that.

For the two days she'd been in Étienne's farmhouse, he had made it clear he didn't want her there. But if that were true, why was he so very much with her *here*? The almond scent of his shaving soap clung to her nostrils. Under the gabble of her workmates, she heard the slight *shush* of his loose linen trousers as he passed through the kitchen, making coffee, bringing her a bowl of soup. If he hadn't wanted her around, he shouldn't have been so kind. And he definitely shouldn't have worn clothes that whispered an invitation with his every movement. The more so since she knew what was under them. *Touch me, touch me*, sang the folds of his shirt. *Stroke me here, and here,* was the sibilant chorus of his trousers.

Between the corset girls' chatter and her heat-generating memories, she was relieved when Madame broke into both by jerking aside the drape. She barked out instructions for a delivery to the Crimson Lantern, one of the posh brothels making up a lucrative, but discreet, fifth of the Salon's trade. Ada and Eileen would go, since no *corsetière* went alone. It slowed production and left the Salon short-staffed at times, but Madame wasn't willing to risk another disaster like Jillian's abduction whilst on a delivery.

'I'm off to Fenwick Fancies for ribbon,' Madame concluded. 'Min, if you'd kindly deal with any custom that arrives, I'd be grateful.'

Since when did Madame use *kindly* and *grateful* with the help? Surely, it was due to the mourning black; it said 'serious', 'responsible'. And, because it was three years old, 'thrifty'. All qualities Madame prized.

Ada and Eileen exited first, then Madame. The second the shop bell stopped jangling, Min hopped to her feet, took her old chair next to Evie, and delicately but firmly moved Eileen's work to the side. She bent closer to Evie to speak in a barely audible voice. It wasn't necessary, since they had the place to themselves, but she had a feeling the ensuing conversation would be conducted as though they were in church.

'Tell me true. *Are* you and Philip Morehouse courting? That must be difficult, with him in the Royal Navy.'

'Pon, he is...' Evie, using Philip's nickname. Another new development. 'He is not in the Navy, *précisement.*'

'Not – precisely.' Min reared back a little and studied her friend. Evie, eyes down, studied her sewing. 'Evie, I talked to Jilly just a few days before I got the wire about my grandfather, and she told me her brother was on the HMS *Ramillies*. She thought the ship was in the Mediterranean. Philip was due for his annual leave, and Jilly thought he might be able to–'

'She is wrong.' For the first time since their odd exchange began, Evie looked up. Her dark eyes were troubled. 'Min, this is most important. You must not say to anyone what I tell you. Philip is not on the *Ramillies* and not in the Mediterranean. He is not in the Navy at all.'

'Jillian doesn't know?'

Since Evie dropped her eyes to her hands and didn't reply, Min had her answer. Her own wavered a little. 'All right.'

Was it all right, that her friend knew more about Philip Morehouse than his own sister? Clearly, things had progressed a long way in two years. Since Evie had first sighed over the cabinet photographs in uniform Pon enclosed with letters to Jillian and which had then been passed around the workroom. Min should have paid more attention. She suddenly felt displaced in time, a traveller gone far longer than a month.

Evie whispered again, in French, as though she needed to add another layer of secrecy to their talk. '*Comment s'est passé ton voyage en France?*'

God bless her workmate. She *knew*. For the past two hours, she must've been nearly combusting with the need to ask, 'How did your trip to France go?' That, despite Min having never uttered a word beforehand about going there. When she'd opened the telegram about Asa Hawkins' death, she hadn't known she *was* going. She was still a week from retrieving her Little Farnleigh post with its poisonous letter from Raeburn. Two weeks from launching her desperate – or ill-judged – quest for Étienne Sansecours.

But Evie... She'd been in the alley behind the Salon on the day Min had first met him, and again on the day, weeks later, when he'd taken her hand and questioned her so carefully about Jillian's disappearance. Min had no idea what the others had made of those encounters, but Evie had obviously gotten the lay of the land faster than a surveyor.

To be fair, after her first meeting with Étienne, Min hadn't hidden her reaction to the nattily dressed giant who'd smiled and taught her to juggle sugared almonds, his hands gentling aside her hair and his voice deliciously deep, dangerously warm. That Evie was now asking how her trip to France and, therefore, to Étienne went, was no surprise.

She put down the peach satin corset, anchoring her last stitch with a quick in-out motion of the threaded needle. 'France was interesting.'

'Min.' Evie laid down her own work and fixed her with a sceptical expression. 'It is I, your friend, Evangeline Broussard. You remember me, yes? "Interesting" is an excursion to the Kew Gardens.' Evie took her hand and squeezed it. 'I trusted you with my secret, Minerva. You can trust me with yours.'

Min's sigh came from a deep place, flowed outward, and took all her resistance with it. 'You're right. I suppose I'd better tell you everything.'

Which she did. It might be the pinnacle of folly to reveal herself. But a single hair from the frightened-of-everything rabbit she'd been before she'd met a man called Dague warned her to do it, anyway. Someone, somewhere, should know what she knew.

Someone, somewhere, should know what she was planning to do about it.

CHAPTER NINE

'You've gone and lost what little sanity you ever had, you French lummox. That's the only explanation for you being back in London.'

Given the heat of the day, the cool glasses of bitter on the table before them at The Judge's Tavern sweated temptingly, but neither Étienne nor Michael Kelly was drinking – yet. Kell was still talking.

'I've lost track of the number of warrants out on you.'

'Ask Scraper. He will know.'

'Ewan doesn't answer to that name, these days, any more than I answer to Stammer.'

'And yet, beneath these skins we have so carefully stitched on,' Étienne waved at Kell's notch-collared waistcoat, then tweaked the lapel of his own more dashing suit, 'we are just as we were.' He finally lifted his pint and took a long swallow. 'Animals.'

'Maybe so. But I'm an animal with a family.'

'Ah, *oui*. How goes *ta femme*, the brave Jillian? And the small son, Andrew?'

'They're fine, both of them. The small son has a small sister or brother on the way.'

'*Félicitations.*'

Both men turned to look for the source of emphatic footfalls. Ewan Exeter, deliberately making noise as he crossed from the door to their dim corner. The noisy entrance was part courtesy, part caution. Neither Étienne nor Kell were men to be crept up on.

Exeter took the empty chair. 'I like this place.'

They all liked The Judge's Tavern. Comfortably shabby, ill-lighted, and blessed with an incurious landlord, it was under the very nose of New Scotland Yard, making it convenient for Exeter to step across from his office. The Judge's was also one of the few public houses where one of them hadn't done something to get barred during the Jacks' years. Publicans had awkwardly long memories.

None of them spoke again, waiting out the unhurried passage of Archie Fowlkes from behind the bar to their table. While he had no interest in his patrons' affairs, Archie knew what they drank, to a man, even if he hadn't seen them in years. In one knob-knuckled hand he carried a pint of bitter and, in the other, a brimming glass of whisky. He placed both carefully in front of Exeter, who nodded.

'Ta, Archibald. How're the missus and the bairns?'

'Right as rain, sir, right as rain.'

'Glad to hear it.' Exeter placed a half crown on the table and raised his whisky. 'To your very good health, Archie, and have one for yourself.'

The coin disappeared under Archie's palm. 'Cheers, gen'ulmen,' he said as soberly as the judge for whom the tavern was named. His departure, like his arrival, was unhurried, and the men at the table had to wait a good three minutes for Fowlkes to take his stance behind the bar and resume polishing it, whistling tunelessly through his teeth.

Exeter used the interval to down his whisky and drain half his ale. When he returned the pint glass to the table, it was with the exaggerated calm that told the other two men their former chieftain was a hairsbreadth from tearing the room apart.

'Dague.' The name came out like frosty breath on a cold morning. 'Or – hold on. Étienne Emmanuel DeLille Sansecours, to use the name on the eleven arrest warrants fluttering around the Yard.'

Étienne turned to Kell. 'You see, I knew he would have the exact number.'

'Felonious assault, robbery with violence, attempted bodily harm, grievous bodily harm – three counts of that. Attempted murder, forgery–'

'I was never a forger.'

'My mistake. Wouldn't want to besmirch such a spotless reputation.'

'And the robbery was yours, if you will be so kind to remember. I was merely guarding the door.'

Kell chimed in, cheerfully. 'I remember that! It was cold as brass monkeys that night and–'

'Dague.' The name was no warmer the second time Exeter said it. He reeled out the rest in his old voice, his Jack voice. 'Slouchin' back 'ere – it's a mistake. Some coves 'as pages o' form. You got the 'ole buggerin' library.'

'And that's not counting,' Kell interjected, 'the charges that followed you from Dieppe. Stripling youth that you were, you hacked off Her Majesty's Customs to the point they'd have brought back gibbeting, just for you.' He took a gulp of his drink. 'Sure you've thought this through, bruv?'

Étienne shifted his body on the tavern chair, which squealed alarmingly. 'Kindly do not insult my intelligence by suggesting I return here on a whim. A matter of importance brings me to England.'

Exeter diverted his gaze from Étienne to Kell. 'Why am I thinkin', Mr Kelly, that after our bruvver 'ere's been livin' like a monk these many years, the important matter involves a skirt?'

'Can't imagine, detective inspector. Though Jilly tells me that

Ada told her that Minerva Hawkins has been missing from Salon Sirena for weeks.'

'Stop gossiping like a pair of laundresses.' The mention of Min's name drove heat into Étienne's face and he was powerless to stop it. Perhaps his former gang associates would think the rising colour was anger. He raised his voice in aid of the fiction. '*Fils des chiens*, will you help me or not?'

The silent reply the question got drove him to his feet so abruptly the table rocked. Both Kell and Exeter grabbed their glasses.

'Hold on, you excitable moose!' Exeter barked. 'Sit down and tell us what you need.'

Étienne sat, counted silently to ten, and spoke again. 'I wish to know everything there is to know about one Charles Augustus Raeburn, the superintendent of a mad–' Étienne caught himself. 'A shelter for those suffering mental derangement. Meeth, Devonshire. The place is called Raeburn House.

'As well, since we have established that *I* am not a forger, I need the services of one.'

'What, pray tell, are you forging?' Sarcasm put a jagged edge on Exeter's tone. 'Art? Currency? Stocks and bonds?' Both he and Kell leaned forward with interest.

Étienne finished his pint, then wiped his mouth on the back of his hand. 'Letters of introduction, one in French, one in English, at least one in German. And a passport, not for travel, but to support my identity.'

Exeter's eyes narrowed, sarcasm shifting to curiosity. 'You won't be yourself, then. Who the buggerin' hell *will* you be?'

'*Monsieur le docteur Henri-Lucien Habsburg, Vicomte de Vaux.* Heir to an ancient title, sometimes lecturer at the Sorbonne. Amateur alienist and author of treatises on maniacal behaviour. Possessor of immense wealth, and son of a lunatic duke.'

Kell fell back in his chair. 'Fuck me.'

Exeter beckoned to Archie for another round. 'Listen, Dague.

Whatever daft caper you're planning, I can get eyes in my borough, even in London generally, to look the other way. But if you're handed in somewhere else–'

'I will not be handed in.' Étienne's flat declaration was followed by uneasy silence. Archie shuffled over with their drinks and the three men waited until he shuffled away again.

Exeter sighed, three parts resignation, one part doom. 'Right, then. Tell us the lot.'

CHAPTER TEN

I'm doing this for the best of all possible reasons. And because no one else will.

Min had said it over and over to herself since she'd first come up with her plan. Somehow, it rang with less conviction now that she was thirty yards and a few minutes from its realisation.

Admittedly, the plan had a few holes. Most of them were in the cloth that stretched between finding her mother and removing her from Raeburn's clutches, but she'd weave those together when she got to them.

She'd been both lucky and cursed so far. When she stepped off the early morning train in Great Torrington, the market town six miles from Raeburn House, it had taken only a handful of queries to find a cabman willing to take her to her objective. He justified his exorbitant fare by the rarity of her request.

'Niver a fare diz I get fer thik madhouse. An' niver a lady. Thought they loonies wuz all raff. One o' they yourn?' He'd sent his good eye – the other wandered and was cloudy – on a journey up and down her clothing and shoes. At the end of the inspection, Min was sure he could have estimated to the farthing what she was worth in fares.

She rewarded his impertinence with a pound note. 'You will take me there and wait while I complete my business. When you return me to Great Torrington, there will be another pound for you.'

The money sealed the cabman's mouth and imparted cheer to his mood. Less to his horse, who required the whip and a ration of verbal abuse to deliver Min to the gates of Raeburn House. She arrived an hour before her appointment with the superintendent.

The cabman let her clamber down from his rig by herself. He then drove his trap under a tree outside the gates, pulled his hat over his face, and slumped, arms crossed. Min hoped the man and the rig would be there when she was ready to leave.

She faced the pair of tall stone pillars at the drive's mouth. The heraldic beasts crouching atop them were of the warning-off variety, mouths agape and teeth showing. She bolstered her resolve by muttering Bonaparte's dictum to them. 'If you want a thing done well, do it yourself.'

She began trudging up the drive.

The drive was long, bendy, and bricked from road to house, which must have cost a fortune. The grounds seemed normal in every way, right to the drive's end, which made a neat loop in front of what even a cynic would call a fine manor. Before she got to the loop, she stepped off the drive and into a ragged circlet of trees edging the lawn. She wanted to observe Raeburn House before breaching it.

She'd never seen an asylum, not close, at any rate. It was certainly nothing like the newspaper and magazine images she'd seen of Bethlem Hospital, still popularly called Bedlam, in Moorfields. That was a colossal structure, not much different from the London Royal, from any public building.

Raeburn House was far smaller. It seemed harmonious and

staid, neither a stark contrast to the well-tended grounds nor disappearing into them. Of weathered Portland stone, it bore a central pediment at the top, some sort of escutcheon inside. An unbalanced number of bay windows marched across the ground-floor facade: two on the right, one on the left, flanking a door under a square portico.

There was a second level and an attic storey above that, with a parade of gables thrusting self-importantly out of the roof and glinting with glass panes. All the windows, even the gable ones, were shut and closely curtained. It seemed a shame on such a fine summer morning, but perhaps the side and rear windows were open to admit light and air.

Sheltering behind an ancient yew with a trunk as broad as a boat, Min listened hard for screams and raving. Nothing rewarded her effort but a warbler, cheerfully singing to itself.

If asked, she'd say Raeburn House was no different than the country manors she'd seen in Devonshire. She almost expected a gentlewoman, basket over her arm, to open the red-painted front door and greet her. *Oh, good afternoon! Do let's stroll among the roses. Afterward, we'll take tea in the drawing room.*

A speck of green, vivid against her mourning black, appeared on her forearm. A lacewing, pursuing its own affairs. She envied it, flitting thither and yon without complex errands like hers. Insect families were never troubled by members in asylums. If a lacewing went mad, it simply flew headlong into a tree or offered itself to a rising trout in a nearby stream, thinking the trout opened its mouth for conversation.

Shame gave her a sharp twinge in her midsection. She shouldn't compare her mother to an insect. Alternatively, the twinge might be due to her corset. She was laced to the point of near asphyxiation, also the high point of style. Apart from the fashionable torture of her waist, she'd divided her hair into four plaits, not her usual one. Fifty-five pins – she'd counted – held her complex coiffure in place on the crown of her head. She'd pinned

Grandmother's best bit of jewellery – a mourning brooch of onyx set in gold, with a robust diamond solitaire – at the high neck of her dress bodice. Her hat was the same she'd worn to Salon Sirena, but she'd added a coy little net at the front. Her gloves of black kid were so tight she couldn't make a fist.

All part of the plan. If she was going to hoodwink Raeburn into believing she accepted his terms, she needed to present herself as winsome, frightened, wealthy, and a bit dim.

She fancied she'd made a good start with the earnest money. And the letter, though she'd struggled for an hour to achieve the right tone.

> Raeburn, if that's your real name.
>
> You are a cruel and villainous wretch! I will under no conceivable circumstances succumb to your extortionate demands, nor will I, for one single instant, allow you to

That went into the waste can, along with her next try.

> Dear Superintendent Raeburn,
>
> Devoted as I know you must be to the relief of suffering, you are certain to acknowledge a daughter's distress, as well as the fragile condition of a patient entrusted to your care. Therefore, I ask, nay, I plead with you to

Finally, after she'd paced the carpet in her bed-sitting room nearly to the floorboards and consulted a Bradshaw for train times, she sat and composed the letter she posted the same afternoon.

Dear sir,

I agree to your proposal, stipulating only that I visit the dowager countess and confirm her well-being beforehand. Consider the notes enclosed, in the sum of fifty pounds, a pledge of my agreement. I shall visit Raeburn House on Tuesday instant, at ten o'clock in the morning.

Respectfully

Respectfully, who? The room had whirled for a few seconds, as though it and life as she knew it were being sucked away by a cyclone, leaving her suspended in a vacuum. Who was she now? Min Hawkins, corset-maker? Minerva Langworth, daughter of an earl? Lady Dunmara, lost Scottish heiress?

In the end, she'd signed as the person she might always feel she was. Minerva Hawkins. Abandoned child of a mother she never knew. A young woman from Devonshire, more familiar with country lanes than London streets. A *corsetière*, just back from France where...

Now wasn't the time to remember what had and hadn't happened in France.

The small watch dangling on a chain clipped to her skirt gave her just two minutes before her appointment with Superintendent and Chief Blackmailer C. Augustus Raeburn. She patted her hair to make sure she wasn't wearing any stray leaves or lacewings. Taking the deepest breath her corset would allow, she crossed the lawn to the asylum steps.

CHAPTER ELEVEN

'He won't kill her, will he?' Jillian directed the question to Kell, but her eyes stayed on Étienne Sansecours and Evangeline Broussard, locked in conversation a dozen yards up the alley behind Salon Sirena.

'Not unless she lies to him.' His mouth quirked as Jillian's head snapped toward him, her mouth falling open. 'Just a joke, Jilly. Dague's never harmed a woman.'

Kell redirected his gaze to the talking couple, their heads close together, hands jabbing and weaving. French talking, then. Not really a point to the way they'd put themselves out of earshot, Kell's French being limited to a few ripe insults he'd learned from Étienne in the Jack years.

Jillian's fretful sigh told him she wasn't reassured. 'All this would be easier if I'd found Min in Devonshire, where she'd told Ada and the rest she was going to finish sorting her grandparents' estate.'

'You're absolutely sure she's not there?'

'Yes, husband, I'm sure. Little Farnleigh's not exactly a metropolis. Unless Min was hiding in a hayrick for the entire day, she's not there. Villagers keep an eye out for the comings and goings of their own, you know. "Her wiz here and gwine in days, then naight a sight of her fer weeks." That's what the butcher said.'

Kell nodded and they both looked toward Evie and her large interrogator. 'Did anyone question why you were asking about her?'

'Fewer questions than if *he'd*–' she jutted her chin toward Dague '–turned up there. The butcher wondered out loud why a London cousin didn't just post a letter. I embroidered my story a bit, told him I had written twice, but Min hadn't replied.

'If her post is being held at the post office in the village shop, everyone will soon know that's not true. Those postmistresses aren't known for being overly discreet.' Her eyes darted to Étienne. '*He*'s certainly in a lather.'

Kell nodded glumly. Jillian paid a moment's wifely attention to his tie, straightening the knot. If he lived to a hundred, he'd never grow tired of her little ways, the ones reminding him he was a husband and loved. He tucked a wayward strand of her copper hair behind her ear. 'You'll be the talk of Little Farnleigh for a while.'

'I'm unimpressed. From what I gathered, the most interesting news before my visit was Goram, the ploughman's horse, dropping dead between the shafts.'

'Min's grandfather... His death didn't make a stir?'

Jillian shook her head. 'Widespread opinion was that he was ancient and overdue for it. Loud and pious proclamations of dismay, of course, followed by whispered assertions that he was a mean-spirited old jackdaw who'd shucked off the mortal coil not a day too soon.'

Because he was lost in his wife's green eyes, Kell missed the sudden silence when Dague and Evie stopped Frenchiversing at each other. The nearing of his fellow Jack's heavy footsteps, along with a voice made huskier than usual by emotion, brought him back.

'She has gone to Raeburn House.'

Jillian emitted a low cry. 'The *asylum?*'

Kell took her hand. 'We've no secrets, Dague. And I wasn't going to let Jilly go to Devon without knowing the whole story. What you told me, I told her.'

The big man nodded. He'd taken off his derby hat and held it in one hand. The other raked through his hair and left it uncharacteristically mussed. Except in the middle of a fight, Kell had never seen Dague anything less than perfectly groomed.

'*Je vais la suivre maintenant.*' A headshake and a correction in English. 'I go to follow her, now.'

'I can–'

'No.' Dague's hand fell heavily on Kell's shoulder. 'You will stay here, with your *bonne femme* and your child.' He smiled down at Jillian, the swelling of her belly testing the powers of her maternity corset. 'Children.' The derby went back on the disordered hair. 'I need the forged documents. Quickly.'

'If old Simon Kaan can't get to them straight away, they'll be worth the wait. Wych Street, over The Oyster. You'll find him in, I reckon. He's not left his mouldy digs in forty years.'

CHAPTER TWELVE

When it came to getting her from the door of Raeburn House to the superintendent, the asylum was a pattern of efficiency. A thin, solemn-faced wardress in a starched apron over a gown the same grey as the exterior walls, answered the first ring of the bell.

Efficiency was just what Min had in mind. She had not the slightest inclination toward *What a fine day* or *Such charming grounds you have here*.

'I'm here to see Mr Raeburn.'

The wardress' reply was a cool nod.

Six steps into the lofty entrance hall, she was transfixed by a pool of colour-shot light on the marble floor. The source was a chandelier, broad as a bed and dripping with pendant bobs, tiers of them. Prisms were scattered on the tiles like coins tossed by a monarch.

Her anger flared and sparked. Raeburn bought crystal light fixtures with the money he bled from his victims.

She silently fumed until a discreet cough brought her back to her mission. The wardress paced away and she hurried after. They halted at a stately mahogany door, half open. A gleaming brass doorknob was matched by a plaque. The plaque read *C. Augustus Raeburn, Superintending Surgeon*.

His consulting room, then. Peering through the opening, she saw a broad space with windows overlooking the park. Might have been a parlour when the house was a house and not some place to hide unbalanced relatives. A man sat at a majestic desk under the windows, reading a newspaper. The wardress tapped lightly on the door and the man looked up. His eyes met hers.

'Lady Dunmara!'

It was her first time being addressed that way in person. Like all first times it was disorienting. She nearly asked, *Who?*

The man who rose behind the desk was middle-aged, of middle height, preceded by a middling paunch. Tugging down a striped silk waistcoat, he thrust his arms into a dark coat he pulled from his chair back. Pomaded waves of thick blond hair, fading into grey, framed a genial, jowly face, made broader by grey-blond side whiskers. His stock was blindingly white, the stick pin surmounted by an emerald. He rushed toward her, smiling, and threw the door wide.

Playing a role, Min thought. *Kind uncle greets niece come home for holiday.*

'Please forgive my negligent attire.' A courteous nod, the straightening of cuffs that revealed heavy gold links. 'I was so embroiled in my work that I lost track of time.'

Work? Min glanced behind him. Apart from the newspaper, the desk was as empty as the Sahara. When she brought her gaze back to Raeburn, she went momentarily mute. What was the protocol for greeting one's blackmailer? She strove for the same tone as her letter: curt but courteous.

'Mr Raeburn.' Well done. Steady voice. Slight incline of the head. Nothing so severe as the 'brow of woe', but a grave, no-nonsense expression. 'I should like to–'

'See your mother, of course, of course. Nothing finer.'

Such bonhomie. She'd had no idea extortion was such a cheerful profession.

'Right this way.' He gestured her out of the room and into a narrow hall that passed along and behind the main staircase.

Getting right to it. That suited Min. Unfortunately, getting to it seemed to involve a lot of walking. Down the hall to the back of the house they went, stopping at the foot of a narrow, uncarpeted flight of stairs.

Raeburn waved Min up, so up she went. And up. Still up. Every tread increased her fear that her mother was housed in some airless chamber at the top of the house, as in a Gothic novel. *Countess in the Attic.*

At the second landing, Raeburn pushed past to beckon her through a narrow door. She found herself in a carpeted upper corridor.

Lushly carpeted, forsooth. Red Turkey, thick and spotlessly clean, muffled their footfalls as they passed one, two, three doors. At the fourth, Raeburn halted and pulled a ring of keys from his coat pocket.

Before she could remind her mouth that she'd decided to be frightened and winsome, she blurted, 'You lock them in?'

'Our friends are not *incarcerated.*'

Friends. A kinder word than some others she'd feared he might use.

'When we feel we must prevent their egress, it is only to ensure their safety and comfort. Take the countess. If left to her own devices, she *wanders.*'

The shocked inflection he gave the word suggested she stripped naked and danced on the lawn.

After quite a lot of attention, the lock gave a loud click and Raeburn rotated the handle, pushing the door inward.

With the same contrived cheer as in his consulting room, he announced, 'Lady Amica Langworth, the dowager countess of Dunmara.'

CHAPTER THIRTEEN

The sitting room was small and well-appointed in a characterless way, like a good commercial hotel. Rose and trellis wallpaper, two gaslight sconces with etched glass shades: both conventional. The sofa and chairs and table lamps, the hearth with a brass fire screen and a bisque chateau rug in front: all unremarkable. The drapes framing the one window were faded red velour, the colour of bricks exposed to the sun for fifty years. Madame would have dismissed it as too dull for her dullest corset design. All the furnishings were clean but unlovely, as though they'd been purchased as a job lot.

In a chair by the window – a barred window, not visible from the front of the house – sat a woman. A dressing gown of soft white lawn, gathered under the bust in the style of the first quarter of the century, fell past her feet and puddled on the floor. The colour was more usual on a young woman, but the smooth innocence of the face above it somehow made it appropriate. If pressed, Min would guess the woman's age as near forty. But if that were true...

Min was twenty-four. Even if the countess had birthed her at sixteen... But no, that was hardly credible, since the countess, according to Raeburn's letter, had suffered several stillbirths before her last and unlikely surviving infant.

'She seems,' she began tentatively, 'terribly young.'

'Of course, she's young!' Raeburn snapped. 'You must understand something,' he adjusted his tone to the amiability he'd exhibited earlier. 'The earl had the most ardent hopes for an heir. Infant deaths being so prevalent and no guarantee of male offspring... well, my goodness. Any man in his position wishes for a young wife whose fertility will span a decade or more.'

'But in Scotland, as you told me in your letter, a daughter may inherit a title.'

'Yes, but who wants that?' The superintendent seemed to realise he'd maligned her and hastened to revise. 'That is to say, that which is possible is not always that which is desirable.' He lowered his voice conspiratorially. 'Scots, you know. Heroic notions from the past. All their leaders are supposed to be William Wallace, claymores aloft, war cries ringing.'

She just avoided rolling her eyes. The topic of succession could be tabled, for now, if only to stave off more fractured folklore.

And also because she wanted Raeburn to stop blathering so she could speak with the singular woman before her. Her face was pale and luminous as a pearl, a perfect oval under an unbound wilderness of auburn hair, streaks of white running through it like water over rocks.

My mother. She is my mother. Thinking it was enough to smother her doubts about the woman's age. After a lifetime of being without kith and kin, she might be steps from reunion with the woman who'd borne her. Joy and fear assailed her.

For a long minute, she and the woman stared at each other, speechless. At least, Min stared. The woman's limpid blue gaze skimmed over her and then wandered the room, as perplexed as someone lost in a London fog. Was that door the inlet to Curzon Street? Could the sofa be the costermonger's stall on Berwick?

She had to get closer. Spotting another chair, she rushed to pull it toward the woman, but Raeburn charged forward with a 'Please allow me!'

As he settled the chair opposite his 'friend', she noted a flicker of movement in the white-clad body. Nothing so definitive as a recoil, not even a flinch. Just a start, accompanied by the sudden drop of the woman's head. Her hands twisted in her lap. With a slight shock, Min noted they were gloved. Who wore gloves with a dressing gown? Was it some mad conceit?

The gloves were white like the gown, nicely crocheted, but not of the fineness one might expect on a countess. The woman's thumb and forefinger worried a tiny, thread-wound button at one wrist.

Having discharged his gentlemanly duty with the chair, Raeburn began a purposeless pottering about the chamber. He kept up a muttered, mostly inaudible commentary as he patted the bare mantel – she presumed a fear of hurled projectiles kept it that way – and levelled two bland landscape paintings. He opened the second door in the room, which Min supposed went into the bedroom, looked in, and shut it.

Drat it all, why wouldn't he leave? The last thing she wanted was a pair of extortionate ears listening to every question, making note of every answer. She'd no sooner thought it, when the same wardress who'd admitted her entered the room and murmured something to Raeburn. He responded with an irritated cluck, waving the wardress away.

'No rest for the weary,' he moaned, misquoting Isaiah forty-eight, verse two. 'It's like this all day, ceaseless interruptions and bother. Do continue your visit with the countess, my lady. She's perfectly harmless, though–' he chuckled, 'you won't get a sensible word out of her.' At the door, he ducked his head briefly. 'I'll be just a few minutes.'

Thank you, heavenly hosts. He'd left the door ajar.

She rose and tiptoed to it. Widening the gap, she pulled back with a gasp. A burly attendant was just outside, leaning against the corridor's opposite wall. Arms crossed and mouth grim, he trained his black eyes on her like a hunting dog on a quail.

'Oh, good!' she giggled breathlessly. 'I was hoping the superintendent had left a–a–' It felt awful to say it. 'Minder.'

She pushed the door until the latch clicked, then waited behind it for a count of twenty. No noises from the hall, so the attendant didn't object to the closed door. Why would he? He didn't care if she and the inmate were shut in, only if the inmate tried to get *out*.

At least, a closed door gave her a chance to converse privately with the countess. And to get a better look at her eyes. There was something familiar about them, familiar but strange. Like a thing she'd once known well, now altered in memory.

She took the chair. 'My lady, I am Minerva Hawkins.' Their knees were only a few inches apart, but for all the woman acknowledged her nearness, she might have been in the hallway with the minder. 'Have you ever heard my name?'

Starting off like a featherhead, Min. If she hadn't been seen since her birth, how would the woman know her name?

'I am twenty-four years of age.'

No response. The blue eyes wandered again.

'I am employed as a staymaker, a *corsetière*, in London.' Extraneous information, but she had to push the one-sided chat along.

'Until five years ago, I lived in a village called Little Farnleigh. It's not too far away. Do you know it?' *Why didn't you ask if she knows Peking or Timbuctoo?*

'I am– I was an orphan. As a child, I was cared for by a couple I called my grandparents. Asa and Mary Hawkins.'

'Mairi.' The word came out as a dry husk, and in such a pronounced Scots burr that at first Min thought the countess was just clearing her throat. Its impact, when she finally understood what she'd heard, was like a blow to the chest.

'*Mah*-ree.' She copied the Scots intonation. 'That was my

grandmother's name, Mairi MacDonald. Once she became Asa Hawkins's wife she went by Mary. Do you know her? She was from...'

She stalled. Where was Grandmother from? She'd not been given to misty-eyed recollections of her origins, mentioning them only twice that Min could recall. 'The southwestern coast of Scotland?'

Was that a nod from the woman opposite? Such a slight movement, so vague. It could've signified *Yes, I know it* or *I've seen it on a map* or nothing at all.

The only reaction she'd got thus far was to Grandmother's name, so she returned to it. 'Are you a kinswoman of Mairi MacDonald, my lady? Are you of her family?'

Nothing. Not even a glimmer of recognition.

She might be going at the problem of identity the wrong way. It might help to first determine if the woman was truly a countess. Just how was she supposed to do that? Was there an examination for countesses?

While the questions went round and round in her head, she couldn't help but keep her eyes on the agitated hands of the woman in white. Constantly twisting and chafing, her fingers worried at the thread-wound buttons of her gloves.

'Do they bother you?' Min reached across and carefully unfastened one button, then worked off the glove. What she saw, when the skin beneath was bared, made her breath catch.

Red, rough, and callused, the hand could have belonged to a farmer's wife in Little Farnleigh. Certainly, it wasn't the hand of a gentlewoman, whose most demanding daily labour would be embroidery or flower arranging. Swiftly but gently, Min unbuttoned and removed the other glove.

Both the woman's hands were battered and nearly raw with ill-use.

A notion so bizarre it might have come from an inmate of

Raeburn House slid into her thoughts. Hands notwithstanding, if the woman facing her was a countess, she would speak French.

Min had learned it in the schoolroom. It was one of Asa Hawkins' few pretensions to class. He liked to distance himself from what, with curled lip, he called 'the labouring folk of Little Farnleigh,' by insisting she study gentlewomanly arts: elocution, watercolour painting, playing the piano. French. A certain winemaker didn't think much of her mastery of it, but she could surely dredge up a phrase and say it correctly.

She gently tapped the knee of the woman opposite to get her attention. '*Madame la comtesse, êtes-vous heureuse ici?*'

It would have eased her heart to know whether the woman was happy here, but the question got even less response than the ones she'd asked about Mary Hawkins and Scotland. Not proof positive, any more than the hands were, but she was inclined to think that if the woman was a countess, Min was Florence Nightingale.

A half dozen objections crowded her brain, of course. Perhaps insanity had affected the countess' memory. Perhaps she was one of those rare gentlewomen who'd not followed the canon of her class and learned French. Perhaps her illness had led her to abuse her hands in some way, through excessive washing or some other mania. Perhaps Min should have asked her to perform a court curtsey or dance the quadrille. *Perhaps perhaps perhaps...*

Perhaps the woman wasn't a countess but *was* Min's mother. That would leave Raeburn's demand for her maintenance intact but deprive Min of any way to meet it. Corset makers were renowned for not having fifteen thousand a year.

Whether or not the woman was her mother, it left the disturbing question of the whereabouts of Amica Joan Langworth, the dowager countess who was listed as an inmate of Raeburn House. She pushed to the side a half dozen frightening thoughts of where she might be. First, she must deal with the white-gowned imposter, who'd slipped back into torpor.

Who *was* she, with her Scots intonation, her strange but familiar blue eyes?

'Well, now, how are you and the countess getting along?' Without a knock, Raeburn noisily bustled into the room.

Min took her time coming to her feet. She brushed down her skirt and adjusted her veil, keeping her gaze down. She needed a minute to get her face under control. It wasn't the opportune time to glare at Raeburn for the tent-sized wool he was trying to pull over her eyes.

When she was sure her expression was bland, she waved airily toward the slumped and apparently dozing woman in the chair. 'You're right, she makes very little sense. And I believe my visit has tired her. I should return another time.'

'Assuredly, you should and you may! Now that we've established the terms of her ladyship's care, I'm sure you will be a regular visitor.' Raeburn held open the door, his free hand gesturing Min through it. He didn't spare a backward glance at the seated figure by the window. 'Just give us a little notice, if you wouldn't mind. She has good days and bad ones.'

'As do we all,' Min said tersely, moving out of the room.

And very soon, you'll be having the worst day of your life, you weasel.

Chapter Fourteen

A full day after Kell assured Étienne that 'they'll be worth the wait,' Simon Kaan had still not finished the forged documents. Worth it or not, Étienne stood close to the thin old man who was bent over a table, back to a window. Light from the window illumined a room so crowded and chaotic he could not believe the forger could find his own hands, much less the supplies needed to replicate vital documents.

He knew it was probably harming his cause to glower, but he couldn't shake the presentiment of time running out. 'How much longer to copy the–'

'I am not a copyist.' Kaan did not look up from the German letter on which he laboured, thick spectacles perched on the very end of his long nose. 'Any fool can copy. I am a *feiner Künstler*, a fine artist. One who does not appreciate the humid breath of a giant upon his work. Sit!' Kaan pointed with his dip pen at a chair some feet away, the seat covered with books and, atop them, a tray bearing a crusty cup and a chunk of bread. The bread might have been fresh when Hadrian's Wall was built.

Étienne picked up the lot and moved it to the narrow bed

against the wall, where it joined a scatter of other books and a sleeping calico cat.

The forger kept talking. 'To copy demands no talent and no finesse. A fool with good eyes and a fresh nib can produce a credible facsimile of the Magna Carta. An automaton could do it. The work I do is of infinite subtlety.' He picked up a magnifying glass and peered through it at the paper over which his pen hovered. 'This letter, for example.' He put aside the glass and touched his pen to the paper again. 'It is pure fiction, worthy of a great novelist. Alexandre Dumas or Charles Dickens.'

Étienne settled carefully onto the chair. It gave a sharp little scream and a crack, which he ignored. He was accustomed to the complaints of furniture when it met the challenge of his body.

'To make this so-credible forgery of a letter from a professor at the *Humboldt-Universität zu Berlin*, where you, most fancifully,' Kaan looked sceptically at Étienne over his glasses, 'have lectured as a visiting scholar, I write in the language and with all the pompous exactitude of your senior colleague.' He laid aside his pen and plucked off his *pince-nez*. Pressing his fingers to his eyes, he spoke behind his hand. 'Herr Professor Günther E.B. von Bayern considers himself Germany's foremost proponent of the inherited insanity theory. He admits a grudging admiration for your monograph, *'Les conséquences de l'abandon'*, on the role of orphaning in madness. The professor notes, in his letter of introduction, that your study is remarkably well-reasoned and persuasive, considering you are an amateur.'

Kaan carefully replaced his *pince-nez*. 'Von Bayern writes in High Prussian, a formal dialect in which I have vast fluency. Fortunately for your other documents, my pen is likewise fluent in multiple forms of English, French, Italian, and Dalmatian.' He picked up his pen. 'I blush to admit I use a dictionary for the last, but calls for forged Dalmatian documents are very rare and it hardly matters.'

Étienne's sigh was so loud the cat woke, widening its eyes at him.

Kaan clucked irritably. 'Your presence is distracting and oppressive. Take yourself for some hours to the library of the Royal College of Surgeons in Lincoln's Inn Fields. My documents will get you in the door of this asylum you wish to penetrate, but you must inform yourself about insanity well enough to pass through and out with your identity intact and your awkwardly large body free of a strait waistcoat.' He took more ink from a bottle and wiped the excess on a spattered rag. 'When you return, bring me a pigeon pie, two boiled eggs, and a quart of beer. You will not subtract the cost from my fee, which will be immense.'

The chair screamed again as Étienne stood to leave the room.

CHAPTER FIFTEEN

'You received the letter first.'

'That's correct.' Min shifted uneasily on the chair. It was the hard wooden specie, but she was happy to have it. She hadn't been told she was in an interview room, but what else could it be, with no furnishings except an ugly table and two chairs? An undraped square high in the wall admitted just enough light to deserve its name of window. It had poultry wire on the outside. Clearly, people in the room were not here for the view.

She'd been in the poky constabulary at Great Torrington for over an hour, and had reeled out her story to Constables Jervis, Amory, and Hill in succession. At last, she'd gotten the attention of the chief constable, Major Fitzsimmons. He narrowed his eyes at her now.

'The short note arrived a day later?' he asked.

'It did.'

'Both were posted to Little Farnham.'

'Farnleigh.' The village was admittedly a flyspeck, but it was in the chief constable's district. She'd have thought he'd know its name. 'My grandparents, that is, the couple I always thought were my grandparents, owned a smallholding there.'

'And they are both deceased.'

'Yes.'

He had the typewritten note pinched between thumb and forefinger and held it up. 'This is the only demand that's been made? No wires, no approaches through a confederate, no contact with other members of your family? Anything like that?'

She shook her head tiredly. 'I haven't any other family and no, just the note.'

Fitzsimmons paced. It was a small room. The pacing took him a few feet beyond the ugly table where she sat. Back again. Repeatedly.

She occupied the time feeling idiotic. Assigning idiocy to herself was becoming a habit, lately.

Fitzsimmons stopped pacing and propped one hip on the nearest corner of the table. It was as if a stork perched there. He was tall, thin, and very closely shaved. His jaw was granite, but he had a beaky nose. A great heron of a man, in a tweed suit so countrified it made him appear he was off to a shooting party.

'The note.' Fitzsimmons held it up again, to what light there was. 'There's really nothing that says it's a demand.'

She didn't want to seem uncooperative, but he hadn't asked a question and, if he had, she didn't think it deserved an answer. Of course, the note was a demand. How could he not see that?

He laid the note on the table and stared at it. They both did, as though it might magically turn into a candle or a dove.

'Not a thing,' Fitzsimmons finally observed, 'that links the note to the letter, as far as I can tell.'

That was, indeed, a problem. One of several to which she probably should have given more thought before she barged through the constabulary door. She could hardly tell the chief constable that her intuition told her Raeburn had written both the letter and the note. Or say that her visit to Raeburn House confirmed – to her – that her intuition was right. Fraud as flagrant as the Fiji Mermaid underpinned both.

If she did say either, Fitzsimmons would give her an indulgent smile and a pat on the shoulder. *Intuition, is it, my dear? Ah, how we do love the ladies and their feathery little heads.*

He picked up the letter. 'The woman to whom the letter refers. The Countess of Dunmara. *Is* she a countess?'

'No. That is, I don't see how she could be.' *Because she has hands like a dock worker, among other signs.*

'And is she your mother?'

'I... I don't believe so, but...'

'But you are not certain.'

Certain? Her hour at Raeburn House had gone by so fast. Whirled around by shock, confusion, and anger, she'd not done the one thing that she ought to have done: shown the 'countess' her sun-and-moon pendant. Not, considering the state the woman was in, that she'd necessarily have recognised the jewellery. And if she had, what would that have said?

It was all so confusing. Where was the real countess? Was the real countess, wherever she was, her mother? If not, did Raeburn know who her mother was, where she was? Was the woman she'd met related to Mairi-Mary Hawkins?

Could she get her fifty pounds back?

'No, I am not certain, Major.'

He nodded sagely and seemed to ponder her answer for a long minute. Then, he asked what she surely should have anticipated his asking before she set a foot over the doorsill of the constabulary.

'Did you not think to present this problem to the police before now?'

'I– it... the note said no police. I was uneasy about consequences. And I couldn't be sure anything in the letter was true. I felt I should visit the asylum and see for myself before I did anything else.'

'Bit risky, don't you think? To go there alone.'

I see you know my friend in France, Major. 'Perhaps.' She sat straighter, trying to ease the jab of her corset busk into her abdomen. 'I came away unscathed, as you see.'

'You're very brave.' At least, Fitzsimmons gave her credit for courage. More than Étienne had. Somehow, the compliment didn't please her as much as she thought it should. A week after leaving France, she'd managed to do just about everything Étienne told her not to do.

'Rum business, though.' Fitzsimmons said it as he folded her papers together the way they'd been when she'd pulled them out of her handbag. He didn't return them, just tucked them into the inside pocket of his jacket.

Should she have told him the papers he had were copies, the originals hidden in her London room? Overall, she thought not. At least in that, she and Étienne were of one mind. *You are wise to make copies. The police will wish to retain the originals.*

The chief constable smiled and stood. 'Let me see if I can find you a cup of tea.' Eyes twinkling kindly over his beaky nose, he left the room.

She tugged up her watch. Nearly one o'clock. She'd offered the hackney cab driver – *may he acquire piles* – a shilling to wait for her while she conducted her police business, but he'd merely laughed. How much longer would this conference at the constabulary last?

And then, what? If nothing came of this chat with the chief constable, she'd be in the same fix she was when she'd arrived earlier today.

Hole in the plan, hole in the plan.

Not that it had been much of a plan to start with. Just a vague scheme to spirit her mother out of an asylum. The scheme suggested she'd read too many novels of intrigue. In them, there were always proofs of identity, bribable servants, a rear exit, a dash for the stables, and a convenient horse or two.

The only two servants she'd seen were the unsmiling wardress and the fierce-looking minder. Neither one looked like the sort of adaptable lackey who would stitch up the master for a few guineas. On her way up the back stairs, she'd glanced over her shoulder to note the long rear hall ended in a door. It might have led to stables. Or a tennis court or a maze or a piggery. Armoured with locks and bars, the door looked as unyielding as the windows she'd seen at the side and back of the house. As to her mother's identity, or the countess's...

How had she thought she and whomever the inmate was would get out? Fly up a chimney like the fairy in that French ballet?

She fidgeted on the wooden chair. Her corset was getting more uncomfortable by the minute. The pins holding her hair in place had turned into tiny rats and were chewing her scalp. She worked a finger into her collar and adjusted the ribbon holding her pendant. Pendants, plural. The ones belonging to her and her mother.

Who was still unknown, in an unknown place. Alive or dead, also unknown, but she just couldn't bear thinking about that.

It continued to rankle that before her daft scheme, she'd had a better one: securing Étienne Sansecours' help. He was the expert, after all. Housebreaking and kidnap were probably no more challenging for him than a round of Snakes and Ladders.

But Étienne wasn't here and any second the chief constable would be back, wanting to swap a cup of tea for more answers.

On that uncomfortable thought, Fitzsimmons entered the room with her tea. The questions began before he even placed it on the table.

'Miss Hawkins, will you accompany me to Raeburn House? I believe we can sort this business straight away. Will you do that?'

She hadn't expected that. She didn't know much about policing, but she thought members of the public were not usually participants in enforcement. Perhaps she was 'helping the police with their enquiries'.

The chief constable put the tea in front of her. It was milky, which she didn't like.

'Here's the thing, Miss Hawkins. Mr Raeburn is rather a fixture around here. Respected, admired, even. And the asylum has always conducted its business quietly. No fuss, no alarms. No complaints.'

Until yours, he needn't have added.

He patted the breast of his tweedy jacket. 'My guess is that there's some misunderstanding involved with these communications. I know you've had a trying morning. But if you'll agree to visit the place just once more, with me as your escort, I'm confident we can set everything right.'

Before she answered, she took a gulp of the tea. It was tepid and heavily sugared. She'd missed lunch and the mug appeared to be all she'd get for now. Perhaps policemen were too manly for biscuits.

She forced down the syrupy liquid and tried to smile. 'Yes, of course, Major. I'll accompany you to Raeburn House.'

CHAPTER SIXTEEN

'Vicious little shrew bit me.' Fitzsimmons was wrapping a handkerchief around his hand. He put out a booted foot and gave her limp body a sharp nudge, as though confirming that a badger one has walloped is truly dead.

Through her pain, she thought *B.G.K.*, with satisfaction. In Jillian's course of self-defence at the Lady Pugilist's Academy, biting, gouging, and kicking were called the First Line. She might now be lying on the floor of a room at Raeburn House, but she'd done damage to the man who put her there.

'Unpleasant, I'm sure,' Raeburn snapped, 'but did you have to be so rough with her?'

She kept her eyes half-closed and her body leaden as the superintendent bent down to clutch her chin, turning her head from side to side. Revulsion rippled through her. The graze of his fingers on her inflamed jaw made her want to scream, but she settled for moaning and tucking in her head, her undamaged cheek pressed against the scratchy carpet.

Raeburn clucked with annoyance. 'I was hoping to marry a woman not quite so damaged.'

'Marry her? I thought she'd agreed to the maintenance.'

Raeburn squatted next to her, balanced on toes and fingertips like a spider, and Min felt the gorge rise in her throat at his smell. Wool suiting, imperfectly washed skin, and sweat, all overlaid with heavy cologne. Stomach acid burned the back of her throat, and she battled it down. She dared not retch. Her captors must continue to think her too groggy and cowed for further resistance.

'She agreed before she got too clever and tumbled to "the countess, your mother" being someone else entirely.' Raeburn rose with a crackle of knee joints. 'And before you planted your fist in her face.'

'At what point did *you* develop such refined sensibilities?'

'At the point, you fool, that we let a countess die of pneumonia. Once she was dead, only a single visit by Earl Dunmara stood between us and prison.'

'I'd be careful whom you called a fool, Charlie.' Fitzsimmons' drawl had an edge of threat in it. The scritch of a vesta on a striker followed, then the quick, sharp odour of sulphur and, more slowly, a whiff of pipe tobacco. 'Langworth was a bigamist. He knew it, we knew it. Only our discretion and his wealth kept all of us out of the clink.'

'And you call yourself a chief constable. It's highly unlikely an earl would go to prison, at least not for having two wives at once. Definitely not years after one is in her grave.

'The second wife was the only one Langworth fretted over, anyway. A flawless beauty from a flawless family, that one. But her fortune was controlled by her father, wise man. Right to the altar and beyond. Putting aside the scandal, do you think Langworth would've gotten close to the dowry if Papa found out his prospective son-in-law had a wife in a madhouse, a possible heir inside her?'

Silence and tobacco made the room feel close for a minute, and then Raeburn spoke again. 'A timely reminder, Fitz. The earl courted trouble if he was found out, but you and I were the ones in danger from the law. We still are.'

The click of a watchcase opening and closing followed Raeburn's remark. 'Our little prize will be fine where she is, for the moment. I've a foreign colleague arriving shortly and must get downstairs to greet him.'

Not in a rush, though. Another interval of silence passed, with only the subtle sounds of Fitzsimmons drawing on his pipe. With her head bowed and her eyelids barely cracked, Min could see only the shoes and trouser hems of the two men. She had a crawling sense they were examining her. Head to toe. Was it possible to repent dressing well? She did.

'Don't you look lovely, dearie!' a woman in the seat next to her had twittered when she'd boarded the crack-of-dawn train to Great Torrington. What she would give now to be in an unlovely nun's habit.

Finally, more sounds and fresh movement. Both men walking, shoes brushing the carpet. A door opening, Raeburn talking again. 'Complications aside, our countess is dead and the earl, too. But as a wife, the daughter's worth both of them together.'

'The notch she took out of my hand says she won't go to the altar without a fight.'

'If she's resistant to reason, a few weeks in the shed with the loobies will soften her. An ice bath or two, perhaps some electric shock. I've a new appliance and am eager to try it on someone not likely to die at the first jolt. She'll come round to the idea, eventually. And once we're wed, all that's hers is mine.'

'*Ours*,' Fitzsimmons said, his voice faint through the closing door.

Chapter Seventeen

Mid-afternoon sunlight flooded the consulting room, making it easy for him to assess the expression on C. Augustus Raeburn's face. The superintendent was in an anxious mood. Étienne's had been getting blacker and blacker for the past week, so he did not care whether Raeburn continued to frown over the letters of introduction, burst into tears, or throw himself from the roof. The last would simplify matters enormously, but one should not expect Greek drama from an English dog.

Whatever resolution awaited, it would be the first and last time he would stand in the man's *sanctum sanctorum*, pretending to be a French alienist and a viscount.

'Uh, my German is not...' Raeburn's voice wavered, then strengthened. 'I've had no reason to employ the language since my days at university. Devonshire's not exactly on the Grand Tour, ha-ha.'

But of course. The superintendent could not translate the elegant High Prussian for which Simon Kaan had demanded from Étienne a bloody fortune. Raeburn had made a pretence of reading the French document, the one from the *Pitié-Salpêtrière Hospital* in Paris, but Étienne would wager he had learned nothing from it. It could have been an introduction or a laundry list.

It was unsurprising that the man's education left him deficient in languages. And in other things, as a boy educated on the parish would be. That was just one of the many interesting things Ewan Exeter's helpful research had uncovered.

He strolled to the window behind Raeburn's desk. Loomed there, as Min would say. The view of lawn and woods pleased him, almost as much as it pleased him to know it unnerved Raeburn to have his light blocked by an enormity of muscle.

Time to advance the plot. He did so without turning from the view.

'*Eh, bien*, you do not read the letters from my colleagues in France and Germany.' His drawl was the quintessence of bored nobility and tried patience. 'But you are aware, I presume, of *Die Herren* Sigmund Freud and Josef Breuer?' The hurried scrape and drag of Raeburn's chair said the superintendent had turned it around and was facing his visitor's back.

Smiling grimly, Étienne spun from the window to bend over the man in the chair, who gasped.

'*Der Psychoanalyse!*' he trumpeted into Raeburn's face. 'That is what they call their new field of study. It is no secret, even to alienists in the wilds of Devonshire who read only English. In a series of articles in Britain's own *Journal of Mental Science*–'

'I-I don't have much t-time for medical journals.' Raeburn waved a shaky hand. 'Managing a madhouse–'

Étienne howled like a man with toothache. 'Do not, I pray you, use that word! It is more than archaic. It is medieval. A survivor of the rack and the thumbscrew.'

Nom de Dieu, this was amusing. If he had not needed to get on with finding Min, he would do this all day. Now that he had shaken the superintendent like a jar of beans, it was time to change his approach. A tiny calibration. The length of a leg on a flea.

With one hand, Étienne plucked off his eyeglasses – a gold pair with clear lenses he'd purchased especially for this role – and with the other he extracted his handkerchief – one of his own, fine linen with a rolled edge.

'Let us discuss insanity as the colleagues we are, *hein*?' With calm deliberation, he left the window and circled the desk. It was a ridiculously large desk and he took his time, polishing his eyeglasses as he went. The circumnavigation forced Raeburn to scrape and drag in a rotation of his chair again.

'My forthcoming study – you will find it most interesting – concerns types of insanity as they are found in institutional settings. I shall include case studies from six asylums in Britain.' He held up the spectacles, frowned, and returned to polishing them. 'And six alienists, of which you are one.

'The list was composed with the help of my good friend and colleague, Dr Thomas Bond, of Westminster Hospital.'

'*Thomas Bond?*' Raeburn all but sprang from his chair with excitement. 'The examiner of the Jack the Ripper victims?'

'The very one, although the lurid press surrounding the murders obscured the subtle character of my friend's work.' He plucked an eyeglass case from an inside pocket of his coat. Like the glasses, the case had been commissioned for the role. Of smooth dark leather, the coat of arms in gold leaf on the lid gleamed softly. The red silk velvet interior was exposed when he opened the case to place his spectacles inside. He kept the lid up long enough to make sure Raeburn appreciated it. *Wealth*, it all said, and *rank*.

As did his flawless suit, the heavy signet ring on his left hand, the gleaming shoes and exquisite tie. *In summa*, a tempting array of possibilities for a greedy parvenu. A man born Charlie Ruggs in a riverside tumbledown in West Yorkshire.

Precise as any surgeon probing a wound for a bullet, Étienne edged closer to the point of his too-long morning in this particular parvenu's company. 'My friend's best work, I maintain, is the typology of the criminally insane. I so often tell him, "Thom," – you will understand, we are long-time intimates and address each other in familiar fashion– "Thom, you are one of the few who appreciates that only those who are charged with the daily care of lunatics can understand the workings of...'"

He broke off to lift the lid of a garishly gilded cigar box on Raeburn's desk. With a short sniff of disdain, he closed the box and finished, "'Their minds.'"

'Thomas Bond,' repeated the superintendent, like an awed parrot. His own mind had evidently stopped functioning after Étienne's mention of the Surgeon to the Metropolitan Police, chief medical witness to the Battersea Mystery and Thames Torso Murders, and consulting surgeon to both the Great Western and Eastern Railways. 'He-he suggested me?'

"'Add Raeburn House to the list, H.L.'" – my name is Henri-Luc, you comprehend – "and Mr Charles Augustus Raeburn, the superintendent."' He shrugged. '*Et voila*. I am here.'

Raeburn all but quivered at his desk, eager as a spaniel. Étienne dashed just the right amount of cautionary water on the spaniel's nose. 'The list is, of course, how does one say? *Une esquisse*. A sketch. My visits to the institutions and their directors will determine which lines are removed.'

He extracted the bullet and closed the wound. 'And which remain.'

The superintendent shot to his feet and gave his visitor a fulsome bow. '*Monsieur le vicomte*. Allow me to show you my asylum.'

A short walk along a bricked path at the back of Raeburn House brought them to two broad, single-storey sheds, roofed with wood shingles. The walls were of clumsily mortared stone. Assuredly, a determined inmate could break through them with a spoon. Perhaps none had yet tried. Or they were not given spoons.

Raeburn beamed the sort of pride that a pigman reserved for

his prize boar. As Étienne let himself be led on a circuit of the sheds, he spotted windows piercing the stone at irregular intervals. No glass, only bars. The howling winds and freezing rain of winter found no impediment, then, on their mission to give the inmates chilblains. He schooled his face not to register the roil of his gut when he also noted just one door in or out of the sheds. In the event of fire, if the door was blocked, those within would be consumed like kindling.

They entered the men's shed first. Outside an oak door as solid as the walls were crumbling, a thickset man stood with arms crossed. Assistant, attendant, guard? Étienne recognised the type. No great height. Bulk, but more fat than muscle. Narrow eyes gleaming with porcine aggression. Himself, he would not soil a *poignard* with the man. A blow with one fist would suffice to cripple. A second to kill.

At the superintendent's wave, the man turned an iron key in a massive lock plate, then tugged aside two heavy bolts, one above, one below the plate. Raeburn was perhaps holding a dragon inside, since the door was further secured by a thick plank running through iron brackets. After much shoving and grunting from the guard, the crossbar moved and the door scraped inward.

Two dozen men lay, sat, or stood in the sparsely furnished interior. The men's faces were blank, their limbs slack as puppets with severed strings. Strewn about the shed in no apparent order were narrow iron cots, a long table, and some chairs. Most of the chairs were broken to greater or lesser degree. The table was liberally stained and splotched.

The smell...

He had encountered less odorous cesspits. Les Pinsons had its fuggy tasks and corners, as did all farms. But the noxious wave that rolled out of this shed was positively stygian. Worse. Fish in the River Styx would leap from the water to fry in Hell rather than endure this stink. He gritted his teeth not to snatch out his handkerchief and cover his nose. As it was, his eyes watered.

Even Raeburn was affected. 'Cawsey!' he bawled at the guard. 'For God's sake, man, when were the slops last emptied?'

Cawsey's reply was unintelligible. He stamped into the shed, where he kicked and cursed his way through the unresponsive men to a row of buckets against the back wall. The latrine, Étienne assumed. No privacy, no seats, and less hygiene than cowsheds he had seen.

Cawsey returned with two overflowing buckets. He carried them into the trees beyond the sheds and presumably emptied them. The procedure was repeated three times. Cawsey made free with his boots and insults each time he passed through the inmates. None reacted with any force. A few rolled slightly away from the vengeful feet. Most continued to stare into space, scratching their rag-clothed bodies with languid hands. One man appeared to conduct a phantom orchestra, his dirt-blackened hands waving gently like wheat in the field when a breeze stirs it.

On the third slops-retrieval journey, Raeburn finally commented. 'Staffing this place is the bane of my existence. It doesn't matter what I offer people. They simply won't work among lunatics.' His sigh was heavy and pained, as though he and not Cawsey was the one toting pails of excrement to the woods.

'I'm sorry you had to see us at our worst, Viscount.' Abruptly, his face brightened. 'But, after all, they are indigents. The poorest of the poor. I doubt any of them has ever seen a toilet.'

That, Étienne felt, was enough chat upon elimination. 'Do you not think of giving them something to do? At Hanwell Asylum, inmates are put to such work as laundry and sewing.'

Raeburn's laugh was so loud and hearty that one of the nearby inmates clapped his hands to his ears. Another mimicked the guffaw with uncanny exactness, then dropped his head to his chest and appeared to fall asleep, as he had been before the sound woke him.

'My dear Viscount de Vaux, I can only imagine the havoc these creatures would cause with access to mangles and boiling tubs.

Even needles would pose a threat to the eyes and ears of their fellows. It's why I keep them sedated, you see. It's really the only way they can be managed.'

No wonder more than half the room seemed to be snoring. A seated man with shaggy hair and a beard to his chest struggled upright and made for Étienne. Halfway there, he lost direction and staggered into a wall. Sliding to the floor, he sat again, legs extended and hands limp at his sides.

'Paraldehyde, I presume,' Étienne said. 'It is more usually administered in the late day. To aid in the sleep.'

'Oh, we give them a topping up with their tea. Does wonders for the peace and quiet around here.' Raeburn brushed a gloved hand down his sleeve, frowning. Perhaps he wished to peel off his clothing and burn it. Contagion seemed to float in the fetid air.

'The women,' Étienne said, turning his back on the horrors in the men's shed. 'I should like to see them, now.'

'Indeed, indeed.' The superintendent rushed ahead of him, out the door. He pushed aside Cawley in his eagerness.

With the crossbar banging and the bolts jangling behind them, he and Raeburn walked the fifty feet to the second shed. No less decrepit than the first, the door of that shed lacked the crossbar and bolts but was double locked. The shanks of heavy iron padlocks ran through hasps driven into the stone door frame. While they waited for the guard to finish securing the other building, Raeburn lectured on his female charges.

'Quite a dull lot at present, I'm afraid. Garden variety hysterics, most of them. There's a syphilitic whore – she always bares her breasts, so you'll see how advanced the lesions are – and an old biddy the locals called a witch, if you can believe it in this day and age. Her fits interested me at first, but she's just an epileptic.

'If only you'd been here last year at this time! You'd have seen an interesting case, a poisoner from Barnstaple. Did for her husband using arsenic salts. She initially was sent to Broadmoor but stabbed a wardress with a bit of sharpened wood in her first month. I then had the dubious privilege of her company here.

'Half a year, I kept that skirted monster, but when I finally got her readmitted to Broadmoor, the staff there were impressed with the change I'd wrought in her. Very impressed, indeed.'

The guard came and wrestled open the women's shed door. Raeburn motioned Étienne through, continuing his story to his guest's back. 'Meek as a lamb, she was when I finished with her. Couldn't remember her name, but no one was asking after her anyway, ha-ha.'

To cover his shock at the sight before him – twenty female inmates of every age and condition, all with flyaway hair and unwashed faces, all staring, stupefied, at him – Étienne posed a clinical query. 'On the poisoner, what did you use? Bleeding? Trephination? Removing the teeth?'

'All useful in intractable cases, I concur. However,' Raeburn came up level and thrust his thumbs into his waistcoat pockets, beaming, 'I have a unique approach relying on electrical current.'

Étienne made his face into graven stone as he faced the superintendent. 'I should like to hear more. And make notes, of course.'

'I am only too pleased to share my research, Viscount.'

The 'viscount' put to one side the command from his brain: attach electrical cables to Raeburn's testicles and see how much current would turn them into *escalopes de veau*. *Later*, he promised himself, *later*.

For now, he concentrated on the women inmates. They exhibited much the same profound lassitude as the men, their faces empty and their limbs slack. But their environment was significantly less squalid. They had arranged their beds in squares of four, like small village commons. He supposed the arrangement gave them a sense of community. The long wooden table in the centre of the room showed signs of scrubbing. At one end was a stack of plates, with mugs to the side. All wood, of course, since broken china could become a weapon. He had used it himself more than once.

The women's privy, if it could be dignified with that label, was screened by a wooden partition. While the shed smelled of unwashed bodies and insufficient ventilation, it did not exude the reek of the men's shed. The women were in ragged and mismatched raiment, but they were clothed. Apart from the bare-breasted prostitute, they had even made some effort at modesty. Buttons were buttoned, shirtwaists tucked into patched skirts, feet shoved into some sort of footwear. It was as conceivable as stoats raining from the sky that Raeburn's 'treatments' had produced their more-civilised aspect. He would wager the entirety of Les Pinsons' next *vendange* that the inmates themselves clung to fragments of dignity, despite their barbaric conditions.

And the women were working. At least half of them held partially completed baskets on their laps. Their hands moved at a sleepwalker's pace, but they moved.

'I see you are making art, here,' he said, unable to keep the irony from his voice.

'Yes, they do very well, very well!' Raeburn was a nursemaid congratulating a toddler on washing its hands. 'Some of them even finish a basket completely. We provide incentive, you see. If a woman completes a basket, she receives an apple.'

An apple. If he were one of the women and Raeburn gave him an apple, he would shove it so far up the superintendent's arse it would come out the other end. An orange would work as well, but he could not imagine how many completed baskets it would take to get one.

Oblivious to the grisly scenarios in his guest's mind, Raeburn burbled on about the artisanal torture before them. 'Mind you, we don't give them dangerous tools, but they manage.'

They were managing to wreck their hands on the splints of ash and elm. Among them, they had only one knife and that a dull one, from the way one woman was sawing hopelessly at a piece of wood. No hammers. Just a small mallet to pound in the nails that affixed the splints to the anchoring stave.

A surge of anger nearly choked him at the thought that some of the women labouring so futilely might be victims of Raeburn's extortionate tactics. The Lunacy Acts had largely halted the practice of committing inconvenient wives to asylums, but some of the women might have been here for years.

He wrestled bile down to deal with matters at hand. Strolling around the room with Raeburn at his heels, he scrutinised the dull faces turned in his direction. *Grâce à Dieu*, Min was not among them. The knot in his gut eased slightly. He had seen all he needed to see of the hellish conditions in the pauper wards of Raeburn House.

'*Eh, bien*. Very well-ordered establishment, Raeburn.' He could have read a book by the self-satisfied glow from the superintendent. 'Perhaps I may view your electrical apparatus, now. I should also like to see any inmates you keep in the house. I was told some rooms exist for those of a better class.'

'Ah, that was true at one time,' Raeburn glided smoothly toward the door. 'Not at present, though. I've not had a gentle in residence for quite a long time.' At the door, he extended his arm for his guest to precede him.

'I see.' Étienne turned his back on the women with a silent *Que Dieu vous garde*.

As he hoped God kept Min. His relief was inexpressible that she was not among the lunatics in the shed. He was far from satisfied that she was not somewhere on the grounds. Or in the house. When he was done with this place, there would not be a single chamber, outbuilding, cupboard, or cake box he had not turned out for traces of Minerva Hawkins.

He had only to wait for nightfall.

CHAPTER EIGHTEEN

The suite into which she'd been locked was the same one where she'd met her 'mother'. In the bedroom, the linens hadn't been changed; they were still tumbled about from the prior occupant. She examined the room foot by foot, wall to wall, ceiling to floor. Lesson Three from Jillian's self-defence training: *Common and Household Items As Weapons.* Nothing useful materialised in this room, not that she'd expected cudgels in the clothespress.

She screwed up her face when she spotted the chamber pot, half full, at the side of the bed. There'd been pots in the Little Farnleigh house. No one in the village, to her knowledge, had an inside convenience. But life in London had accustomed her to toilets, flushing ones, at that. The Salon had a curtained alcove for the purpose and her bed-sitting room in St Christopher's Place had a washroom and toilet up the hall.

Still, needs must. She gathered up her skirts, used the pot, and slid it under the bed.

Several hours passed while she alternately paced, stretched out on the rumpled bed, and sat in the sitting room chair where the 'countess' had sat, watching dusk advance through the barred window. The room would grow dark quickly. She tried the gaslights on the wall. Either they were disconnected or locked, since she could not produce even a faint hiss of gas. The one oil lamp, on a table under the window, required matches. She and the room had not a one.

She'd at least been able to keep her pocket watch, though Raeburn had confiscated her handbag. And her hat, which had been dislodged and then snatched away during the scuffle with Fitzsimmons.

Pity she'd lost her accessories. She had a lovely long pin in the hat and a small folding knife in her bag. As she considered whether her shoelaces, tied together, would serve for a garrotte, a sharp rap at the door made her jump.

'Slops!' A bark from the hall. Not a man's voice, a woman's. The wardress?

Desperation and inspiration joined hands in a merry little dance. The lock in the door was stubborn. It had taken Raeburn a full minute to open it. There was no reason to think it would take the wardress any less.

With mumbled oaths and rattling coming from the hall, she pelted to the bedroom and hauled out the chamber pot. When the door opened, she was ready.

The wardress was nimble, she'd give her that. As the contents of the pot made a yellow arc in her direction, the wardress hopped smartly to one side. Min went past her like cannon shot and made for the stairs. Holding up her skirts with one hand and gripping the rail with the other, she hurdled two and three treads at a time, risking her neck to get to the bottom. She tore down the long hall and made the marble-floored entrance hall.

Where she ran smack into the burly guard who'd blocked the door of the room upstairs when she and the supposed countess were in it.

He spun her around and gripped her about the middle, trapping her arms. She tried stamping on his feet, but he just laughed, holding her off the ground. She struggled furiously, mixing invective with backward kicks at his legs. No question he liked his work. She felt his enjoyment prodding her in the backside.

Raeburn appeared, his swift foot taps telegraphing annoyance. 'Lady Dunmara. Must you be such a bother? You're only making things worse for yourself.'

Jillian's voice in her head again. *You can always fight back. Your body knows how.*

Her choices were vomit or saliva. She'd always thought spitting was something one had to learn, like whistling or the cello. She was wrong, apparently. Given enough provocation, she could spit like a cobra. The wad flew into Raeburn's face.

He extracted a handkerchief from his jacket and wiped his cheeks. His voice was calm, making it more horrible when he said, 'Put her in the shed, Cawsey.'

'With the men, sir?' Cawsey's leer was in the words.

'No, you dolt, the women. For now.'

CHAPTER NINETEEN

The largest part of the criminal profession was waiting. As he settled against the broad trunk of a tree in the fringe around Raeburn House, Étienne reminded himself of how coolly he had always done it. Waited for the tide, as a smuggler must. Waited in a boat for the spout lantern onshore to blink an all clear, so contraband could be offloaded. Waited in an alley for an enemy of the Jacks who was owed a beating, or a crooked copper who was owed a bribe.

But this waiting in the shadows at the rear of Raeburn House... His heart hammered with multiple anxieties. Min's location, her condition. The various means by which he could force Raeburn to reveal her whereabouts if he did not find her on his first pass through the house.

Torture was not something he relished. It was an infrequent necessity, always repugnant. He could do it – he had tortured two men to reveal Jillian Morehouse's location after she had been taken and was in imminent danger of death – but it left unfillable holes in him. Fanged creatures lived in the holes. They emerged now and then, to dine on his soul.

Where the hell was the *sangfroid* that had hallmarked his early career in crime?

He closed his eyes. Now was the time to calm himself as he had done in his past, with small and routine night noises. In Dieppe, those had been the whispering waves, the laughter from a dockside tavern, and the yowls of mating cats. In London, the yowling cats had yipping dogs for counterpoint, and the clip-clopping of hackney cabs ferrying late revellers back to their lodgings.

The night concert in the grounds of Raeburn House was not far advanced, but already it offered an interesting programme. After bidding the superintendent adieu, he had accepted the reins of his horse from Cawsey. He had then ridden out the gates to the road, where he immediately turned into a screen of trees at the perimeter of the asylum's grounds. There, he had loosely tethered the beast close to the road but away from sight. She was a dappled grey mare, barely visible among the trees, even less so as the light waned. Now, she whinnied once, to remind him of her existence.

The small noises closer at hand were rabbits, moving out with cautious rustlings to feed. From a distance came the scream of a fox, looking to feed upon the rabbits. A low hoot from the tree above was owl with the same agenda. It hunted prey more suitable to its size. Field mice, perhaps, or a scuttling rat.

He had never thought of himself as a predator. Perhaps he was. His rare musings on his ancestor painted Robert de Lille as a knight errant, but what were the Templars, in truth? Predators, all. Whether they hunted for the glory of Christendom or the order's enrichment was a matter of opinion. They tore apart their prey with the same limb-rending efficiency as the fox and the owl. As him.

He shifted to one side and patted the ground where he had been sitting. Good, still dry. If moisture had been trapped in the soil, the heat of his body would have brought it out, and he would not like the Vicomte de Vaux's fine suit to acquire damp trousers.

Couilles du diable, he was hungry. Another change he must lay at the feet of age, like the eyeglasses for reading and the pewter threads in his beard. In years past, gripped entirely by some lawless adventure, he had often gone for a day and a night without thinking of food.

When he got Min back to Les Pinsons, he would kill a chicken and make *coq au vin*. He had a *bourgogne* to serve with it, rich and red and earthy. It would bring out the flavours of the mushrooms and...

What was he thinking?

There would be no more meals with Min at Les Pinsons. He would stay in Britain, risking his outstanding warrants, only long enough to get her to Scotland. That would be the end of it. The end of them.

If everything Raeburn claimed in his letter was true, Min was a countess. A countess did not belong at an obscure vineyard in France, dining with a wanted man.

A clamour from the house brought him to alertness and, an instant later, to his feet. Three, no, four people emerged from the rear door of Raeburn house. One, the grey-gowned wardress, remained at the door, holding aloft an oil lamp. The flickering light played over three bodies struggling down the back steps and onto the bricked pathway to the outbuildings. The lamplight and a fat-faced moon let him identify the three. Raeburn, the guard Cawsey, and–

'*Min.*' He hissed it on an involuntary step forward, reaching inside his jacket for a *poignard*. He could take the men on the spot, take them both. In seconds, they would be bloody pieces on the path.

Several things, all related, stayed his hand. The wardress was still standing at the top of the back steps. His longstanding disinclination to leave witnesses had ensured that none of the warrants Ewan Exeter said were fluttering around New Scotland Yard had *First Degree Murder* scrawled across it. But he neither killed women nor engaged in wholesale violence. Raeburn was a dead man, but the wardress and guard, however loathsome, were servants. A man of his repute did not kill servants. If he could avoid it.

And there was Min. For her to believe him an assassin was one thing; for her to watch him kill three people, another. Once he got her safely away, he might never see her again, but he would not have her last image of him be that. He would find another way to–

The trio were midway between the manor and the shed closest, the women's. He had an excellent view of Min's foot as it lashed out and caught Raeburn a fair blow between the legs. The man doubled over, clutching himself.

Très bien, renardette. Raeburn believed he had collared a doe rabbit. He faced a small, dangerous vixen.

Half rising, the superintendent's choked words carried on the still air. 'Hold her, you idiot! Hold her fast!'

Cawsey, arms belting Min, lifted her off the ground. She flailed and screamed, but he had her trussed like a hen for market.

Raeburn brought a pair of manacles from his coat pocket and limped to Min's side. He locked the cuffs around her wrists. 'Stop fighting. *Now*. Or I will chain your ankles, too.'

The threat did what Cawsey's brute strength did not, and she quieted in the warder's arms.

Raeburn straightened his coat and adjusted his tie. 'You may release the countess, Cawsey. She's a clever young woman and will give no more trouble.' Cawsey let his arms fall away.

Even bound, Min remained stiffly upright and defiant. 'People know where I am, Raeburn. If I'm not back in London by tomorrow morning, they'll come looking. Some of my friends are not what I'd call law-abiding. I hope you've made a will.'

'How romantic!' the superintendent crowed. 'The first sweet verses of our engagement.' His head jerked in the direction of the women's shed, and Cawsey reached for the padlocks.

The moment his back was turned, Min bolted. She made it a dozen yards toward the wood before the warden caught up with her. This time, he dragged her back with an arm around her waist, his other hand at her throat.

The knife in his hand shone dully in the moonlight.

Savage joy flared in Étienne like a torch, burning away any reluctance about using his own blades. On the guard, on Raeburn, on anything and anyone who stood between him and Min.

The superintendent sighed noisily, coming up alongside his captive. 'Gracious, you're a troublesome wench.' He reached into his inside coat pocket. When he withdrew his hand, it held a syringe.

Time to move. Étienne strode calmly from the shadows, his long legs closing the distance to the doctor in seconds. '*Bonsoir, Monsieur Raeburn!*' he shouted cheerfully. 'Lovely evening, is it not? Ah, I see you have secured the wench.'

A yard from Raeburn, he lowered his voice to a snarl. '*My* wench.'

CHAPTER TWENTY

Raeburn's face blanched so starkly Min saw the change even in moonlight. Two seconds ticked by, and the scene went off like a grenade. Raeburn wheeled and raced for the back of the house as Cawsey jumped back from her and streaked for the trees.

Étienne reached under his coat and came out with two *poignards*, one in each hand. 'Stay here, Min.' He set off for the wood at a run.

Stay here? Where did he think she could go with her wrists bound? Why had he pursued Cawsey and not the superintendent? What if Raeburn came back? She looked frantically around for a weapon. A stick, a brick, anything. Noises came from the vastness into which the two men had disappeared. Cursing, crashing. A hoarse shout, abruptly severed.

Then, nothing.

Fear shrilled in her ears. Cawsey had gone into the wood armed. She had boundless respect for the Jacks' – tradecraft – but the guard was an ox. An ox with a knife. An image leapt into her brain. Étienne on the ground, hurt, bleeding, unconscious.

Panic fired her veins and she beat her bound hands on her

thighs, whimpering. 'Oh, God, no, no...' She mouthed a desperate, inaudible prayer, then gave up on religion in favour of shouting.

'Étienne!'

The only answer was the night's deathly quiet. Min unravelled, screaming for all she was worth, '*ÉTIENNE, ÉTI-ENNNNE!*'

'*Minerve, je t'en pris.*' He appeared from darkness, tucking his blades into his coat. 'You will bring Scotland Yard with that voice.'

Her sob of relief caught in her throat. Before she could get a word past it, he enfolded her in the safety of his body. Hard chest, thumping heart, powerful arms, the scents of almonds and wool. Quite inappropriately, her bound hands were trapped at his groin. She tried to keep from touching him, but he was very warm there.

As though she'd been thrown against him and bounced, she sprang backward. She was suddenly, painfully, aware that she'd done not a single thing he'd told her to do, other than going to the police. And how had *that* worked out? Now, he was here in England, exactly where he should not be. She sensed another uncomfortable conversation coming.

'H-hello, Étienne.'

'*Minerve.*'

He took her hands – they were icy, his were warm – and began inspecting the shackles. She hoped he'd brought lockpicks. Surely, they were regulation kit for his former profession. 'Why did you go after Cawsey instead of–?'

'The guard had a blade at your throat. Raeburn was unarmed.'

'But he could've gone back to the house for a weapon!'

'Most assuredly, he could have emerged with a trebuchet. But Monsieur Raeburn is of a type I know well. With all speed, he will flee to save himself. He witnessed *le vicomte* disappearing before his eyes. He will have no desire to meet his replacement.'

'If'n you sent Cawsey ta hell, they be no scritchin' from me.' The wardress, her lamp a bobbing orb, appeared like an aproned Diogenes. Étienne shoved Min behind him and reached for a *poignard*, but the wardress merely gestured toward the wood.

'Evil meggot abused th' women. Even old'uns. Even Sal, me sister.

'Er's th' one keeps her teats out. Still me sister. Er's why I come 'ere, but stayt on fer t'others. Somebody got to do fer they.' She hawked up a blob and spat on the ground. 'Agnes Broadripple.'

With that, she put her lamp on the ground. She used her ring of keys to release Min's wrists and then opened the padlocks on the shed door. In the doorway, she turned to address them both.

'Raeburn be affways ta Torrington by now. Ee be arter Fitzsimmons, t'other evil meggot.' She hoisted her lamp and entered the shed. Min heard her talking to the women, her Devonian accents as thick and soothing as honey.

Immediate crisis past, reaction shuddered in Min's blood. Her voice quavered. 'C-can we please leave, now, Étienne?'

'Who is this Fitzsimmons?'

Oh, blast. He would ask that. 'A corrupt policeman, the chief constable in Great Torrington. He's Raeburn's partner.' And a man who liked hitting women. Good job it was probably too dark for Étienne to see the evidence Fitzsimmons had left on her jaw. That would be another uncomfortable conversation, one that would happen once the sun was up.

She glanced at the open shed door. The 'countess', standing in the opening, was no longer in the white lawn dressing gown. She wore a plain, baggy dark dress with a large rent in one shoulder. Lighted from behind by Agnes' lantern, her streaked auburn hair was a burning bramble. Her light eyes fixed on Min.

'We're taking her.' It came of its own accord from her lips.

He followed her gaze. 'Who is she?'

Hung for a sheep, hung for a lamb. 'The dowager countess. My mother. You remember, the letter said–'

'Min, please listen. We are now fugitives for several reasons. In the beginning of this affair, my plan was to eliminate your blackmailer. Simply. Discreetly.

'Finding you came here alone, I am forced to other measures. I employ a tissue of lies and forgeries to gain access to the asylum. Once here, I discover you are a prisoner. You are damaged.' He waved at her jaw. So much for waiting until daylight to discuss it. 'And in manacles. There is now a corpse in the trees thirty yards away. A witness just there.' He jerked his chin toward Agnes. 'And the blackmailer himself is free to invent a story reflecting unfavourably and dangerously upon me. A strategy most effective for him, you agree? And effortless, when one has the chief constable of the district in one's pocket.

'Now you tell me there are *two* countesses who must make an escape. Not being a prognosticator, I did not bring a second horse for the second countess.'

It wasn't easy to squirm standing up, but she gave it her best. 'I do appreciate all those points.'

'I am pleased beyond measure. And you have found your mother, a cause for celebration. Later, when we are fifty miles from here, we will celebrate as the natives do in this part of England. Sausages, perhaps.

'But before we are fifty miles away, we must be five. *Quickly.* Your mother...' He flicked a glance at the spectre in the doorway. 'Looks unwell.'

The wardress pushed past her to face Étienne. Confrontationally, Min would say, with her lamp throwing amber light on his face.

'Er'll do. Raeburn took one oss, but they be ither in stable.' She waved the lamp toward some outbuildings, throwing wild shadows. 'Cart oss, fer when Cawsey needed ter 'aul somethin'. Ee's not much ter look at, ol' Rags, but ee'll saddle up an' carry two women.' She gave Étienne's body an entirely too exhaustive survey. 'Or one hill o' muscle like yerself.'

Étienne strode off in the direction of the outbuildings, talking heatedly to himself in French. Agnes waited until he was out of sight, then turned the lamp toward Min. 'Yer laidyship–'

'Minerva, please, Agnes. Or Miss Hawkins, if you like. Would you mind lowering the light?'

Agnes complied, holding the lamp away from her skirts. She glanced at the woman in the shed doorway. 'Er's Morag.'

Morag. A Scots name. No surprise. The woman's *r*'s rolled like water over rocks.

'Er's yer mither's maid.'

A maid. Not a countess, but she'd already worked that part out. Not her mother, either, she guessed. 'Am I the dowager countess' daughter?'

'Ye were, miss, till nine yar ago. Thik were when countess died.'

CHAPTER TWENTY-ONE

Nine years. Min shut her eyes. If she dozed for a bit, she might wake from this bizarre dream.

The superintendent's lies had successfully extorted 'maintenance' for a countess nine years in her grave. He had every reason to believe that a slight adjustment of the lies would keep the money flowing.

'I knew she had died. Raeburn said it was pneumonia. Is that true?'

'Somethin' like, miss. Twuz afore my time 'ere.'

'Where is she–' she had to force out the word, 'buried?'

For answer, Agnes looked uneasily toward the wood.

'And my grandparents...' *No.* 'Asa and Mary Hawkins. How did I come to live with them in Little Farnleigh?'

Agnes turned the lamp on Morag, who seemed to be asleep standing against the door frame. 'When er's back t'erself, ye'll 'ave tale from er.'

Min didn't wish to appear rude, but the woman in the doorway looked unable to string six words together. 'Are you sure she's... coherent?'

'Will be, in a bit. Raeburn doped er.' The recollection of

Raeburn's syringe made Min's stomach flip. 'Er don't usually come in fer it, but ee wanted er witless fer yer visit. Mostly, er works round 'ere.'

'Doesn't she try to escape?'

Agnes shook her head. 'Er was 'appy enough when countess lived. 'An' er's been 'ere a long while.'

'A long while' was putting it mildly, if Morag had been at Raeburn House since before Min's birth. She was desperate to know more, but Étienne was returning across the lawn. He carried a saddle over one arm and led a bridled black-and-white elephant behind him.

'Yon big man,' Agnes said softly. 'Ee yorn? D'ye trust ee?'

Was he hers? She wouldn't say yes, but for her life she couldn't say no. 'I trust him completely.'

Agnes nodded. 'Ye'll want vittles fer road.'

Off the wardress went, lamp aloft, toward Raeburn House. As she passed Étienne, she gave him a few words. He gave a few back. The elephant, which she now saw was a massive horse, contributed a whuffling opinion.

Étienne drew level with her and began silently installing horse tackle. From his silence and the stiffness of his posture, he was still angry. The horse... Min's head didn't reach its withers. Its hocks were shaggy and its feet the size of dinner plates. She took a precautionary step back.

Next to the Hawkins' smallholding in Little Farnleigh was a farm with a horse like that, brown with white stockings. The horse in front of her was piebald, black and white, and outsized the one in Little Farnleigh. *It's a Shire.*

Truly, she was coming unstitched. Too many emotional states in too little time. Hope to indignation to fury to terror. The result was that she'd identified a breed of horse in mere seconds, but couldn't seem to take in what Agnes Broadripple told her about the late countess and Morag. And herself. It was as though she'd arrived at Raeburn House a cat and was now a lampshade.

He'd got the horse saddled. It really was massive. It would help to lean against it for a minute or two, just until the landscape stopped spinning, but Étienne was in the way. Adjusting stirrups, tightening the girth, murmuring sweet French nothings into the horse's ears.

She must at least veer from the mental track she was speeding along before she ended up in a shed like the one behind her. 'You said there was a corpse in the wood. Is it Cawsey's?'

'*Merci*, Étienne, for saving me from the very bad man.'

'Thank you. I promise you, when I got up this morning, I didn't... That is, I couldn't know... I didn't want you to kill anybody.'

The look he turned on her was both incredulous and exasperated. 'Minerva, you were in my house not one hour before you said, "I need you to kill a man."'

'Yes, but I didn't understand, then. What killing meant, what it meant for you. I just–'

'I did not kill Cawsey. The world is a cleaner place now that he has a place with Satan, but I did not send him there.'

'But, if he's dead...'

'He had a knife, as you saw.' He put one stocky finger on her collar, pushing down the top edge to brush the skin where Cawsey's knife had pressed. Her eyes shut and she took in a sharp little breath. His touch sent a hot spark along her throat, leaping over her collarbone and waking her nipples. They rose to greet it. *Hello, Étienne's fingers*. Stupid as a newt again.

He released her collar and turned back to finick with straps, talking over his shoulder. 'The guard ran. It was dark. He tripped over the root of a tree. The knife was beneath him. He fell upon it. *Voilà*, death by misadventure.'

Death by misadventure. If she and Étienne and Morag couldn't elude Raeburn and Chief Constable Fitzsimmons, would death by misadventure be their lot, too? The three of them were liabilities, loose ends, walking threats. They knew what Raeburn and

Fitzsimmons had done. The neglect and abuse of inmates, the extortion, the abetting of bigamy, false imprisonment, possibly worse. Her jaw ached, a reminder of threat and vulnerability.

She inhaled deeply, letting the breath out on an apology. 'I'm sorry. Not for Cawsey, though I know I should be.' Asa and Mary Hawkins would have been horrified at her unchristian attitude, but nearly everything she'd done since meeting Étienne would have horrified them. 'I truly didn't think Raeburn... I wasn't expecting what happened.'

He spun to face her, his expression so sharp that she flinched. 'Tell me, Minerva. What did you think would happen when you came here alone? You read Raeburn's letter and the note. A child of six years would have seen the author was an arrant villain.'

Her own anger flared. 'Well, see, there's the problem. I don't turn six until February. And I just told you I didn't *expect* any of this.'

'As I did not *expect* to be riding through the wild reaches of Devon this night, accompanied by a madwoman.'

'Morag is not mad!'

'She is not the madwoman to which I refer. And no countess is named Morag.' His expression moved from flint to fire. 'Who is she? Do not lie to me again.'

'Oh, now I'm a liar as well as a five-year-old. Feel free to slight me, Étienne.'

'If I am to risk, as you English say, life and limb, I deserve to know for whom.'

'Fine. If you must know, she is – was – my mother's maid.'

'Your mother was the dowager countess?'

'Apparently so.'

'You are the heir, then? The Countess of Dunmara?'

The answer was just one word. Why it took fifteen seconds to leave her mouth she didn't know. He waited until she mumbled.

'I did not hear you, Minerva.'

'Yes, all *right*, yes!' She balled her fists. If only she were a man, she'd dot him one on the nose. 'I'm the Countess of Dunmara. What difference does it make?'

He threw the piebald's reins over its head. 'The difference is everything. A difference to you, to me, to people you do not yet know. To this night and tomorrow and next week. And it is a difference made whether you accept it or continue to live in a land of fairies where you do whatever you wish without considering the effect on others.'

'How *dare* you? You are being grossly unfair and insulting. And... and discourteous!'

'*Ah, je vous demande pardon, madame la comtesse.*'

She wasn't even aware she'd raised her hand to slap him until he grabbed her wrist. In less than an eyeblink, he had her against him. Under him, within him. And he was everywhere in and around her. The enclosure of his arms was so right she went completely limp. If he hadn't held her upright, she would have fallen to his feet.

But she didn't fall. She *climbed*.

She latched her arms around the back of his neck and hung on as though he was a rope ladder and she was scaling the side of a ship. Before their mouths even met, his hands dragged down her body to her hips. When they dragged back up, her skirts came with them.

He took her mouth at the same time she parted her thighs. An instant later, he lifted her so she could wrap her legs around him. Those purposeful hands of his got under her buttocks and pulled her tight.

The union of their bodies was water after thirst, bread after hunger. All of a piece. She couldn't distinguish the hot invasion of his tongue from the grind of her pelvis against him, or the deep groan he made from the lightning jabs of pleasure in her core. *Me* and *you* were thrown into the night. *Separate* was a distant memory. They fused to each other like solder onto steel.

She was wet between her legs; he was hard between his. She'd seen his naked, upright member in France, but feeling it push, huge and relentless, at the place it wanted entry...

She took one hand from his neck and worked it between them, fighting her bunched skirts to find his trousers placket. Fumbling like the virgin she was, she still managed to get two buttons undone. Her heart nearly left her chest when she thrust fingers inside and felt warm, bare flesh, the slight rasp of hair.

His voice was harsh above her, pleading in French, in English. 'Stop, *Minerve*, stop, *pour l'amour de Dieu–*'

That was when they both heard a sharp whinny. Not the Shire's. A different whinny from a different horse, its shoes clacking on the bricks of the drive.

Étienne swore filthily and pushed down her skirts, her legs with them, and put her on her feet.

'Mount the horse,' he told her roughly, shoving her at the Shire.

Mount the horse mount the horse mount the... She'd told him she was reared on a farm. He naturally assumed she could ride. She should probably have stipulated that the Hawkins' farm was so small it didn't have a horse. And, presently, she was reeling and panting from nearly giving her virginity to a man in vertical intercourse.

She somehow got her left boot toe in the stirrup and her hands on the saddle. After watching her hop up and down a few times like a lame rabbit, Étienne bent and put his shoulder under her derriere. He straightened, vaulting her into the saddle, where she wobbled, whimpering.

'I don't think I'm going to like this.'

'*Bon*. It will be incentive for you to avoid similar occasions in the future.'

Agnes, leading a grey horse Min reckoned was Étienne's, came up alongside. With one hand, the wardress passed the reins to him. With the other, she gave him a long cloth bag, knotted at one end.

'Fer road. M'lady's handbag's inside. Don't think Raeburn took aught from it.'

Aught, *yet*. Min was sure if she'd remained at the asylum much longer, Raeburn would've taken a lot more from her than a few pounds and a tortoiseshell comb.

Étienne acknowledged the bag with a nod and flung it over the pommel of the grey's saddle, then jerked his head toward the sheds.

'Raeburn House will almost certainly close, now. You must alert the authorities posthaste. In the meanwhile, the inmates–'

'I'll see ta they till they's sorted.'

Morag had melted out of the shed to stand, empty-handed, a few yards away. There were advantages to being an asylum inmate if one was leaving in a hurry. Nothing to pack, not so much as an apron or a spare pair of shoes. Agnes crossed to the Scotswoman, giving her a few low words and an encouraging pat on the shoulder.

Étienne bent at the Shire's side, lacing his fingers. It was enough of a prompt for Morag who, despite her lethargic appearance, moved swiftly to take the leg up. She vaulted neatly onto the pie's back, behind Min. The horse seemed to take that as a *walk on* and threw up its great head. Étienne fisted the cheek strap of the bridle, ordering him to stand. In French, of course, but a fencepost would have obeyed.

How in the name of heaven was she going to manage the animal on her own?

Scrabbling the reins into one hand, she used the other to unclip Mary Hawkins' brooch from the neck of her dress. Even in moonlight, the diamond solitaire at its centre gleamed boldly. She handed it down to Agnes.

'Take this. It'll keep you for a few months, a year, even. Until you can get yourself and your sister somewhere better.'

The wardress's face creased in the first smile Min had seen on her. 'Plymouth.' She gave the word wistful reverence, like Xanadu or Camelot. 'Always wanted ta go there.'

CHAPTER TWENTY-TWO

They took to the road. Étienne kicked the mare into an easy canter. The piebald matched the mare stride for stride.

Min was all compliance at the start, but he saw a hundred questions in her face. Now was not the time for her to ask nor for him to answer. She had given him the only answer that mattered, as far as he was concerned. From the start, he had suspected that Raeburn would not have risked such a serious crime as blackmail, nor asked such an exorbitant sum, nor increased his jeopardy with false imprisonment, without some surety that Min was truly the heir to a title. At the asylum, she had found her own proof – some proof, at any rate – that Raeburn was right.

She was a countess. An estate and a future awaited her in Scotland. Her task was to accept that. His task was to get her there.

The immediate and more urgent challenge was to put distance between themselves and Raeburn House. As long as the blackmailer and his tame chief constable prowled Devonshire in search of her, Min was in grave danger.

They struck out in a south-easterly direction, following the River Torridge. It was not until they reached the village of Meeth that they slowed. The horses were blowing, by then, and needed to rest. The two women would also need rest. Min was clearly no horsewoman, and the woman Morag looked as though she had spent the last week in a laudanum bottle. He could only hope neither would fall off or, if they did, he would notice before the horses left them too far behind.

Meeth was quiet, not even a cat on the wander. Leaving it, they came to a fork, where the well-travelled old coaching road acquired a narrow branch. He took it.

In no time at all, the branch strayed toward an ancient wood. For nearly a mile, it coursed along the perimeter, trees on one side, farmland on the other. A dog barked half-heartedly at them for a bit. A donkey with its head hanging over a stable half-door brayed at the mare, who gave a superior snort.

The branch remained wide enough that they rode abreast. A convenient arrangement for the launching of questions, objections, complaints. He could not avoid them indefinitely. Perhaps it was as well to get them over with.

She began conversationally. 'Where are we going?'

Ah, that. Her reasonable tone would be short-lived. He enjoyed it while he could. 'Scotland. You are a Scottish countess, yes? The Countess of Dunmara.'

'Correct on both counts, I admitted under duress. Isn't Scotland to the *north*?'

'That depends on where one starts.' The charged stillness from her told him he should not have been ironical.

'From where *we* started. Would you say Scotland was north of north Devonshire? I would.'

'Scotland is indeed to the north of Devonshire, not only the north of the county but the middle and every other part.' More ill-advised irony. She would make him suffer later, but it was irresistible in the moment.

She looked to the right, the left. The rear, as well as she could with Morag affixed to her back like a limpet. Finally, she looked up. For nearly a minute, she studied the position of the moon.

Clever, clever Min. As the English said, his goose was cooked.

'I'm hoping you'll explain why we are we moving *south*.'

'Because we take a different route.' He urged the mare into a fast trot. Behind him, Min brayed like the donkey, but only briefly. It is difficult to hurl insults and remain upright on a trotting horse.

Two miles beyond his entirely unrevealing revelation of their itinerary, even the faintest sounds of civilisation disappeared. The track felt it had flirted enough with the wood and plunged in. Trees crowded close and muffled the sounds of the horses' hooves, the slight squeak of their saddles. Everywhere, the dripping of damp from leaves and the rustle of night creatures wove spells around them. Reminding them they did not pass through the wood; it *allowed* their passage. Such dark enchantments were capricious. It might expel them any second.

They were fortunate in the horses. Both were good and uncomplaining. No fits of temper, no troublesome rebellions. They trotted when they were told, walked when they were given rest, cantered when they were fresh. Turned right and left as ordered by the reins. A horse had a simple life, he reflected. It was never required to explain itself to the police. Or to Minerva Hawkins.

Explaining himself to her was not a pressing matter at this moment. She was not speaking to him. The silence was restful to his mind. That would change. After some short time, he would be annoyed with her. Then, he would experience guilt. Finally, the absence of her voice would be so painful that he would provoke an argument, just to hear it again.

He must hear it again. There was so little time.

He had always known that speech with Minerva was a fleeting pleasure, like the *beaujolais nouveau*. Unlike the *beaujolais*, no grand, mature conversational wine would follow the youthful wine when it was gone. Soon, when she was in her rightful place in Scotland, he would take leave of her. Whatever words they said to each other at that farewell would be the last. He was carefully avoiding even one thought about his life beyond them.

It was enough for now to fix his mind on this route he had hastily mapped in his head. South by land, west and north by sea. Safe for some reasons, dangerous for others. It put him in the way of things he had forsaken, or that had forsaken him, long ago. Some of those were deadly. Who could say what would happen when his past and present crossed? At least, if he died along the way, he would not have to face a final parting from Min.

Gallows humour, the English called that.

Onward in a silent, single file they progressed, ever southward. The track was a white scar in the earth, illumined by moonlight that came and went through breaks in the canopy.

'Sir! Sir!'

He pulled up the mare. Impeded somewhat by a pair of saddlebags behind and Agnes' long sack in front, he still twisted enough to see why Morag was shouting. Some yards to the rear, the Shire horse was planted in the track. Min was half off, her one foot caught in the stirrup. Morag was struggling to haul her back into the saddle by her clothing. Both women were thrashing about, reins, mane, and saddlery tangled in petticoats and legs. *Merci à Dieu*, the wise and stolid horse did not let himself be pulled to the side.

Étienne was off the mare in an eyeblink. She was not as wise as the Shire. He dropped her reins to the ground to signal her to stand, hoping for the best. It was the work of a few seconds to extricate Min's foot from the stirrup. The tangled mass of her clothing took longer. Why did women wear such dangerously elaborate attire? In the end, he simply plucked her off the horse and stood her on her feet. In gratitude, she swatted furiously at his hands and was free with her opinion.

'I'm fine, you interfering giant! Leave me alone!'

The other woman had removed herself from the Shire without assistance. He was pleased to see she seemed more alert than when they had left the asylum. That would be helpful. He had not looked forward to ferrying a drug-addled female all the way to the coast. One uncooperative spitfire was trouble enough.

'You have the truth of it, Minerva,' he snapped. 'If I had let the horse drag you by your ankle for a mile or two, it might have improved your temper. We would all have been grateful.'

She ignored him and applied herself to the straightening of the bodice, the dusting of the skirt, the realignment of the hairpins.

By all means, let us be fashionable and neat. One never knows, in the hinterland, when a social occasion might arise.

He frowned about the wood. It had been thinning for some time. Through the straggling sentinels at this outer edge, he saw broad, down-sloping fields. Beyond them, the sun just showed its face on the cusp of the horizon. An English dawn, shy and polite in a pink dress, accompanied by the trill of a wren.

Idiot. This escapade was transforming him into a bohemian poet. Soon, he would frequent absinthe bars and scribble verses on the tabletops. He must finish the job at hand and go back to Les Pinsons before he lost his mind and his manhood altogether.

He examined the brightening horizon again, and the sun. Dead ahead. The track was leading them more to the east than he had hoped. That must be corrected when they were in the clear.

He waved toward the sunrise. 'We will cross that field. On the other side, we will take rest and food.'

CHAPTER TWENTY-THREE

'We will cross that field. We will take rest and food.' General Sansecours commanded and his troops obeyed! Not that a woman who'd barely stayed on her horse should even think of countermanding his orders. Didn't stop her from resenting his being so up himself.

Liar. All right, she envied his self-possession. The past month had left her feeling like the litter of someone's desk, swept onto the floor. She couldn't determine which scrap was a clue to understanding herself, him, the thing that grew and pulsed between them, and which was a laundry ticket.

In lieu of a handy water closet, they had all gone off behind separate trees and returned to their mounts. Daylight chose that moment to lighten their surroundings, and Étienne chose it to be observant about her face.

'Explain this.' He grasped her chin in his thumb and forefinger and turned her head to the side.

'It's nothing.' She actually didn't know if it was nothing or something. English forests were sparsely planted with mirrors. And now, he was drilling holes in her with his angry gaze. He'd probably do it all day if she didn't explain. 'Fitzsimmons was throwing his fist around and my face got in the way.'

The next thirty seconds were a compact and impressive demonstration of why crossing Étienne Sansecours was a bad idea. He became not a column of fire but an ice storm.

He released her chin and stared into the trees. She had the feeling he did it to prevent her seeing what was in his eyes. After another laden half minute, and in the same tone as *I will rise at six* or *I will have a muffin, thank you*, he said, 'I will kill him.'

Truly? He wouldn't kill her blackmailer, but he'd murder a chief constable who'd handed her a facer? He was the most infuriating man. But if she said *please don't kill anyone* again he'd say *she* was infuriating and then off they'd go, bickering like Ada and Eileen.

She compromised. 'Let's not talk about killing before breakfast.'

She pushed past him to stand at the piebald. He helped her into the saddle, then swung Morag up behind. He mounted his own horse. *Monsieur le Général* didn't seem to care for remaining long in the open, and so they set off across the field at a faster pace than she'd have liked.

The sun was full up by the time they left a crease in the hayfield – timothy and clover, a knee-high crop – and entered another wood, not as dense as the first. She'd call it a grove or a spinney. Immature trees, mostly rowans and field elms, with graceful swayings of willow to one side. A river was close. She smelled its mossy freshness.

By the time they dismounted, she was sure if she never saw another horse again it would be too soon. Morag slipped off the pie and to her feet with no more fuss than rising from a chair. Min was frozen to the saddle. Every muscle ached and she was sure she'd lost two inches of her spine to the road. She got her feet out of the troublemaking stirrups. Then, she sat, unable to move her legs.

Wordlessly, Étienne strode over and hauled her from the saddle like a bag of oats. She mumbled thanks and limped stiffly to a tree. For the next little while, she leaned against it while he and Morag went about making camp. The maid seemed to have awakened from her drugged state, though she still lacked initiative and hardly spoke. Whatever Étienne told her to do, though, she did, and capably. Gathered dry wood and tinder. Started a small fire with the box of vestas he handed her. The tinder combusted on the first match. She was fairly sure if Morag had only flint and steel, or even two pieces of toast, she could've done just as well.

Étienne unsaddled the horses and hobbled them loosely, so they could graze within sight at the edge of the field. His every movement was unhurried and efficient. The rope with which he made the hobbles came from his saddlebags. There were undoubtedly other useful things inside, things she imagined all people on the fly needed.

She'd probably have stocked the bags with a hairbrush, a sponge bag, a pair of fresh stockings, and a sewing kit. The last might have been of some use, since the shoulder of Morag's baggy dress would not magically repair itself. Riding astride had also burst a side seam in her own skirt.

She picked at the split silk, making it worse. Her fingers were as stiff and sore as the rest of her. On the whole, she should probably be more gracious about Étienne's leadership. She would have run them straight into a bog. Or more crooked policemen. It was doubly wrong to be resentful when she was the cause of all their trouble, the reason the three of them were in the 'wild reaches of Devon' instead of going about their lives.

She just wasn't accustomed to feeling so useless. And guilty.

Étienne, with his uncanny ability to know what she was thinking, came to her tree. He placed his palm against the trunk and loomed the way he did, while she, *weakling petticoat!* was pathetically grateful for the sheltering arm.

'The discomfort will leave in a few hours. You are simply not accustomed to riding the horse.'

'Well, no. In London, trains and hackney cabs have actual seats in them.' She forced her fingers away from her skirt and crossed her arms. If they were trapped, they couldn't reach for him and pull him to her. She lifted her chin in Morag's direction. '*She* seems to be doing all right.'

'She is Scottish.'

He said it to provoke a smile, and she almost produced one. 'Does she play the bagpipes, too?'

'When we are bored enough, we will ask for a brief demonstration.'

The fire was going well, embers rising and dying as they flew upward. A campfire, making a jolly crackle and snap that was completely at odds with her feelings.

'Minerva. You are certain your mother does not live?'

'Raeburn said she's dead. He was talking to Fitzsimmons, so it wasn't just some lie he was making up for me. Agnes Broadripple confirmed it. She died of a lung complaint years ago.'

He nodded, mercifully not adding hollow condolences like the ones Madame and her workmates had ladled out at Salon Sirena. It was convenient that she'd already been wearing mourning when she discovered how numerous the dead in her family were. Shameful, that she couldn't summon more than a hazy regret for any of them.

'Did you really forge papers to get into Raeburn House?'

He took the non sequitur in his stride. 'The forgeries were done by someone else. They involved some letters of introduction, only. And a passport. All necessary to present myself to the superintendent as an alienist from Paris.'

'Did you use an alias?

'You have an obsession with aliases, Minerva, but yes. *Monsieur le docteur Henri-Lucien Habsburg, Vicomte de Vaux*. The title is now extinct.'

'Blimey. Viscount for a day.' She unlocked her arms and pushed both hands at her hair, wishing she had a mirror. Or perhaps not. If she saw herself, she might be tempted to an alias, too. Scruff-Bramble, the Queen's Croquet Ball. 'I'd like it if my title was erased like yours.'

'Never say so. For you, it is the rarest and finest of outcomes.' Leaving one hand against the tree, he dropped the other on her shoulder. 'I spoke sharply when you had your mishap with the saddle. I regret it. You asked for none of this, *mignonne*. It came like a sudden storm, or a plague. Nothing is your fault.'

'I just... I just don't understand what I did to make all this...' She looked desperately into his face, seeking answers she already knew weren't there. 'How did I get here?'

He didn't answer. To her everlasting humiliation, her eyes stung and overflowed. She sagged against her tree, covered her face with her hands, and wept. It was quiet and messy. He stood braced over her, letting her get on with it.

He could have held her. She wanted him to, wanted to be enclosed in his safety and strength the way she'd been during those soaring seconds at Raeburn House after they'd argued, then kissed. More than kissed. They'd tried to join their bodies, cell by cell, making one being from two.

There was no repeat of that. Eventually, her tears stopped. Her eyeglasses were completely fogged. She unhooked them and pulled up the hem of her dress, not caring that she exposed a white wedge of petticoat. He'd seen it before.

She cleaned the lenses on the black cloth and put the glasses on again. It would kill her to say she was still thinking about their kiss, so she improvised.

'Thank you.' *Again, and always.* 'I'm sorry to be such a leaky spigot.'

'Stop worrying.' He cupped her elbow and tugged her gently toward the fire. 'A meal will improve your mood.'

CHAPTER TWENTY-FOUR

They ate sparsely, bread and a wedge of cheese, portioned out among them. Thirst was a torment, but they took only two long swallows apiece of cider from a stoneware flask Agnes had provided in the bag of victuals. Meal over, they composed themselves to rest.

It was always difficult to sleep in daylight, but the grove was as shaded as a young wood could be. And they had been in the saddle long enough for their bodies to surrender for a few hours. The fire Morag had so deftly built was not strictly necessary, but it drove off the perpetual English damp and was cheering.

Bedding was also not strictly necessary, but he found himself grateful for the Scotswoman's woodland craft in that regard, also. She had gathered great armfuls of bracken, interlacing the leafy fronds to give some measure of comfort. At least, they would not lie upon the bare earth. At sixteen, when he fled Les Pinsons, he had for weeks slept on hard, cold ground, even harder and colder doorways and cellar steps. It was a thing the spine did not easily forget.

Tomorrow, they would find a clean stretch of river. Some river. Their only map was in his head, an Ordnance Survey of the county he had studied while waiting for Simon Kaan to finish his work. Most instructive, but it was difficult to be sure of landmarks relative to their current position. He had not, at the time, appreciated how his simple mission would become so complex.

They were in Devonshire, however, a terrain as stippled with rivers as a tabby cat was with stripes. They would find water to drink, even bathe. There would be more food, since rivers meant villages and towns.

All would materialise, just as soon as they put more ground between Raeburn House and themselves.

How did I get here? Min's question came slinking back. It worked its way inside as he shed his coat, jammed his collar and tie in a pocket, and rolled everything to make a pillow.

Nor was it deceived by a lengthy debate in his mind regarding the retention of his shoes. Questions that are primed to keep one awake are undeterred by quibbles over the relative desirability of fleeing or fighting in one's stockings.

He stretched out on the bracken bed. Futilely, he tried not to notice that Min, with much rustling and muttering, had moved her own pile of cabbage over until she was an arm's length away. Did she want to talk? Was she hoping he would reply aloud to the question now hovering silently over them both? Perhaps he could feign sleep to avoid it. His mind whirled like a flywheel; feigned sleep would be the only kind he would have.

How did I get here? To that, he had no reply. Did not know one, could not speak one. A man who had success with women would probably do better. That man would give her the lies that Ewan Exeter poured out with such ease.

It perplexed him that he had never become such a man, since he had known women from early manhood. Knowing and understanding them, though... They remained separate and largely irreconcilable states.

He lifted his head to see how Morag fared on the other side of the low-burning fire. She had curled into a ball. From the sound of her breathing and the stillness of her body, she was already asleep. He had done that time and time again, in his past. Dropped wherever he was and slumbered, in broad daylight or darkest night, untroubled as a log.

On smuggling runs, he had slept in a lugger, even with an inch of icy seawater in the bottom. In his early years with the Jacks, he and Kell had slept soundly on the floor under thin blankets, guarding the inside of whatever door they had shut at dawn on whatever gaming hell they operated. It was a twisted blessing, to enjoy the best of sleep between doing the worst of things.

The closeness of Minerva Hawkins might be keeping him awake. She groaned softly as she shifted, trying to find a restful position. Despite what he had told her, she would be in pain for days after the cruel ride they were making, but what other choice was there?

He was to blame, of course. If he were another man, an ordinary man, he would not have *mandats d'arrêt* arrayed like a ring of pikemen, waiting to drive their weapons into his chest. That other man would travel openly with her, bringing her to Scotland with the delicacy of returning a chick to a nesting box.

And yet, that other man would not be able and willing to do whatever was necessary to keep her safe. That other man would not know evil well enough to defeat it. Would not lay down his life to protect her when her enemies came.

Because they would come. Min was too valuable an asset for them to abandon their scheme simply because of the fracas at the asylum.

The not-ordinary man lay alongside her, wakeful. And furious, that he could not simply pull her into his arms and comfort her. If any comfort could be found, considering where they were. Who they were.

How did I get here?

He had reached the age when, in idle moments, he thought of his gravestone. Min's question would make a most excellent epitaph, the best and most durable of any he had heretofore considered. The other questions of his life had been transient. *What shelter can I find? Who pursues me? What can I steal?*

Is this woman mine? He had been not yet eighteen when the uncomfortable answer to that arrived with his first *affaire de coeur*. New to London, he had gone there to evade the Dieppe *Gendarmerie* after a smuggling operation gone bad. He had little money and imperfect English. But he had a certain presence. Big, canny, *dangereux*.

One evening as he loitered with intent to rob in Covent Garden, a skinny, redhaired whore – for that was what he thought she was – sidled up and reached for his arm. He grabbed her hand and nearly twisted it off. Somehow, through her Cockney screeching and wild gestures, he learned she had made him not for a punter but something else altogether. Her name was Beatrice.

She wished to be called Trixie, both a nickname and a descriptive, since tricksy was what she was, through and through. She was a year older and had been on the game since she was thirteen. She made her living by bearing-up, thieves' cant for using a woman as a decoy to rob a guileless cull. She had recently lost her partner to Newgate and saw no reason why Étienne, whom she briskly renamed 'Stevie', could not take his place.

The rig was simple. Notwithstanding, it was not every pair of thieves could do it, since it relied on looks, timing, and acting that belonged on Drury Lane. Trixie tore the neckline of her dress low enough to expose the curve of one lovely breast. Since she used the same dress every time and stitched the tear lightly back in place afterward, opening it again took no effort at all. She then blackened her eye socket with a little soot and grease and put a streak of sheep's or chicken's blood on her cheek.

Spouting false tears like a ruptured drainpipe, she waited with him in the deep shadow of some alley until she saw her mark. A well-dressed passer-by, not too young or muscular.

Stumbling out of the alley into the mark's arms, she stuck like a cocklebur, wailing about the horrid cabman who was hired to take her home from visiting her sick mother in Lambeth, but instead had driven her down a dark lane, then assaulted and robbed her as she tried to leave his conveyance. After a minute or two of that, the cull invariably offered her money, either to relieve her distress or get her off him. That was when Étienne roared out of the alley, enraged to see his 'wife' in the embrace of a stranger. The cull could not empty his pockets fast enough to quell the rage of the 'husband'.

'E offered, din't 'e?' That was Trixie's rationale. What the cull offered was never what he gave up, in the end. That usually included his watch and any other valuable trinkets he might have on him. Trix argued that she and Étienne needed it more. 'Them rich coves,' she would tell him when they went back to her squalid room to divide the take, 'they got mountains of it. Never a one but can't spare the grain o' sand we takes orf 'im.'

Not a sentimentalist, his Trixie. In the game or anywhere else. After they'd coupled on her grimy bed, he tried more than once to put his arms around her. 'Leave orf,' she always said, pushing away his hands. 'I'm tryin' ta sleep.'

Ah, Trix, *la pauvre*. He had never learned her *surnom*; she might not have known it. They were together a few months, perhaps six, when she found a partner she liked better. Older. More powerful, not in muscle but in underworld connections. He lived in a house, a genuine house, with a sitting room and gas lamps and a kitchen.

Étienne, back on the streets, returned to asking himself, *How did I get here?*

Two feet away, the woman completely unlike Trixie had gone quiet. Stealthily, he shifted his weight by increments so he could roll on his side without too much noise from the vegetables beneath. Min's eyes were closed, long eyelashes lying on her cheeks like little wings. Her hands were curled into fists, folded spectacles in one of them, and tucked under her chin.

With this occasion, he had watched her sleep thrice. There were husbands, he was sure, who had done that less often with their wives. He would lie quiet, now, for the pleasure of it. And because he was savouring her like the last anise *confit* in the tin. When it was gone, he would still remember the taste.

Also, he would keep watch because his dark memories, once they started up, were discordant notes that lodged in his head. There would be no sleep until the tune got to its end. He would most certainly rather stare at Min than the trees overhead while it played.

Even after Trixie had dropped him into the streets again, he was not bitter. He bowed to the inevitable and looked around, not very successfully, for another means to keep body and soul together. One night, he was squandering his last pence on ale, drinking it slowly against the outside wall of a dank tavern in Whitechapel. A tall, good-looking man, his eyes the colour of smoke and his short hair like ash, leaned against the wall next to him. Too close.

Étienne figured he was a *sodomiste*, and before the man could offer money to let him suck his cock, he grabbed the man's throat with his free hand and made ready to crush it. He considered the man might have a weapon, but he would be dead before he could reach for it.

Choking and unable to form words, the man held out one hand, open. On the palm were four gold sovereigns, more money than the most committed Whitechapel deviate would offer for sex with the Archbishop of Canterbury. More money than Étienne had seen at any one time in his life. He loosened his hold on the man's neck, just enough for him to speak.

The words were hoarse, but empty of fear. 'I've work for you, mate. Payment in advance.'

He had just met Ewan Exeter. Nineteen years old, forty in crime years, he was barely out of Borstal. He had celebrated his release by robbery with violence, though he did not share the details with Étienne as he moved their talk to a bench inside and bought the next round. The 'work' he offered was the Jacks, and the night was the first in five years of nights.

A half decade of darkness. An eternity of wrongdoing. For which he now paid the crushing price. A fair-skinned, chestnut-haired young woman, born in the gentle country twenty miles from where they now lay, had wept, begging him to explain how she had gotten here.

For Min, he did not know. He could not explain, though her tears made deeper cuts in his heart than a *poignard*. And for himself?

He was here because of her.

CHAPTER TWENTY-FIVE

They left the wood at the edge of the hay field at noon, by her watch. The hours of travel that followed were better in some ways, worse in others. She woke to muscles that had a lot to say about what captured spies suffered under torture. Bad enough on its own, but her clothing was in on the abuse. It fought every inch of her skin, and her undergarments chafed maddeningly. Apparently, they'd been waiting until she arrived on Britain's Lower Lip to express their hatred for her body.

She'd loosened her corset before lying on her lumpy heap of leaves for six hours. She couldn't and wouldn't lace herself tightly again. Or at all. While Étienne tended to the horses and Morag spread the ashes of their fire, she went behind a tree, unbuttoned and shed her bodice, and unhooked the top of her skirt placket. The hell-spawned corset came off and she sighed with relief.

The irony didn't escape her. A corset maker so angry at her own workmanship that she'd cheerfully drop it on the ground and leave it there. Perhaps a family of field mice would shred it for bedding. Birds might weave the laces into their nests. Reluctantly, she decided to roll it up and take it along. One never knew when a corset might come in handy.

She was about to walk away when she spotted the black silk ribbon lying at her feet. Reflexively, she patted her throat, even though she could see the dull shine of the pendant trapped in the dark coil on the ground.

She picked up the necklace. Tucking her corset between her knees, she tied the ribbon around her neck, making the securest bow she could. She didn't want to knot it, but it was slithery stuff and liked to come undone. If they reached a settlement large enough to have a jeweller's shop, she'd buy a chain.

A jeweller's shop? What was she thinking? They'd be lucky to find a settlement that had a well.

They mounted the horses. That was to say, Morag mounted, not the Shire but the dappled mare. The Shire and Min eyed each other with distaste.

'You will ride with me,' Étienne said. Before she could object, he heaved her, squealing, atop the pie and leaped up behind her. How could such a big man be so agile? She barely had a second to speculate when they started off.

He'd shed his coat and vest. His powerful arms, in shirtsleeves, encircled her. His massive thighs bracketed her hips. His fists, reins in them, rested casually in her lap.

She flushed hot, then cold. Coherent thought flew away like a startled bird and she was overwhelmed with sensation. It was impossible. They could not do this.

Except that *he* obviously could. They hadn't gone a quarter mile before she realised the protuberance against her lower spine was Étienne's erection.

She was simultaneously so befuddled and excited she couldn't utter a sound. But then, what does one say in a situation like that? '*Pardon me, sir, your manhood is impinging upon my person?*' It wasn't as though he could move it anywhere; it was attached at one end.

They should change places. She could ride pillion, like Morag had done behind her. She'd put her arms around his waist, if they reached. Perhaps she could just hold on to his braces, like the hanging straps on an omnibus.

'A man cannot control some things,' he rumbled, his mindreading trick enlarging her shock by a factor of two. 'Pay no attention.'

By all means. She would do that. *Distraction, distraction.*

Morag provided it, asking, 'Air we gettin' close?'

Sitting her horse in apparent ease, the Scotswoman nodded when Étienne replied, 'We have yet some distance to go.'

Morag smiled and began singing softly to herself in Gaelic. She was altogether more alert and responsive than when she'd been at Raeburn House. She persisted in calling Min 'my lady,' but the honorific might just be a relic of her long years as a countess's maid, like a sailor's rolling walk or a gambler's habit of tumbling dice in his pocket.

The query led Min to one of her own. Trying not to move any more than was strictly necessary – a hopeless strategy, since the horse's gait bounced her against Étienne's groin every few seconds – she asked over her shoulder, 'Where exactly are we going? And please, don't say Scotland.'

Plymouth was his answer. She sorted through what she knew of the town. Almost nothing, beyond the *Mayflower* and Charles Darwin. The name certainly had none of the magic Agnes Broadripple had given it but meant something to Étienne. There were other *cachettes*, he explained, his label for hideouts, but only Plymouth held a former associate, a smuggler, whose discretion could be relied upon.

Discretion. Do I really want to know why?

'A day more of travel,' he said. 'Two, at the outside.'

Two more days. Anything could happen in two days. To avoid more wriggling, she addressed the shock of black mane between the piebald's ears.

'Can't you just put me on a train, Étienne? Surely, we're not that far from the railway.'

'I will not permit that you travel with no protection other than a maid. Nor can I accompany you, since Fitzsimmons will have police looking for the three of us at every stop. Morag's capture would profit Fitzsimmons nothing. Yours, a great deal more. For dragging me before the courts, Fitzsimmons would be a hero.'

She gave up arguing her case. The road stretched on and on for several hours while they saw no one and heard no voices but their own. When she was about to scream from the tedium, they halted outside a village so small it hadn't even a roadside stone with a name.

Her spirits sank when Étienne pointed the Shire into a lacy fringe of trees alongside an old chapel. She'd been hoping for a room for the night, a hot meal, even a bath. Not, apparently, features of No Name Village.

Once both horses were well-hidden among the drooping branches of ancient yews, Étienne sent Morag to the village. She was armed with the empty flask, some coins, and strict instructions about what to say and not say. A well with a bucket and a creaky hand crank in the churchyard produced water for the horses. Étienne went about that while Min paced, stretching her aching limbs.

In a half hour, Morag returned. She brought a sack of pasties, a few apples, and the flask, filled with cider.

And a newspaper. While the women sat on a fallen log to tear into the food, Étienne stood, reading *The Western Times*. Min was glad she'd eaten before he passed it down to her.

'Front page,' he said.

Disturbing News from Great Torrington

From the Constabulary at Great Torrington comes a report of abduction and murder. A known French criminal, Edouard Sansecours, overcame a warder at a lunatic asylum, Raeburn House near Meeth, and made off with two female inmates. The warder's lifeless body was discovered in an adjacent wood by constables investigating the incident. The victim appeared to have sustained a fatal knife wound to the chest. A valuable horse was also stolen.

It is believed the abductor retains his two captives and is making for the southern coast. The police inquiry will remain active until the women are freed and their murderous abductor apprehended. Major Arden Fitzsimmons, chief constable at Great Torrington, asks the public to be vigilant. News of sightings or any other intelligence about the party should be sent forthwith, by wire, to the Great Torrington Constabulary.

As though struck by magic, she transformed into lichen. Immobile, stuck to the log, she couldn't speak or move. The newspaper remained in her hands, but she no longer understood the words on the page.

Morag finished her meal and stood, handing the half-empty sack to Étienne. She began wandering through the churchyard, running her hands over the broad, wrinkled trunks of the yews.

Still too stunned to think or speak sensibly, Min finally said, 'The papers got the story fast.'

'The miracle of telegraphy.' The corner of his mouth quirked. 'I was sure Fitzsimmons and Raeburn would hasten to enlist the press and the public.'

She shouldn't have doubted him or the circuitous escape he was leading them on. She would have stumbled into the snare set for her like the stupidest rabbit in England.

'They got your name wrong.'

'A stroke of luck. The four Edouards in England will be made most uncomfortable in coming weeks.' He finished the pasties from the bag in large, efficient bites, chasing them with a lengthy draught of the cider.

'I'm not an inmate, either.'

'The chief constable could hardly describe you as the victim of an extortion and kidnapping plot engineered by him and the superintendent. Such candour from criminals, while refreshing, is unlikely.'

'How did they know we're heading south?'

Étienne's answer was a particularly eloquent French shrug. 'We were seen by someone. A tramp, a stockman, his wife, their dog. Or the *journaliste* consulted a seer.'

He stretched, arms to the sky. 'We are too close to the river and still too much to the east. From this hour, we will avoid towns and villages. It is summer, a good time to see the pretty Devonshire country. We will take the smaller lanes.'

Could there be any lanes smaller than the ones they'd taken so far? She dropped the newspaper on the ground. A small, speckled apple nestled in the lap of her skirt and she reached it up to Étienne. She'd lost her appetite completely. She might not know her county's roads and rivers with any specificity beyond Little Farnleigh, but in a general way she was well-acquainted with Devon's rutted tracks and burdock-infested fields, its unfriendly farm dogs and unfriendlier farmers. Encountering them as a fugitive wasn't something she anticipated with glee.

She sighed gustily and stood, brushing off her skirt. The dust of the road was turning it into a slate colour instead of the rich black it had been when she buttoned herself into it a week ago. Not quite a week. A handful of days, each of them defying the laws of time to last for a year.

Étienne picked up *The Western Times*. Folding it, he walked to the mare. First, he gave the horse the apple, along with a pat and some French endearments. The newspaper went into his coat, the coat across her withers.

He gave a low whistle in Morag's direction. She skipped out of the trees and hopped onto the mare like a girl who'd won top prize in the village gymkhana. Min clambered awkwardly aboard the pie, Étienne pulling himself up behind her.

They moved away from the road that had taken them into No Name Village, Étienne in the lead. She had no idea how he knew where to go, or even if he did. Hers not to reason why, etcetera. If she had to choose between wandering around Devon with him and meeting Fitzsimmons and Raeburn again, the 'known French criminal' won the coconut shy in a clean sweep.

What with fatigue and the heat and the additional worries the *Western Times* had dropped on them, Min thought surely the body of the man behind her wouldn't be so – responsive. But they'd gone not a mile southwest from the village when she felt what a novelist would call 'the proof of his desire' nudging her in the back again. Unlike the first time, Étienne didn't remark on it. Was he being a Frenchman, worldly and jaded? Did he think she had merely added his response to her storehouse of natural history, like the moon pulling the tide and birds mating in the spring? It was alarming that he would think her so blasé.

Even more alarmingly, she didn't know if she wanted to jump off the horse into the nearest ditch or turn around and beg him to use his proof as Nature intended.

The miles and the hours dragged onward, and she couldn't make up her mind.

The route to Plymouth – if they were still going there; she'd rather lost the plot – got longer instead of shorter. Étienne's small-lanes diversion was to blame, since after No Name they came across so few human settlements they might have been Ancient Romans, exploring Brittania.

After hours of meandering through trackless countryside in a generally western direction, they turned due south, onto a genuine road. Not a broad or paved one, but a well-worn wagon track that showed decades, possibly generations, of traffic on hard-packed, Devon-red earth.

Two questions burst like flushed quails from her sketchy mental map of the environs. Were they close to Dartmoor? Did Étienne intend to cross it? She shivered at both possibilities.

The moor had always been a refuge for fleeing felons, bandits, escaped prisoners of war, and Gypsies. Is that what her life had become? Good Lord, she'd gone from Mayfair to a desolation of tors and bogs in a matter of weeks.

Once she got past the first shock, though, she found she couldn't generate the dismay Dartmoor probably deserved. She was weary to her bones. She'd even stopped worrying about the compromising position she and Étienne were in atop the pie.

Tiredness and the long shadows of late afternoon lulled her into a drowse. She lay back against his chest and let her eyelids droop. He was safety and strength. He would never let her slide off the horse. Just as he'd done in the kitchen at Les Pinsons, he'd catch her. She'd been nearly asleep then, too, but not so deeply that she hadn't felt him lift her from the chair at the table and bear her away. To his bed.

Where she wished she was now. Lying on clean white linen. The room growing dark, darker, as the day wore out its welcome and settled to sleep along with her.

Suddenly, the body behind her went so rigid she was almost propelled off it. Étienne gathered the reins higher. She roused herself to look around. They were in no part of the county she recognised, and the road stretched ahead with nothing but more road. When she'd shut her eyes, hedges of hazel and hawthorn had been crowding it on both sides, fields visible in the breaks. Now, the road was a ribbon laid down on dull green moorland, dotted with small clumps of trees and not a single farm or house in view. Ada would call the scene 'the yawnin' arse crack of nowhere.'

'Where do you think we–' she began, but Étienne's hand, rough, warm, and smelling of leather, covered her mouth. The pie sensed its rider's urgency. Head high, its ears pricked and swivelled.

With a '*Hue!*' so low only she and the horse heard, Étienne kicked it into a gallop and off the road, the mare following closely. Min might have been a sack across the saddle for all the Shire cared. It simply drove forward while she gripped the pommel. The two horses plunged noisily into a scanty patch of trees some fifty or sixty yards from the road.

Morag was off and lying flat on the ground before the mare quite stopped moving. Étienne slipped off the pie, pulling Min with him. He all but flung her to the earth and lay half atop her. The horses stood where they were, unmoving, quiet.

'Do not make a sound,' he said unnecessarily into her ear. Make a sound? She couldn't have spoken her own name, though her heart pounded so violently she was sure it could be heard in the road. They lay like foxes in a covert, listening.

Then, she heard them. Horses. More than one or two. A small group, nearing. A hundred years ago, those sounds would have meant highwaymen. Even now, they heralded people she didn't want to meet. The man with her, even less.

His body lay across her. The weight both comforted and imprisoned. She couldn't move her torso, but she turned her head, seeking his eyes. He didn't return the look. Focused entirely on the road, his face was drawn with tension, his jaw set like iron.

She couldn't raise herself sufficiently to see the approaching riders. She fought to discern, over the rushing blood in her ears, whether their pace slowed as they neared. It didn't seem so, but just as Étienne had wrenched the three of them off the road because he'd heard a distant noise, the party of riders might have spotted some glimpse of them. Might veer toward them in an instant.

'*Sept.*' Seven riders, his whisper said. If they had weapons and knew how to use them, they would be like a small army when they attacked. She and Morag were all but useless, not even a hatpin between them. It would be Étienne defending them alone, one against seven.

He didn't need to tell her again to remain still. She was frozen with terror. More than when Fitzsimmons struck her in the face, or when she heard Raeburn coolly discussing how he would torture her into marriage. More than when she'd collided with Cawsey at the bottom of the stairs.

Despite the paralysis of her brain, her body absurdly yearned into Étienne's. His weight atop her on a patch of marshland wasn't how she'd imagined it, but it was still him, his power, the heavy promise of his limbs. Her face was just under his jaw; her breath grazed the sprouting beard there and on his upper lip and chin. The dark-shadowed visage joined with his barely leashed ferocity, with all and every aspect of him. *Danger, danger.*

The man she knew as Étienne Sansecours had stayed behind in the village with the yews in the churchyard. The man who protected her with his body was *Le Dague*, the notorious criminal the police of Britain were avid to put in chains.

The mounted men were closer. So close she heard the collective rumble of hooves and the squeak of leather. Dread ushered a macabre troupe of actors onto the stage of her imagination. Violence, pain, horses screaming and wheeling, seven against one. The men charging, Étienne's knives flashing, his magnificent body bleeding out on the earth. The men falling upon her and Morag.

She closed her eyes and focused on the steady breath and thudding heart of the man who pressed her to the earth. The scent of him filled her nostrils; she took it deeply into her lungs and held it there.

If my life ends today, I'll have known what this was like.

CHAPTER TWENTY-SIX

Foutu! What were seven mounted men and nine horses doing on this seldom-travelled path? Here, there were no wayhouses, no inns, no villages. Smugglers knew it as a way into and across Dartmoor. Tin, spirits, tobacco, sugar, lace: for decades they had been cached in barely accessible spots dotting the moor. Most of the seagoing end of that trade had withered before he was born. He had heard that what smuggling now persisted served inmates and guards at Dartmoor Prison. Some of the same contraband as before, some new, like knives. And untaxed goods still came from Ireland, or down the coast from Scotland, even from across the Atlantic. The old Dartmoor caches served new masters, new uses. As did this back road in and out, apparently. A good smuggling route never really died.

Was that the purpose of these approaching riders? The time of day argued for smuggling. Innocent travellers would be tucked up at an inn, not plunging at dusk into the barren landscape of Dartmoor. If they were smugglers, there was no label broad enough to call them innocent, but were they simply going about their business, unconnected to him and the two women?

Nothing about his former life called to Étienne. Even so, there had been a time when he could have shown himself, given a sign or two, and been accepted – warily – as a confederate. The French branch of the firm, so to speak.

To show himself now would probably mean death for him. For the women... He would not think of that.

The riders did not slow as they cantered across the axis running from the trees to the middle of the road. Not a single glance in his party's direction, not the slightest change in the riders' pace. With the two riderless beasts carrying large packs, the men would be focused on delivering their goods without hindrance or discovery. They kept their eyes forward, their pace brisk. They would probably feel as much consternation as he to know they were being watched.

He did not recognise a single man. They were young, except for the one in the lead. He had forty years, maybe more. Hatless, his dark hair streamed behind him. Not so large as Étienne, he was still formidable. Broad in the shoulders, tall in the saddle, he projected authority from atop his roan stallion. Étienne knew without seeing weapons that the leader and all his men bristled with them. Not men he should wish to meet in an unlighted street.

Or on the isolated wastes of Dartmoor.

The men's passage took less than a minute but felt like an eternity. When the hoofbeats died away, he counted to 200, then got to his feet and extended a hand to Min.

'We will edge the moor and approach Plymouth from the other side. It will add another day, but it is better that way.' He looked around the patchy trees, blackthorn and rowan, oak and birch. The dense shadows deeper within beckoned to him. He would wager they promised water, a spring, perhaps. The Scotswoman also squinted into the grove, probably thinking the same.

Min's gaze was fixed not at the wood but at him. His heart warmed and then chilled at the wholeness of her trust. He made himself smile. 'We will be safe here for the night.'

CHAPTER TWENTY-SEVEN

In the end, they probably got to Plymouth before Agnes, but not by much. Étienne pushed them hard in the final miles, so that when they arrived, they were hungry, dirty, and worn to stumps. A day and a half after they'd seen the horsemen on the fringe of Dartmoor, they fetched up at The Eel's Pocket. The name was painted in red-on-blue hoarding over the whitewashed, two-storey café cum hotel. Étienne reminded her that it belonged to his *confrère*.

It wasn't elegant, but neither were they. In a one-on-one match with The Eel's Pocket for shabbiness, her party would come out ahead. Étienne put on his coat, but his once-fine suit was creased in a hundred places. His collar and tie were stuffed in his coat pocket. His waistcoat had lost a few buttons and the survivors were fastened awry.

Her dress was streaked with mud and so spattered with dust it looked like the dappled mare's coat. She didn't have a hairpin left to her name.

Morag, if she really had been a retainer, was evidently attached to a family careless of its help. Her ragged dress appeared a day or two from disintegrating completely. She fretted at the neck of her bodice and scratched her scalp constantly. Min suspected fleas. Or flower bugs. Perhaps an invasion of beetles. Both Morag's hair and her own offered uncombed, unwashed nests for the full range of Devonshire insects.

She twisted Étienne's gold signet ring on the third finger of her left hand. He'd made her put it on, band side up, outside the town. Even his smallest finger was big enough that the fit was precarious. She'd torn a narrow strip of cloth from her petticoat and wrapped it round and round the signet side to hold the ring in place. She wasn't sure why she was wearing it, but it would be unthinkable to lose it.

He had posted a letter from the last village they'd skirted – Modbury, she thought – so they must be expected, but they hovered on the cobbles for a few moments. She jerked in surprise when he roared.

'*Bordel de merde!* This used to be a good whorehouse. Now, look! It's an ugly hotel.'

A short, barrel-chested man charged through the door and at them. Surprisingly, he stopped at their feet, grinned, and hauled up Étienne's hand with both of his, wringing it like a pump handle.

'Strike me blind, yeh French bugger. Yeh bigger every time I sees yeh.'

'You forget things because you are old. How many years you have now, Sammy? Two hundred?'

'Sammy' laughed hugely and the two men cheerfully cuffed and pummelled each other, the way men did. Min had never known Étienne to be any smaller than at present, but she'd not dispute the other man's age, which was probably fifty. Or his profession, a clue to it winking from the gold ring in the lobe of his left ear. His nut-brown face was seamed with lines and the lack of hair on his head was made up for by a curling white beard that fell to the third button of his striped shirt. His eyebrows matched the beard. Under the brows, sharp black eyes weren't so nailed on the 'French bugger' that they couldn't roam over his two bedraggled female companions. The eyes quested for information she hoped she wouldn't have to supply.

The welcome buffeting ended with the men standing a little apart. She didn't hear any mechanical noises, but she sensed her companion gearing up before he tilted his head toward her and said, 'My wife, Minerva.'

Like that, was it? She couldn't say the ring hadn't given her fair warning, but it was still a shock to hear it aloud.

The bearded man's bow was more accomplished than she'd expect from someone who looked like a buccaneer. When he straightened, he pressed his palms together at his chest.

'Samath Rao. *Vanakkam. Eppadi irukkindriirga?*'

'He asks if you are well.' Étienne's translation did nothing to help her respond. *No, Mr Rao, I'm not very well at present, thank you for asking. I am indescribably filthy and so tired I can barely stand. I also believe I've acquired fleas from my 'maid', whom no one has introduced because she's, well, a maid.*

She condensed her rambling thoughts into an oblique sentence. 'You have a charming establishment, Mr Rao.' *Does it pay as well as smuggling?*

A shrug and an even broader grin from Rao. His teeth were white and irregular, a few missing. 'My late wife Siobhan, blessings upon her! Give me six daughter and no son. *Ay, de mi!* Of course, I open a *pension de famille*.' The speech was a sea voyage with stops at several ports.

Étienne lowered his voice and faced away from the open door when he spoke. 'Old friend, my wife and I need a room. Something quiet, *tu sais*.'

'I know, sure, yes, all good,' Rao nodded. 'And the other one?'

'My wife's maid. Is there a place for her?'

'I got cupboard–' At Étienne's start, Rao's hands came up. 'Not for cheese and wine! But in kitchen, like, with box bed. Had boy here till silly bugger run off to join Army.' Rao lifted his chin toward Morag. 'Safe in there, her. Lock on *inside*.'

Trust a couple of outlaws to know the horror of any other kind of lock.

'Our horses,' Étienne began, but Rao cut him off with a shrill whistle, two fingers in his mouth. The sound was still echoing in the narrow street when a flat-capped boy of about twelve, barefoot, in ragged pants and a loose shirt under a too-large waistcoat, dashed from around the corner of the hotel and skidded to the Shire's side. His face glowed with admiration as he ran a bony brown hand across the pie's neck.

'Daughter number six, Chaya.' Rao snatched away the cap to release thick black curls. 'Hate dress and smell like horse.' Scowling, the girl yanked back the cap and stuffed her hair under it.

Rao jerked his chin up the lane and the girl hopped like a grasshopper into the pie's saddle, despite him being nearly twice her height. She held out her hand for the mare's reins and then deftly turned both beasts around, moving them up the lane and out of sight. She sat the Shire easily, her slender back straight with pride.

Rao shook his head. 'Can't do nothin' with that one. Lucky I own livery stable.'

He beckoned them into the cool, dim café. The smell of food was stronger there, and Min's stomach leaped hopefully. A half dozen men sat at tables, some drinking, some eating, none giving their straggling party much notice. It was Plymouth, after all, where odd people came and went with the tide. Too much scrutiny was considered impolite. Not to mention unhealthy.

Étienne glanced at her. His hand steadied her shoulder just as she started to sway with exhaustion. 'Sammy. You have a washroom?'

'Two of 'em, I got, one each end of hall. Bathtubs, you bet. I send hot water to both. Plenty, for washing one moose and one pretty but very dirty little monkey.' Étienne frowned, but Rao laughed, then pushed an iron key into Étienne's hand. 'Number

Four.' He pointed upward with a dark finger and winked. 'Next to outside stairs.'

Inside locks and outside stairs. Rao should rename his hotel The Smugglers' Rest. Her stomach chose that moment to growl so loudly it probably startled people in the street.

Rao just cackled again. 'Send food, too. Everything better with food.'

CHAPTER TWENTY-EIGHT

He insisted she wash before him. If she'd been offered a Roman bath, it wouldn't have felt any better than the washroom's big tub, filled with buckets of hot water by two dark, giggling girls in calico dresses who left as she entered.

A less soothing fixture than the tub was a small mirror, affixed to the wall. After her bath, when she wiped the steam off both her eyeglasses and the mirror, she got her first good look at Fitzsimmon's handiwork on her face. Aubergine, she'd call the colour the bruise had darkened to. If it were a corset, Evie could have dyed the laces beautifully.

She hated to put soiled clothing on a clean body, but she'd not had the foresight to pack a Chinese silk dressing gown in her handbag. Her nose crinkled, but she donned the battered mourning gown again.

The door to Number Four demonstrated that her conversion from *corsetière* to criminal accomplice was coming along. She didn't consider for an instant that Étienne would leave the door unlocked, and he hadn't. He opened it to her knock.

A tea table occupied the middle of the room. It was covered with dishes, half of which were emptied. She steadfastly avoided looking at the bed that filled most of the remaining space. And the man who occupied what was left.

The night was not cold, but he had built a fire in the room's small hearth. She knew he'd done it so she could dry her hair. It was a kindness.

He took her shoulders and steered her to a chair at the table. 'Eat.'

Oui, mon Genéral. The full dishes were complete strangers to her, their colours as dazzling as a Renaissance still life, *Exotic Viands in Ochre, Yellow, and Green*. The aroma was intoxicating. The expression 'so hungry I could eat a horse' came to mind. Her stomach suggested horse was welcome on any menu she was presented today.

'I looked in on Morag.' He spoke from the half-open door. 'When last seen, she was, as the English say, "nattering away" with the cook. Tea and pastry were involved. The cook praised Morag's appetite. Praise also went to the large washtub in the scullery, which was employed to make your maid, in Cook's words, "clean as a new pin".'

Min sniffed. 'Morag's not my maid. And I'm not a countess.'

'She is. You are. We will debate the fine points when I return from also making myself clean as a sewing tool. Put your soiled clothes outside the door. They will be laundered and returned.'

Her mouth was already full, so she nodded. After he left, she realised that if her clothes were outside the door, she would be wearing nothing at all.

'Thank you for the loan of your shirt.' It hung nearly to her ankles, a moot point since she was sitting up in bed with the covers pulled to her breasts. Nor was there much light. The fire had burned low and she'd lighted only one oil lamp on the small table next to the bed.

'You found it, then.' Étienne spoke to the back of Number Four's door. He'd just shut it – firmly. She steadfastly ignored the sound of the bolt being shot.

'I did. It was on a hook, very appropriately facing the wall to protect my modesty.'

'Are you modest?' As nonchalantly as if he'd not just locked them in together, he faced her. He'd not only bathed but shaved. The smooth chin and upper lip startled her a bit. In the past few days, she'd grown used to seeing him swarthy as a pirate. Casually, he began unfastening the buttons of his shirt, starting at the top. His cuffs were already undone, flapping loose around his wrists.

'Believe it or not, before Agnes Broadripple nearly caught us out on the lawn of Raeburn House, I'd never done an immodest thing in my life.'

'Modesty is too highly prized.'

'Says the man who sleeps without a nightshirt.'

In one motion, he pulled his shirt off. A jungle of illustrated skin emerged. She'd seen it before. But only his forearms, in detail. The rest, when she'd stumbled into his bedroom and finally emerged from the bedlinens, was only half-seen, a flash of forms and colour in moonlight.

Apart from the ink, his torso was... astounding. She'd seen a photographic image of Donatello's *David* in an art book once, before Asa Hawkins had swept it out of the house during one of his periodic moral purges of the library. Poor David. He'd been immortalised as a spindly youth with skinny arms and a weak chest.

The man disrobing before her had biceps bigger around than her waist. His pectorals were twin engines of power. Her mouth went suddenly dry. *Just the spicy food*, she told herself.

He folded his shirt and placed it on the seat of the only chair; his coat and waistcoat were already draped over the back. 'There are some who say that for health and honesty, we should all go about unclothed.'

'Yes, but they're German.'

He began unbuttoning his trousers.

'Let me give you some privacy,' she squeaked, and dove under the bedcovers. They weren't so thick she couldn't hear him laughing.

'I will douse the light,' he said. 'To protect your modesty, since we have determined it is profound.'

There were shuffles and clicks as he turned down the lamp on the bedside table. A rustle of cloth against skin. That would be him divesting himself of his trousers. They'd established beyond any argument that he would not be donning a nightshirt. A few seconds later, a muffled concussion beyond the end of the bed shook the floor.

'You may leave your burrow, now, little fox. The room is quite dark. I will pass the night on this small rug at the bed foot, like a faithful hound. Take care not to tread upon me if you rise to visit the toilet up the hall.'

Take care, yes, she would do that. She would be careful as a cat crossing Piccadilly Circus. She emerged from the bedlinens. To have something to do other than acknowledge a big naked man in the room, she unhooked her spectacles and folded them, not rushing. The bedside commode was covered with an embroidered white cloth, the lamp on it still warm. Carefully, she placed her spectacles next to the lamp, fluffed her pillow, and propped herself up against it.

A tense and lengthy silence ensued. Perhaps they were frayed by their expedition across Devonshire, like wilderness explorers must be after a trek. Suffering the effects of sleeping rough, eating badly, fearing always.

Now, they were on clean sheets, well fed, and safe. They should fall headlong and instantly into sleep. Instead, a mutual awareness of the bed and each other grew until the dark was filled with imps of conjecture. A hundred tiny pitchforks prodded her until she had to say something.

'Étienne. Are you awake?' The words came out so small and his answer took so long, she thought he hadn't heard her. Finally, a heavy sigh issued from the floor.

'Yes.'

'Do you want to talk about Scotland?'

'No.'

That came out fast enough. 'Do you... do you want to talk about us?'

At that, he sat up. Her eyes were getting used to the dark and the window curtains over the bed were open a handspan, admitting weak moonlight. Even without her eyeglasses, she discerned the shape of his head through the iron spindles of the footrail, the tousle of his wet hair above.

'There is no "us", Minerva. There is only you.'

'Oh, there's an us, Étienne. We were both there on the lawn at Raeburn House...' Was there a respectable word for what they'd been doing? '...embracing. Or don't you remember.'

He clasped the top of the footrail, his fist filling the space between two spindles. She could just see his eyes. It was a trick of the moonlight, she knew, but flecks of gold glinted from the brown of them. 'Minerva. When I am old and dying among the vines of Les Pinsons, I will give my last moments to that embrace. No matter how long I have lived, no matter what I have done, it will be what I choose to remember.'

Sorrow and longing contorted her face, sending a flash of pain through the bruise. Everything she wanted and couldn't have rose like a river at flood. In seconds she was breathless, drowning.

She began to cry like the sniveller she'd become. Crying and wailing and generally falling apart in a strange bed in a strange town, all because of the strange life that she'd never asked for but was now hers.

'I-I don't want to go to Scotland. I don't want to be a countess. I want to go home, I want to...' She sobbed into her hands.

Linen rustled and the mattress depressed as Étienne lowered himself to sit beside her. Heat and the scent of almonds and a deep voice came with him.

'Min, *je t'en pris*. I beg you, don't weep. You destroy me when you weep.'

And then, he was kissing her. Not the fierce and consuming kisses on the lawn. Gentle feathering kisses across her wet cheeks, brushing her jaw, careful of her wound. Murmurs in French, in English, all in the warm rumble she loved so well. *Ma chère, ma vie*, my dear, my life.

He worked his fingers into the loose braid of her bath-damp hair, teasing out the thick fall until it tumbled over her shoulders. Pressing a handful against his face, he inhaled deeply of her scent.

There was no place on his body she did not want to touch, to stroke, to please. She fingered the angles of his face. Gripped his shoulders, lay her palms upon his chest, delighting in the crisp hair over hard flesh.

Her fingers went to the buttons of the shirt he'd lent her. He helped her loosen them and stripped it from her body. She pushed down the covers or he pulled them away. All at once they were naked, skin to skin.

They lay down and pressed together, inevitable and right as the tide.

CHAPTER TWENTY-NINE

Slow, I must go slow. He must somehow remain master of his body; that was the most important thing. She was a slender, untried maiden, and he was a rutting stag. The hot weight between his thighs drew up, his tool surged against her belly. His blood sang with the need to spread her lovely long legs and take her all at once. *Slow, slow.*

'I want to be inside you.' Tears of the Holy Virgin, what was he saying? That was not being slow, that was sounding a war trumpet and charging her maidenhead. 'I mean–'

'I want you inside me.' She tried to wriggle beneath him.

'Wait, Min, wait.' *She wants it that badly, perhaps you should...* No. 'This first time, it will hurt, *p'tit.* Only this once, I swear it. But I can make it...' He drew his hand down her body, past her lovely white breasts with their impudent nipples, past her fluttering stomach. 'Let me touch you a little.'

'Only if I can touch you.'

Oh, yes, do that. Touch me here, and there, and... He slapped the mouth of the drooling rake in his head. He put her hand to his cock and she fisted it. It bobbed at the touch, a gentlemanly nod before it did something sudden and wet.

'Like this?' Her grip slid up and down, regular and firm.

Oh, Christ. She had the face of an angel and the fingers of a courtesan.

'Am I doing it right?' Some untranslatable noise came from his mouth. Not missing a stroke, Min kept talking. 'I hope so. I did the milking at home.'

He made the noise again and comprehended its meaning. Desperation. Wired to ecstasy. Packed into a bomb that was ready to explode.

'One moment, Min,' he strangled out. 'Let us engage in radical politics.'

'What – *now?* I don't want to–'

He turned in the bed. Demon lover that she was, she managed to keep her hand on his cock the while. 'In 1779, the revolutionary Théroigne de Méricour named this thing *soixante-neuf.*'

'That's a funny–' As he slid into position, Min got her first close look at what an anatomical text he had read called *the organ of generation.* 'Bloody hell.'

'Just continue what you were doing, *ma chère.* I will busy myself some short time with *ton minou.* Your little pussycat.' He nestled his face between her legs.

The next few minutes took him somewhere he knew he could not be. Somehow, on the road of a life that should have led directly to hell, he had diverted to heaven. There was no other explanation for the trembling, silken thighs bracketing his head. The unutterably sweet sounds from Min as he licked and suckled her. The sea salt taste of her loins, the pliant flesh under his mouth. The heat of her, the rising excitement under his tongue.

He wanted to roar his manhood to the world. She was his, *his.*

Not roaring, groaning. Whimpering, almost, as she added her mouth to those fingers that had so pleased the cows of Devonshire. He squeezed shut his eyes against the onrush of his climax. *Not yet, not yet.*

Evidently, he had been possessed by some delusion when they

were first naked. Had thought they would enjoy themselves in this position for a space and then explore other numbers on the erotic scale. If a bewigged founder of the French Republic could invent them, he could, too. Eleven, twenty-seven, sixteen... He had no idea what any of those were. But he had a profound willingness to make them up as they went past *soixante-neuf*.

There was not the flimsiest chance of his making it that far.

With a sort of steam welling in his head, he thrust a finger into Min. She cried out and bucked against his hand. He thrust again, again, and felt sudden, fierce contractions inside her. Not for one instant did she stop gripping and pulling his cock, while she pulsed and flooded around him.

Sensation put a match to his spine and he went up in a searing torch of pleasure.

Chapter Thirty

She splayed her fingers over her face and spoke through them. 'I can't believe I screamed. Everyone in this hotel probably heard me.'

He rescued his shirt from where it had hidden from the past hour's action and used it to wipe spend from her breasts and stomach. 'For some little time, I left my body, so it is possible we both screamed. Possible, as well, that everyone in the next few streets heard us.'

She groaned. 'That doesn't bother you?'

He picked up her left hand and fingered the ring. 'You are my wife, remember? Even in England, which is the Greenland of passion, it is not unusual for a husband and wife to enjoy each other in bed.'

'That's as may be. But the English are a less *exuberant* people.'

'Perhaps you have French blood.' He ran a finger gently over her lower lip. 'Yes, without a doubt, this mouth is French. I hear it say, "Give me a thousand kisses, then a hundred, then a second thousand, then a second hundred."'

'That's not my mouth; it belonged to Catullus. I had a good Latin tutor until Asa Hawkins discovered he was teaching me erotic poetry and sacked him.'

'*Oui*, Catullus, I know him well. French on his mother's side.'

She clucked derisively, but perhaps she did have French ancestry. She knew almost nothing about her mother the countess and less about her father the earl. She could be part Esquimo and the rest Norwegian.

She rolled on her side, facing him. He, on his back, promptly pulled her knee up so her leg was across his groin. The warm mass of his cock began to swell as he rubbed her thigh against it. His recovery was impressive, but then, maybe all men were that way?

Before she got a collar on it, the question lunged. 'Are you– Is that, I mean, are you always so... ready?'

'No.'

She waited, but he didn't elaborate. Fair enough. She wasn't prepared to hear his intimate history with women, anyway.

'May I ask something else?'

'How many times a night? That depends on–'

'No!' She'd find out soon enough, in any case. 'That wasn't my question. It's about why we're here.'

'In The Eel's Pocket?'

'In Plymouth.'

His sigh had that long-suffering quality that was becoming familiar. 'It was necessary for us both to leave northern Devonshire, Min. You, because I cannot permit you to be within reach of that *canaille* Raeburn again. Or his jackal, Fitzsimmons. And me, because of–'

'The warrants?'

'The warrants.'

'I know all that.' She put her hand on his to stop the rubbing. He kept it up, anyway. Not that she didn't like it, but she wanted a different answer to the same question. If he kept up the rubbing, questions would be over for the night.

'What I mean is, I understand why we didn't just go to Great Torrington so you could put me on a train to London. And I agree, it was prudent to leave that whole part of the county. But

ANNIE R MCEWEN

apart from a charming hotel owned by your former – colleague – why are we in *Plymouth*?'

He dropped his chin, casting a critical glance at her from under dark brown lashes. 'Samath Rao is not only a hotelier. He is an expert seaman, and he knows the coastal waters like a fish.'

'Because he's a smuggler.'

The leg rubbing stopped and he agreed with the label by not disputing it. 'What is important, is that Sammy Rao has been to Scotland many times by sea. The way is as familiar to him as the streets of this town. You are still going to Scotland, yes?'

She wriggled up in the bed to half lie on his chest, her head over his heart. It was a steady thump under her ear. 'I suppose so,' she said glumly.

'You must do more than suppose, *ma douce*. At Dunmara, an entire life waits for you, a fine life. If what I learned about the estate is even partially correct, you have a home, a grand house. There are lands and tenants and...'

'I don't want any of that.' She knew she shouldn't let it out, but out it came. 'I want you.'

He went silent and still. When the words finally came, they were the gentlest of knives, cutting her heart to ribbons. 'Min, we cannot be together. We have only this night. No more.'

'Because you're a wanted man.'

'That is reason enough that you should remove yourself from my side with all speed. There is nowhere in Britain that being with me would not put you in danger.'

'I'm not patriotic. We could live abroad.'

He pushed her knee aside and took her hand from his shoulder, putting it on his tool. It wasn't quite the size it had been, but definitely getting there. She wrapped her fingers around him and he enclosed her fist in his, then began moving their overlapping hands in a slow, strong rhythm. He grew harder, thicker. Her breath came fast, and she yearned for more.

'Ah, *oui*, that part works well enough.' His voice was ragged

176

and ironic. 'Others do not.' He pulled her hand from his cock, now rigid and proud against his belly. Below, his balls were tight, drawn up to his body. Bending his far knee, he held her fingers under the taut sack and pressed them against a hard ridge of tissue.

'There, do you feel it?'

She nodded, confused. Was he somehow different down there than other men? How would she know?

'It was many years ago, at Les Pinsons. My two older brothers – half-brothers, we had different mothers – were savage as feral dogs.' He replaced her hand on his member and straightened his leg. 'To beat me was a diversion for them, one they copied from my father. I cannot recall, after so much time, what they were beating me for that day in the wine shed. It could have been anything or nothing.

'I was not then the size I am now. Not yet experienced in *savate*, the style of fighting I later learned from *les contrabandiers* along the coast. Nor had I ever touched a *poignard*. But I was not weak. I had been growing larger and stronger every year. My brothers began to be wary of me. I did not know until that day, but they made certain they had always a weapon nearby, something more sure than their fists.

'I picked up Leo, the oldest of us, and threw him on his back. I was crouched upon him, ready to slam his head onto the floor of the shed. But in the waist of his trousers he had a *hippe*, a hooked knife used to prune the vines. He drove it up, two-handed, between my legs.'

His low laugh hadn't a speck of real humour in it. 'He sought to geld me, my brother. His aim was poor, but the hook went deep. I was fevered for many days. When a doctor finally saw the wound, he said something had been destroyed, some small cord to my balls.

'I tell you this disgusting tale because it is yet another reason this thing between us is impossible. I cannot give you babies, Min.'

'Babies? Have I ever mentioned cradles, nappies, teething

rings?' She checked her indignation. It was wrong to be flippant about something he seemed to think was a gigantic disability. 'You can call me unwomanly, but I don't give a toss about babies.'

'Ah, you say that, now. But you will change.'

No, I won't. I want you, Étienne, just you. And us, just us. She couldn't say it aloud. In the time it took her to come up with something she could, he'd rolled her onto her back and started stroking her breasts. Stroking and cooing and – *great roaring trumpets of Jericho* – sucking them.

If she lived to a hundred, she'd never forget that sensation. The first time, a man's mouth on her nipples, circling them with his tongue. Lightly biting the soft flesh around them and then settling on the rising, sensitive peaks, one at a time. His fingers plucking and rolling the one not in his mouth. She writhed and whimpered, so helpless with arousal that she couldn't decide what to do with her hands.

In desperation, she grabbed his free hand and put it between her legs. She didn't care what he did there, as long as he did *something*.

He, being a man and Étienne, knew exactly what to do. Already nearly levitating to the ceiling from his attention to her breasts, Min let out a small shriek when he dipped a finger into her drenched sex. With maddening slowness, he tunnelled the finger, then two, inside. Fully embedded, he went to work with his thumb on the outer part. The little nub that had brought her to screaming release before was swollen and hard again, and he knew just how to stroke and rub it to make her wild.

She clutched at his shoulders, sobbed, arched against him. On the edge of her shattering completion, he withdrew and got to his knees. She lay there like a landed fish, mouth open, legs spread, gasping for breath. Staring at his – she would call it what it was. *His cock.* Cock, cock, cock. Huge, fully, frighteningly, exquisitely erect.

He picked up his crumpled shirt again. Shaking it out one-handed, he slipped his other hand under her hips and lifted her enough to slide the shirt beneath.

Oh, of course. He won't want to stain The Eel's nice sheets. The clinical fact of penetration hadn't come to her until that moment. Had he done this before, taken a woman's virginity? Even if he hadn't, it was generally known there was blood. Fear and desire raced through her, a riptide carrying her away. Did she want it? Was she ready?

Pushing her legs apart, he knelt between them, falling forward to brace himself on one hand. The waters of panic calmed. She wanted him. He would make it right.

He took himself in hand and went into her, slowly, slowly. An inch, stop. Another inch, stop. She squirmed and panted and tried to take him deeper.

'Min,' his voice was gravel, 'stop wriggling like the small snake. We can enjoy pleasure of ten different sorts in this bed tonight and yet you can leave it a virgin.' He gave her another inch of his glorious maleness, and she began to feel stretched inside, a bit uncomfortable. Still pleasant, still very, very exciting.

He bent to her ear, his mouth hot against her. 'But if I enter you just a little more, you will not be able to change your mind.'

Change her mind? If he thought that, he didn't know what her mind was like when it was made up. She'd never wanted anything so desperately as him inside her. Completely, nothing held back. Begging all night was acceptable to make it happen. She looped her arms round his neck and peppered kisses on his throat and chest.

'Please. *Please*, Étienne.'

He settled onto her, reaching below her buttocks to grasp them firmly. Her mind and memory flew back to Dartmoor. To him lying upon her in the grove, shielding her with his body. The same weight, the same danger, the same hunger inside her.

His words made promises. His body, taut with control, made more. 'We will go easy and slow. Don't be afraid.'

Well, figs to that. They'd gone slow over two-thirds of

Devonshire. She braced her feet on the bed and thrust up and forward, hard, onto his shaft.

Ow, ow, ow. Above her, Étienne's body went rigid as a plank, but he swore lavishly in two languages.

She shut her eyes and counted to ten. Did it again in French but forgot what came after eight. *Not so bad. I can do this.* In fact, the pain was receding. No longer a stab, just a soreness. She wiggled a bit. A slight lift of her hips, a gentle grind.

The parts of her body that had startled into flight at the first shock came back. Her breasts, incredibly sensitive, rubbing against the broad, hairy male chest. The downy hair of her legs against the slight rasp of his more furred ones. The heat of the place they were joined. Everywhere, the brush of skin on skin.

He kissed her eyelids, her forehead, the bridge of her nose. His breath came rapid and warm against her face. 'God in heaven,' he rasped out. 'That was not as I had planned it.' A kiss on each cheek, almost formal. As though they were meeting for the first time. In a way, they were. 'Are you well?'

She nodded, knowing he would feel it against his collarbone. Her capacity for forming words was greatly diminished, might be gone forever. No great loss. Her body still had so much to say. She inhaled as deeply as she could with a large male body on top. He took the hint and reared up, bracing himself on his elbows.

'Look at me, Min.' Not an order. The General was asking, now. 'Please, my love. Please look at me.'

And so, they began. Eyes locked, bodies locked, they mated as though they'd been formed as halves of a whole. Like the pendants on her necklace, fitting perfectly.

In less than a minute, she learned all the truths of them together. Every feeling she'd had in her life had been one feeling closer to this. Every step had brought her to this bed, this man. He knew to hook one arm under her knee. She knew to open wider, welcome him deeper.

The peak he'd given her with his mouth was coming again, a

deeper version, one borne on a flood of heat from her inmost core. Controlling, even slowing it, was not an option. It took her like a pirate taking a ship, no hesitation, no prisoners, bearing her away.

'Oh, God, oh Christ.' He groaned the words. 'Never, never in my life... so tight, so good... *Minerve, Minerve...*'

They released together, her sobbing incoherently, him shouting her name.

CHAPTER THIRTY-ONE

Some time in dark stillness passed. If she left her body and looked down on it from above, she'd see a puddle where her parts had once been. Two puddles. Étienne had exercised just enough locomotion to fall to one side. He was awake – she saw the gleam of his eye when she used what was left of her own locomotory talent to turn her head – but his breathing had slowed to the point his chest barely moved at all.

Her lungs might have given up on breathing. She couldn't feel them. Or her hands and feet. The place between her legs throbbed a little. It was very wet, though, and that helped.

Her brain and her body chose that moment to argue. Body was simple and direct; it counselled sleep. Brain wanted some assurance that what had just happened would happen again and again. That again and again, she would be in bed, some bed, any bed, with the man who'd made it happen. That Étienne was wrong when he'd said they had only this one night.

Body's advice was sound, so she promptly ignored it. She spoke to his profile. 'I... we can overcome the difficulties. Your past doesn't have to determine our future.'

The comment was free-floating, disconnected. He understood it, anyway. Had his parts been arguing, too? 'My past will not disappear, Min. You knew what I was before you went to Les Pinsons.'

'I did, but–'

'You went there *because* of what I was.'

'You've changed.'

'Not to the police.' He untangled their limbs and straightened the bedcovers, pulling them over her and tucking her in, while he lay naked outside. 'Is this our life, Min? Argument broken by intervals of–' His fingers chafed in a representation of sex and she blinked at the crudity.

Muttering in exasperated French, he fussed with the covers again, untucking them and sliding beneath. Argument or not, she couldn't help pressing against him. He wrapped arms and legs around her and sighed.

'Tomorrow, we go to Scotland. We will be a long time in a boat, and you will need to be rested before we set out. Go to sleep, Min.'

Despite his orders – and how quickly he'd gone back to giving them – she didn't sleep for hours. He did, after just a few minutes. She heard his breathing grow deeper and slower. An indistinct murmur and he rolled onto his back, one arm thrown over her and the other under his head. He was as still as a rock after that.

Perhaps he'd lain with a regiment of women, and everything they'd done was familiar. To him. She couldn't sleep for the newness of it. The sound of a man breathing. Heavy limbs half on her, half off, fully and sweetly imprisoning her with weight and size. The heat of the slumbering body. *Her* man's body.

She lifted the edge of the blanket, inhaling deeply. He was a sleek, hot tiger, smelling of semen and power. Animalian, musky. Sweat and their sexual essences dried together. She lowered the blanket and wondered if it was peculiar to get excited again by all that.

It was still early. The moon, a waning half, not yet risen fully. By tilting back her head she could see through the half-open window that it had just crested the nearby roofs and was growing brighter. A white sail, crossing the black water of the night by slow degrees.

Étienne was right; she should sleep. But she remained a wakeful observer, assessing everything he'd done and said. After he'd dragged her down to the cold stone of what could never be, he'd astonished her utterly with two words.

Our life.

He'd said them, she'd heard him. He couldn't take them back, she wouldn't let him.

It was something to think about. She did that, while the moon went about its disinterested voyage. High, higher, high enough at last to send a shaft of silvery light through the glass. An adjacent building blocked part of it. The rest fell on just half the bed, his half. She lay in shadow, untouched by the bright ribbon diagonally striping him like a military sash.

The sum of things she knew about Étienne Sansecours was not much more illuminating than that narrow beam. Making wine was his present profession. His other, earlier career was a monument to vice and violence. He had killed. Certainly, he had told scores of lies, violated dozens of laws, and done things even he had trouble living with. She couldn't argue with any of that.

But loving him – for surely that's what she'd been doing since they'd first met – was the immutable force in her, loving the irresistible nature of him. No moon pulled more strongly than she did. No mountain rose more solidly than him.

No cliff was more dangerous. With him, she perched on its foremost edge, a thousand feet above fathomless waters. If she fell, as she was falling now, she would never rise from the vast ocean of his secrets. He had shared one with her tonight, just one. He might never share another. It wouldn't change a thing if he didn't. She trusted him with her life.

Closing her eyes, she slept.

Chapter Thirty-Two

In the hour before dawn, he half-filled the washroom tub with cold water and climbed in. Every swipe of the flannel that took Min's scent from his hands, his limbs, his groin, earned a pang of regret for its loss. Clean, he dressed roughly from his pack. Chambray trousers and a coarse shirt, his old boots. His fine suit and shoes had been brushed clean but were much the worse for their crossing the county by its byways. He rolled the clothes tightly and crammed them into the pack. He would have left the suit for Sammy, but his old comrade would fit twice into it with space left over.

The daughters had sponged and folded Min's clothes and left them outside the door of Number Four. He brought them inside, stacking them on the lone chair. Her drawers and camisole were on top. The daughters had laundered and neatly pressed them, which made him smile. He held up the camisole, a pretty thing in white with mother-of-pearl buttons and a pink ribbon drawstring at the neck. If she were his to keep, he would buy her silk undergarments, embroidered by nuns.

His to keep? Like a winsome puppy or a ginger cat he found in the lane? He shook his head. With what still lay ahead, it would be a miracle if she did not attempt to murder him.

He had asked if one of the daughters had a serviceable frock for his 'wife'. Lifting the undergarments, he discovered a dress the depressed shade of dried kelp. He laid it across the foot of the bed. She would hate the colour.

For a long minute, he stood, losing himself in admiration for her slim and lovely body, splayed half in, half out of the sheets and blanket. She'd tucked one hand under her head, and a loose rope of chestnut hair snaked downward in the angle of her bent arm, into her armpit, nesting with the tiny fluff of redder hair there. Her breast on that side was exposed, the nipple achingly soft and pink. He would never forget the taste of it on his tongue.

His body responded with the eagerness of a boy seeing a naked woman for the first time. He considered taking off the clothes he had just donned and sliding into the bed. A debate between his cock and his common sense ensued. His common sense won, by a thread. He turned from the bed and left the room.

An hour later, Min descended to the café and joined him at a table. Number Two daughter had laid out a breakfast of rolls and coffee. The daughter might have been Number Three. They were all nearly identical doe-eyed beauties, close in age.

After the punishing journey to Plymouth, followed by their first night of 'married life', he was prepared for Min to be what Michael Kelly, as near as Étienne could make out from the Irish, would call a prashuck, a mess.

She was quite calm, and unnervingly quiet. He poured her coffee. It wasn't the coffee he would have liked to pour, fragrant and strong from the pot in the kitchen of Les Pinsons. The Eel's was drinkable, just.

She lifted the cup to her lips. Before she drank, she asked over the rim, 'Morag?'

'She is well. I asked her to join us, but she is happy in the kitchen where the cook and Daughter Six–'

'Chaya.'

She had remembered the name of a daughter of the house, one she had barely met, and pronounced it perfectly. His heart clenched with pride and loss. She would make an excellent countess.

'Yes. Chaya has become a particular friend. It seems they both like horses.'

He had waited for her so they could eat together. Picking up her roll, he buttered it the way she liked, the way he had seen her butter bread at Les Pinsons. He was being weak as a lovelorn swain in a horrid novel, but the thought he would never do such a gentle, homely task for her again tore his heart into small, hopeless pieces. They flew up like embers and disappeared, leaving him hollow as a drum.

They ate in silence until Sammy entered from the street, noisily stamping his rubber boots. He brought sea smells with him and wore an oilskin coat. 'Tide's turnin', Frenchy. *On y va*, yeah?'

Étienne answered as he rose. 'Ten minutes.' To Min, he said, 'I will get our things. Tell Morag it is time to go.'

Morag might call every horse her friend, but the sea was evidently her sworn enemy. They had barely put out in Rao's ketch-rigged Brixham trawler – as plausible a fishing boat as any smuggling craft could be – when she began vomiting over the rail.

Eight men, most of them burly, dark, and jovial like Sammy, capably crewed the trawler. Étienne was merely an extra set of arms and legs, but he perched with Min on a heap of fishnets on the forward deck, in case he was needed.

The boat rode high in the water as they skirted the southwestern coast. Minimal cargo, then, though some high-value items were light. Or the *Siobhan* might be making the first leg on an outbound run, picking up a duty-free load from the Isle of Man or Anglesey. She might even be fishing, a mission he doubted and would not suggest aloud to anyone onboard for fear of being laughed back to France.

Whatever happened on the trawler or at either end of its voyage, he cared nothing for the details. If Sammy wanted to enlighten him, he would. Theirs was an old but steadfast friendship based on favours given and received. Not the least of them was ferrying Min to the Scottish coast. There, another trusted confederate – one wired by Sammy after Étienne had explained the need – would arrange for someone from Dunmara to take Min the short distance inland to the manor.

Her manor. Her new home. Scotland was not an impossible distance from France, he supposed. But now, to him, it seemed he was taking Minerva Hawkins to the moon.

They sat, not speaking, on the nets. Her face was pinched with the cold salt air, but she sat straight as a soldier, not curling into him for warmth. He understood and respected her small act of defiance; fate and he had left her little else. Even so, he made sure some part of him touched some part of her every second. His thigh against her knee, his hand hooked under her elbow, his fingers brushing wind-whipped hair out of her eyes. He could tell himself that it was to reassure her, but that was a coward's excuse. He touched her because he must. Because their time together shortened with every wave passing under the boat and every snap of the sails above.

He thought she might bring up the subject of their latest argument again, but she did not. It was yet another painful thing he must do.

'*Minerve.*'

For the first time that day, she smiled, gently mocking him

with exaggerated French. '*Oui, É-ti-ennnne?*' He could not return her jest. There was no laughter left in him, even to please her.

'*Tu comprends*, we part at the Scottish coast.'

'How many times must you say it?'

'Until I am sure you accept.'

Or until he accepted. A wager for which the odds were poor. Perhaps the repetition would irritate her so much she would be happy to see the back of him. '*Oh, him! He's such a bore, I'm glad he's gone.*'

'I understand, Étienne. *Je comprend!*'

It was her last show of spirit. No more resistance, no more wild suggestions and resentful accusations. His Minerva, goddess of strategic warfare and victory. It killed him that the fight had gone out of her. That he had driven it out.

After a few minutes, she allowed her weight to rest against him. He encircled her shoulders with his arm, bringing her close. Her body was unresisting and soft under his arm. She was surely exhausted. Neither of them had slept more than three hours in the past twenty-four.

'We have a long way to go. You should–'

No. Stop that. He would not give her another command. There had been too much of that lately. Reining her this way and that like one of the horses. He had done it to move her away from harm, but it grated against her nature, which was not to be controlled. Their last hours together should not consist of him ordering her around like a subaltern.

He began again. 'If you wish to sleep, I will make sure you do not miss a single breathtaking moment of this voyage.'

'Will there be whales?' Her slurred murmur said she was nearly asleep already.

'Not yet.' There were often whales, along with dolphins and sharks, in the northern coastal waters. 'I promise to wake you the second I see a spout or a fin. There is fine fishing in those waters, too. Perhaps Sammy will let you help with the...'

But she was snoring softly before he finished.

CHAPTER THIRTY-THREE

She had no memory of going belowdecks, but she woke in a narrow bunk in an equally narrow cabin. For quite a long while she lay there, deeply confused about where she was. For a few horrible seconds, she thought she'd been taken back to Raeburn House and locked up somewhere, a cupboard or a cell that unaccountably tilted one way, then the other. She heard waves slapping just outside the cabin wall and remembered. She was aboard a boat.

Going to Scotland. Where she would step out of her old self and become the Countess of Dunmara, a thing as exotic and unlikely as being crowned the Queen of Sheba.

The door... Maybe it was called the hatch? Bulkhead? Capstan? She knew nothing about ships except they were better on top of the water than under it. The door-thing opened, and Étienne stood in the gap, a dark shape against the light. Where were her eyeglasses?

He answered the unspoken question by crossing to the bed and handing them to her. 'You have been asleep for a day and a night, Min. We are nearly there.'

Wobbly as a top, she sat up, putting on her glasses. She tried to smooth her hair. It was like a fur bonnet, frizzy and massed at the crown of her head. When she pushed her fingers through it, she discovered it was less of a hat than something a troop of pixies had camped in overnight, filling it with snarls and knots. 'Where is "there"?'

'The Scottish coast. Near a village called Tayvallich. Dunmara is not far from there.'

'Any chance we can turn around and go somewhere else? I should like to see America.'

He made no answer to that. 'There is a chamber pot under the bunk. I will bring you water to wash, and some food.'

'Tea,' she said numbly. 'Very, very strong tea.'

He nodded and left her to pluck the elf locks from her hair.

Being too demoralised to think coherently was a blessing. Two hours later, when she was trundled into a dinghy and rowed ashore in Scotland, it taxed her intelligence just to stare at Étienne, seated across from her. It was a foolish thought, but perhaps if she memorised every line of his body and stitch of his clothing, she could keep him. *You're as deranged as one of those poor creatures at Raeburn House, Min.* Was she thinking she could take him with her, as a child takes a favourite doll on a journey?

She twisted the gold ring on her left hand. She'd tried to give it back, but Étienne refused. It wasn't a promise for the future. He'd made it clear they didn't have one. But it was inexpressibly sad to think it was nothing more than a memento of the past. A souvenir, like an engraved silver spoon. *Étienne and Minerva, 1894.*

It said nothing good about her that she didn't remember Morag until they landed. The dinghy scraped on the gravelly sea bottom and Étienne jumped out to help drag it ashore. She twisted around and saw the Scotswoman hanging over the gunwales. Her face was a shade of green not too different from the dress Min was wearing.

The dress. She hadn't asked which daughter had given it to her, but it was a reasonably good fit, if a little short at the ankles. She picked up a fold of the skirt and rubbed it between her fingers. A subtle calico print, much laundered and faded. Still, a dress was a dress, and with six daughters, she imagined Mr Rao's clothing budget was taxed. She would post him funds for a new dress. Six dresses, one for each daughter. Except Chaya. For her, a new pair of trousers and a matching cap.

She shifted the cloth bag on her lap. It was the one from Agnes Broadripple. Her mourning attire was inside, along with the bonnet, her handbag, and her corset. She'd be perfectly content not to wear any of them again.

Thought vaporised in the sensation of Étienne picking her up. Always with the same ease, like she was a parcel of insufficient weight to even make his muscles twitch. He carried her to the beach and put her on her feet. Her boots immediately sank into soft sand and water welled around them.

It was only then she saw he was barefoot, his trousers rolled to the knees. He was also sinking into the soggy sand, and she memorised that image along with the rest. The tops of his feet, now that she saw them in sunlight, were tawny, as though he often went without shoes. Perhaps in the vines at Les Pinsons?

She should have asked him that. There were a hundred things she should have asked, and now she never would. Tears welled like the water around her boots.

To stop herself from bawling like a child, she scrutinised the cliff that rose from the beach not very far from where they stood. It was neither too tall nor too steep, and steps were carved into the face. Not a difficult climb at all. Even the landscape was on the opposing side, making it easy for her to walk away from her old life.

She scanned the top of the cliff. Against a dull pewter sky, she could just see the outline of a cart or wagon, a man leaning against it. Someone hired to cart away a bothersome woman.

She faced Étienne. 'Will you... I don't want to...'

'I will go with you to the top, of course. And Morag will be right behind.'

Which she was, being helped from the dinghy by one of Rao's crew. The Scotswoman's bliss at stepping onto more or less solid ground was as visible in her face as if she'd backed a winner at Epsom Downs. A maid again, she promptly took the cloth bag from Min.

They climbed the cliff stairs in a file, not talking. He made her go first, in case she fell and he was forced to catch her. Falling was unlikely, as the mortared stone steps were broad and solid, but she gave leaping from the top a think.

When they reached the wagon, she stood to the side and examined it. Her mood suggested it should be a funeral coach drawn by harpies, but it was an ordinary wagon, drawn by an ordinary horse. It might have last been used to haul cabbages or potatoes to market. Morag, who'd scampered up the cliff behind them, climbed into the back without help and waited, knees drawn up, chin resting on them. She appeared to doze. Probably she hadn't slept on *Siobhan* as much as Min. Vomiting tended to keep a person awake.

The driver was a man around thirty, red-haired and sturdy. As ordinary as the horse and wagon. He didn't speak, only straightened, turning alert and curious eyes on her. She considered asking him how he knew Samath Rao and the *Siobhan* but thought better of it. She'd rather had her fill of smugglers, lately. The driver continued to look appraisingly at her until he met Étienne's gaze. He looked quickly away, then.

She faced Étienne and waited. Time drew out, second by second. He didn't rush her, but deferring their disengagement wouldn't make it easier for either of them. Besides, the trawler could only idle so long within sight of land, where everyone and his dog could get a look at it. The longer it dawdled, the more chances that someone would notice and make awkward inquiries.

How many words were there in the English language? Even counting the ones she didn't know and the ones irrelevant to the occasion, like *teakettle* and *omnibus*, there were theoretically a vast number she could call up to say goodbye to Étienne Sansecours.

Not that one, though. Not *goodbye*.

She raised a tiny white flag of a smile. 'I never saw the whales.'

His returning smile hurt in the gentlest way. 'They were shy. As were you, when we first met.'

With that, it was two years ago. They were in the alley behind Salon Sirena. Ada was scowling, pressed against the closed door to the workroom. Min and Evie were standing against the brick wall, staring wide-eyed at two men. One of them, Michael Kelly, was there for Jillian. The other was Étienne. He held out a bag of sugared almonds and smiled at her, just as he was smiling now. A smile wholly, unreservedly, exclusively for her.

He would never smile for her again. Before grief made speech impossible, she choked out the question she'd sworn to herself she wouldn't ask. 'Will you miss me?'

'Not at all. You are a constant aggravation.'

Her laugh became a sob. He opened his arms and she flew to them. They held each other for a while. A minute, an hour.

He had to be the one to put her away from him; they both knew it. It was done with the care of moving a crystal vase to a different spot on the mantel. *There, you'll be safe, now.*

Too late, she could have told him. *I'm all in pieces.*

He took a step back. Another. They clung to each other's hands as long as they could, until he released his hold and his fingers slid away. She still held his gaze. Finally, with every cell in her body screaming resistance, she shut her eyes.

If she watched him turn his back and leave, it would forever be the image she took away. But with eyes shut, she'd remember the image before that. His eyes, the same colour as his hair, whisky with glints of gold. His sad, fugitive smile, brushing her like a feather borne on the salt air between them.

Cruelly, her hearing still worked when her eyes were closed. The sounds of him descending the cliff steps were knives, scraping away her flesh.

The sounds finally faded. She opened her eyes and blinked away tears. The driver reached out to help her into the wagon, but she ignored his hand. She would guard the imprint on her skin of Étienne's last touch for as long as she could.

Still trying to be helpful, the driver cupped her elbow. 'Guid day, yer ladyship,' he said cheerfully as she clambered into the cart with Morag.

Christ and the Apostles, she'd be hearing that every ten minutes, now, in the rolling accents of Scotland. She didn't correct him, even though she'd ruthlessly been saying, *Miss Hawkins, please* or *Minerva will do* to everyone who'd handed her the honorific since it became obvious, *to them*, that it was hers. She made no response at all to the driver's greeting, which wasn't like her. If nothing else, Asa and Mary Hawkins had reared her to be polite. Perhaps when she surrendered to the title she'd become imperious and rude, like titled personages were rumoured to be.

Perhaps not. She sighed resignedly. 'Good day. Thank you for taking us to Dunmara. Is it far?'

'Nay, not at all, my lady. Three miles, as the boobries fly.'

Boobries? What were those? Creatures hailing her from the crowded pantheon of Scottish magic? Pucas, kelpies, selkies, the nuckelavee. She'd have to learn them all, along with Tam Lyn, the elven knight held in thrall until he could be rescued by his beloved, the Fairy Queen.

The wagon started off with a jerk and Min clutched the side. She was no Fairy Queen. But she'd said farewell to her knight to end the danger he'd put himself in to get her to a life he thought she deserved. Said farewell to save him from Newgate.

Because Newgate was to thrall what Hell was to a fairy glade. She would have done anything to keep him out. Letting him go might not be enough, but it would have to do until some greater magic came along.

Chapter Thirty-Four

Numb and cold, like he had been packed in ice for a few hours, Étienne took the oars from Sammy's crewman and rowed the dinghy back to the trawler. He could think of no fix for the gaping hole Min's leaving had made in his chest, but he had to do something to divert his thoughts or he would go mad. Whatever Sammy had planned for his men, he would be one of them until he was not needed or some terminal outcome found him. He could not make himself care one way or the other.

Sammy had agreed to ferry Min to Scotland at least partly because it fit into an existing smuggling operation. He had said not one word about the odd goings on with Étienne and Min. Why his former associate wished to put his wife and her maid ashore in Scotland while he went off with the *Siobhan*'s merry little band for some indefinite time...?

Most men would have wanted to know more about that, but inquisitive men did not last long in free trading, and Sammy had been at it for many years.

The two of them leaned against the rail as the trawler tacked northward in the Irish Sea. They smoked, a vice in which he rarely indulged, but he did it now to be companionable. As they passed a pipe back and forth, Sammy explained the operation.

'In Devon, call they a barrow.' He took a long draw and blew out smoke in a perfect ring. 'Milkin' stool.'

Étienne took the proffered pipe and pretended to suck from it. Even not inhaling, he appreciated the aroma of fine tobacco. Smuggled, of course, from Virginia via Ireland. 'In Dieppe, we called it *le tripode*.'

'Same thing, aye, sure.' Sammy took back the pipe and used it to stab the air. 'First leg, we go from Plymut' with cabbage and marigolds.'

Cabbage and marigolds. That explained the high perch of *Siobhan* in the water. Paper currency and gold coins were very kind to weight and space.

'Second leg,' a stab at the air again, 'we put in at Tobermary, where some friendly Scotchies make best whisky you ever drink. Cabbage and marigolds go to Scotchie friends, whisky barrels go in hold.'

The barrels would make *Siobhan* ride a bit lower, but when stowed in the hidden compartments within her hull, they would be as invisible as air to Revenue officers. Unseen was untaxed. When he nodded his understanding, Sammy continued.

'Third leg, Isle of Skye. We meetin' some Norwegian fellas.'

Smugglers from Norway. That could mean several things, most of them smelly and space-consuming. Before he could ask which one Sammy was swapping whisky for, his friend passed over the pipe with a grimace and an answer.

'Furs.'

Bordel de merde. He hated smuggling furs. At some point, they usually required overland transport. Furriers in Paris had their own sources from Russia and the Baltic. That meant London would be the final destination for Rao's fox, sable, lynx, wolf, seal, ermine, even bear pelts. All with the minimum of processing done before shipment. In addition to the risky handover to land transport, furs left maggots and a stink that lingered in the hold for weeks, if not months.

Still, there was high profit in them, if one had the right connections. And the *Siobhan* was not his boat. If its owner wished to douse it in perfume of dead animals, it was his decision.

'I can take first watch,' he told Sammy, who shook his head, white beard waggling in a cloud of smoke.

'Got plenty crew. You sleep. Need you later for palaver with Norsemen.'

Hard luck. His Norwegian was as rusty as iron machinery abandoned to the elements for years. Maybe the wheels would turn once he got started. He climbed down the ladder to the cabin where Min had slept, rehearsing words and phrases. *God dag, jeg heter Étienne.* Good day, my name is Étienne. *Flytt ikke. Jeg har en pistol.* Don't move. I have a gun.

If he'd had a gun, he might have turned it on himself when he peeled off his shirt and boots and lay on the bunk, pulling up his legs to fit. The blankets smelled entirely and implacably of Min.

CHAPTER THIRTY-FIVE

During the boobrie-length journey to reach Dunmara, about three quarters of an hour, Morag kept her head on her knees and was as mute as the sand on the beach. Min silently wailed her despair. She had never felt so unequal to anything in her life as she did to what awaited her when the wagon came to a halt at Dunmara's gates.

She took a long moment to hunt through her memories for referents. She could certainly recall the fine houses she'd seen in London. It was a little game she and Evie played on their Sunday afternoons. Dressed in their best, they wandered Arlington Street, Park Lane, Grosvenor Square, inventing stories of who they were, where they lived. All the houses they saw had iron fences marking them off from the pavement. Many had gates. Keeping the riff-raff out, keeping the quality in.

Dunmara had gates of iron. Stout, rather than ornamental. There was a gatekeeper. Of sorts. An ancient retainer who got no wages, her driver said over his shoulder, but paid no rent. The gatehouse was the size of a hackney cab, planted where the rough track from the coast met a gravelled drive to the house that would be hers.

The driver hailed the tiny cottage, and the keeper tottered out.

He came straight to the wagon and peered in the back, his watery blue eyes glancing off Morag and settling, for a long moment, on her. She nodded, aware she looked like a weary vagabond. Perhaps she'd be turned away and not have to be a countess at all. *Nay, nay. That canna be the countess, not that ragamuffin. Tak her back where ye found her.*

No joy. The gatekeeper grinned, showing gums top and bottom, and cackled something. It might have been Gaelic, English, or Mandarin.

Morag, whom she'd thought was asleep, lifted her head and spoke. 'That's Hamish MacDonald. He says to call him Bodach. It means "old man".' It was the most words Morag had strung together in days.

'Old man' reached into his coat, which looked like it had been slept in for a year of nights. Extracting a string-tied packet of post, he shoved it at her, then faced the driver. The two men began a spirited discourse in the lingua franca.

She examined the packet. The envelope on top was from Gordon and Blackford, Solicitors, Glasgow. She could almost see them, Gordon older and white-haired, Blackford younger and ambitious. Sober, black-suited men in faraway offices.

It gave her a profound shock followed by a frisson of unease to see the direction on the envelope: *The Right Hon. the Countess of Dunmara.* The first letter the solicitors had sent, the one she'd opened in Little Farnleigh, had been addressed to Miss Minerva Hawkins. The contents had been largely incomprehensible, peppered with references to 'heirs whatsoever' and 'the remainder'. It also mentioned the College of Arms, a body she'd barely heard of before that moment. The letter went on to say the firm was examining 'certain proofs of parentage', along with the late earl's 'articles of succession'.

Despite the circumlocution, the letter's conclusion had been earthshakingly clear. She, Minerva Hawkins, appeared to be the heir to the title and lands of Dunmara.

Despite the direction, and on the off chance they were writing now to say it had all been a terrible mistake, she worked the envelope out of the packet and ripped it open.

No joy, there, either, though many people might think so. Four pages of typewritten lines and numbers gave her Dunmara's accounts to date. Everything was there for the past year, from roof tiles to baskets of mussels, timber cut and sheep sold. At the bottom of the last sheet was a summary of the estate's net worth and the amount of funds she could draw upon at any time from the British Linen Bank in Glasgow. The numbers, in black and white, took her aback.

She shuffled through the pages again. The accounting must be a yearly itemisation of outlay and income for the estate, no matter on whose shoulders the title sat. It was nothing she had the strength to deal with now. She'd see to it later.

A screech of rusty hinges announced the end of chatting between driver and gatekeeper. Dunmara's gates swung open. The wagon trundled onto the drive, neatly raked and smoother by far than the road that had gotten them from the coast. The gatekeeper hobbled back to his cottage, leaving the gates open.

The drive was short and made a loop at the top, where the wagon stopped at wide stone steps. The driver dismounted and came round to help his passengers, her first.

When she was on her feet, he bounded past her up the steps and applied a key to a door the height of a small barn. Since he appeared to be ready to stand there indefinitely, key in his outthrust hand, Min met him on the porch.

'Callum MacDonald,' he said, rolling the Ls almost as much as the Rs. 'Anything ye need, just ask fer me.'

She took the key, giving him what she'd decided to call her 'countess nod'.

'*Fàilte gu Dunmara*, my lady, welcome. Ye're hame.' He tugged at his forelock, then jogged down the steps to his wagon, where he gave her a short bow before mounting.

A courteous man, but altogether wrong. No part of her was home. Home had rowed away from her an hour ago.

Morag, carrying the canvas bag, scurried into the house with the speed of someone who knew where she was going and was pleased about it. Min wasn't as ready. She might need to wait for an invitation, like a ghost. Eileen had read Coleridge's 'Christabel' and assured the Salon's workroom it was so.

To give herself time to get used to the idea the place was hers, she went back outside and began a circuit of the grounds around the manor. She wanted the measure of the estate, or at least the house and the visible outbuildings.

It took her only a few minutes' walking to agree with Étienne. It was grand.

Even after he'd said it, she'd clung to some notion Dunmara House was a ruin. Some part of her had hoped for that. An ancient pile of decayed walls and crumbling towers. Bats in the attic. Rats in the bedchambers. A wreck about which she could throw up her hands and say, 'Well! Nothing I can do with this. I'll just go back to...'

Not France, since she was unwelcome there. Not England, where Raeburn and Fitzsimmons lurked. Above all, not Little Farnleigh. The little village was too crowded with her ghosts to admit one more.

Whether she was dismayed or happy about it, Dunmara Manor wasn't a ruin. A broad brick residence of fine proportions, it looked to be in good repair, though the lawns were patchily scythed and apparently hadn't been rolled in years. To one side and somewhat behind the house, three buildings clung together, as though for companionship. Stables, wash house, dairy?

On the house's other side, an arcade supported ranks of espaliered trees. Fruit trees, she surmised. Despite it being summer, they were gaunt and bare with neglect. At the back of the house, a half-glassed building stood. An orangery, she presumed. A former orangery; much of the glass was broken.

As impractical in Scotland's climate as she could imagine, a pair of peacocks strutted on the lawn next to the drive. Hopefully, there was a barn or aviary for the birds when winter arrived.

She'd see to the peacocks. And the lawn and the fruit trees and the orangery and the outbuildings and the accounts. God knew she hadn't wanted it, but it was hers, now. She must see to everything.

CHAPTER THIRTY-SIX

The furs were as smelly as Étienne had feared, the Norwegians and their boat *Njord* almost as much. After first greetings, he was relieved to find he didn't have to use his tarnished language skills. The Northerners spoke English well. Better than Samath Rao.

Whisky barrels went from the *Siobhan* to the *Njord*. Furs made the journey in reverse. Business was concluded to everyone's satisfaction. Drinking, at which the Norwegians and Sammy excelled, commenced.

Never had he longed so keenly for his cellar at Les Pinsons. Like tobacco, he had never developed a taste for spiritous liquor. He used a sort of legerdemain to make it seem he was downing whisky cup for cup with the other men until the Norwegians somehow rowed back to their boat and Sammy stumbled below to his bunk.

It was as well he had abstained. The next morning, he woke fresh and alert. And he was the first of the trawler's crew to spot the storm.

Initially, it was just a smudge on the horizon, a broad, disk-shaped dark cloud with bunched white froth on top. He surveyed it warily through Sammy's marine binoculars. An hour later, it had

207

grown broader, darker, and nearer. By then, the glasses were unnecessary. A grey sheet of rain hung from the cloud's underside, brushing the surface of the Irish Sea like a lady's skirt train brushed the floor.

There was little sun, but he cupped his hands around his eyes, anyway, narrowing his field of vision to examine the cloud. It might not overtake the boat. *Siobhan* lumbered a bit, as trawlers did, but with the wind that was already slapping the sails and making them billow, she might put safe distance between herself and danger.

Still, he worried. They'd gone right up into the North Channel, almost to the Firth of Clyde, to meet the *Njord*. Squeezed into the strait, the storm was gathering power. As he assessed its breadth and velocity over a period of minutes, he had a sinking presentiment that *Siobhan* could not outrun it.

He shook Sammy awake and roused the crew. Sammy assessed the storm as he had and came to the same conclusion: the storm might outrace the boat. Fighting cock that he was, Sammy thought *Siobhan* should try. With a cargo of illegal goods, there was nowhere safe to put into land. They would run south, ahead of the tempest, for all they were worth.

A game effort by vessel and men. Not game enough.

After several hours of wretched, straining warfare against water and wind, the storm was victorious, the boat a battered loser. *Siobhan* only escaped being pounded to bits by being driven slantwise onto a deserted stretch of Irish coastline. She did not founder, but stuck fast aground. The trawler's main mast was cracked, the sail shredded. He and Sammy figured they were in the general vicinity of Dundalk. A stroke of luck, if they were. Boatbuilders and outfitters were plentiful in the port.

Alas, contraband furs were plentiful in *Siobhan*'s hold.

Sammy shook his head disconsolately, water drops flying off his beard. 'No help fer it, Frenchy. Got to dump they furs.'

In his Dieppe days, Étienne's less reasonable comrades would have gone ashore and commandeered overland transport, at gunpoint, if necessary. They would have intimidated farm families with threats of revenge if they talked, buffering the threats with a few casks of brandy or bales of tobacco to convert their victims into accomplices. They would then have loaded horses and wagons and melted into the countryside at night, surfacing at a place where the cargo could be sold or moved again over water.

Samath Rao was not that sort of smuggler. At his order, *Siobhan*'s crew heaved bundles of hairy profit overboard until not so much as a squirrel tail remained in the hold. Villagers on the Irish coast would be hauling fur out of the surf for months. Nothing would tie the bundles to *Siobhan*, though there would be abundant speculation. With good fortune, the smell of the boat would be gone by the time it limped back to Plymouth.

Sammy shouldered his loss without complaint. Smuggling was an enterprise of soaring ascents and deep abysses. He and one other crewman stayed aboard in case the rising tide floated *Siobhan* off the bottom. Sammy distributed currency to the rest.

'Yeh boys'll have to leg it, now. Bring back help, yeah?'

They went, all but Étienne, in the hopeful direction of Dundalk. He was bound in another direction altogether. He dared not remain with *Siobhan*. Curiosity about the grounded ship might lead to officials. He would not have Sammy burdened with bribing them. Or, worse, dragged off in manacles along with his wanted French crewman. What would Daughters One through Six do without their father?

He told Sammy his plan: to make his way south along the coast, hoping for a broadminded boatman to take him across the Irish Sea. On England's southwestern coast, he had contacts enough to spirit him across the Channel to somewhere in France. Anywhere would do, even Dieppe, the place he had sworn never to set foot in again.

If the Irish coast didn't produce what he sought before he got there, Dublin might. Some former associates of the Jacks possibly remembered and did not entirely hate him. Trusting the honour of thieves was never his first choice, but he would try the city if he must. When the cork is pulled, the wine must be drunk.

Sammy listened with the discerning ear of a man who had been on the run more than once. At the end, he shared what intelligence he had on the coastal villages and towns. Which ones bristled with English police or Irish rebels. Which ones were considered too insignificant for the English to oppress and too lackadaisical or riddled with informers for the rebels to organise.

He also offered the crewman left aboard, a youngster named Abel, to accompany him. Étienne refused. 'Better for me to go alone, old friend.'

Sammy's eyes narrowed. 'Mebbe so. Yeh hot as a farrier's nail, yeah?' The hotelier-smuggler surveyed the shore for a moment. 'What yeh want done with beasts?'

The dapple grey mare and the Shire, both technically stolen. He gave not a fart for Raeburn's ownership of the Shire, and he had left a surety of four times the mare's worth with the livery stable in Great Torrington. Good animals, both, and he would not like to see them sold to bad owners or go for hired cab horses. Still, horses meant hay and oats and shoeing and other expenses.

He swung his pack off his shoulder and dug in it for a small, heavy, leather pouch, one of several. Many years earlier, he had learned that when the road is uncertain, a wise traveller carries gold, though he also carried a roll of English pound notes and another of French francs.

He handed Sammy the pouch. 'Keep the horses. For Chaya.'

Sammy slapped the pouch against his palm and laughed, irrepressible as always. 'She love yeh forever, Frenchy.'

They clasped arms. Étienne took the dinghy to shore, then passed the oars to Abel, who rowed it back to the trawler.

After exchanging waves with Sammy, he alternately climbed up and slid down a sloping bluff until he gained the top. To the west stretched verdant Ireland. To the east was the sea, *Siobhan* not quite in or out of it. South was a serrated coastline, with almost no towns and only a handful of sparse and suspicious villages. Eventually, he would run across the boatman he needed. Or a mail coach. Or a railroad.

Or a Royal Irish Constable who took particular note of bulletins about wanted men.

He was glad Remy could handle the grape harvest alone.

CHAPTER THIRTY-SEVEN

Her first night in Dunmara Manor had been long and cold. Sleeping in the bed of either of the two late countesses had felt ghoulish, so she'd put sheets from the linen cupboard on a bed in a guest room. The bed, the room, and the sheets were cold, and everything gave off a faint odour of damp. All the guest room had to recommend it was a south-facing window and a bedside copy of *A History of the Highlands and of the Highland Clans* by James Browne, Esq., LL.D, Advocate. Considering the speed at which the clan histories put her under on her first reading, it would be an age before she got through them.

Morag spent the night somewhere in the house, she wasn't sure where. But after helping her juggle bedsheets, the Scotswoman had said 'Goodnight, my lady,' and disappeared into the house's upper floors.

To Min's surprise, she did not spend the night sobbing. She might just be in shock, from which she would emerge in a few days to tear her hair and threaten to throw herself off the roof. But after that black last day, waking on *Siobhan* to Étienne telling her they'd arrived in Scotland, being rowed to the shore, saying and not saying goodbye...

After that, she'd recovered a small, stubborn spark of hope. She would blow on it until it flamed into a plan. The plan would carry her forward, as her plans always did. Somehow, some way, she would be with him again.

It was still an hour to dawn, but she might as well make a start on the thousand things to do in the manor. She got downstairs and into the kitchen without mishap and fired the coal range. While she waited for the kettle to boil, she rummaged about until she found paper and a pencil, not too dull. She then sat at the kitchen table and considered staffing the house.

Morag said there had been staff but, for the former lady's maid, it had been years ago. She remembered housemaids, three or four. A housekeeper. A cook and some help in scullery and garden. A groom or two. A butler?

Securing staff would be the bare beginning. Once they were hired, they'd have to be managed. She quailed at the prospect. Assigning duties, making sure they were fulfilled, coping with illnesses and tardiness and flirtations between the housemaid and the gardener...

The very idea that Min could manage a grand house was an unfunny joke. She'd been a Devonshire nobody and then a corset maker in London. She could train up pea vines and make Victoria sponge. Her sewing skills were excellent, and she could sing a handful of hymns very creditably. She knew the whole of 'The Charge of the Light Brigade' and could recite it with vigour.

She'd never met a butler, any more than she'd met a Yeoman Warder at the Tower.

It was intimidating. Worse, it was unfair. Previous countesses had surely arrived with a retinue of their own and moved into a house already fully staffed. They didn't sit at the kitchen table as she was doing now, with the household accounts from a solicitors' office on one side and a blank sheet of paper on the other.

She supposed she could simply take the staff titles from the wages listed and transfer them to the blank paper. Perhaps Morag could ask around for the servants who'd been at the house when the earl had been alive. It had only been months, not years, since they'd been employed. They weren't migratory geese. There were few manor houses in the district to which they could have flown.

A more attractive alternative for her first morning at Dunmara was to postpone staffing decisions until she'd explored the house and grounds more exhaustively. Or she could send Morag or the gatekeeper to a telegraph office, if there was one in Tayvallich. She didn't think she could bear another day in the same clothes, and the dress Sammy Rao's cook had given Morag had seen better days in 1885. A wire to Evie might produce some clothes from her room in St Christopher's Place – if the landlady had not already given them to the rag and bone man.

Any road, there was no harm in sitting at the kitchen table until shops in the village were open, drinking the tea in front of her. She'd made it from the kettle she'd put on the stove she'd fired herself. Who needed domestics?

She was feeling content with her last choice, wiring for clothes, when Morag stumped into the kitchen.

'My lady,' she began without even a *good morn ta ye*, 'ye maun speak wi' Nanny.' The Scotswoman's uncannily familiar blue eyes were bright with intent.

'Nanny who?' Min was fractious before her second cup. When she hired servants, she'd need to warn them.

Morag made a dismissive noise; it sounded like *arrr pfumpf*. 'Nay, nay. Nanny's no a who, she's a MacDonald.'

The Browne book earned its keep. Clan MacDonald. First to play the bagpipes. Red and green tartan.

'You and her and Callum and Bodach. All MacDonalds. Why are there Highlanders here? We're barely *in* the Highlands.'

Morag shrugged. The motion nearly sent her shoulder through the threadbare seam of her dress. 'We've no got a' the Highlanders, my lady. On'y MacDonalds. Nanny's th' one to tell ye hist'ry. It's why ye maun speak wi'–'

'What we *maun* do is get some other clothes before what we're wearing rots off our bodies and we're left to go to the village grocer in our underclothes.'

Morag made the odd noise again, followed by, 'Nanny'll be waitin'.'

It might be a good time to practice aristocratic *hauteur*. She levelled a look at the Scotswoman that said she liked her a bit better when she was drugged and silent.

Unaffected, Morag planted her hands on her hips. Among other signs of recovery, she'd pulled her hair away from her face and into a tight braid, the better to show off a stubborn Highland chin. 'If ye doona speak wi' Nanny th' noo, I'll address ye as Yer Majesty in front o' a' th' folk in th' village.'

'What, all forty of them?' Min sighed heavily. 'Fine, we'll go. After I've had my second cup.'

She'd unfairly maligned Tayvallich's population. From the bustle in the principal street, it appeared to be more like a hundred and forty. Morag said there were more people scattered in the crescent of countryside that led down to the shore. They were in farms (several of which belonged to the earldom), drovers' camps, a quarry, and a timber enterprise (also the earldom's). And hallelujah, the village proper had a post office. The sign alongside the door read *Money order Savings bank Insurance business Parcel post & Telegraph*.

Nanny MacDonald lived at the top of the street in a picturesque hovel. Travel guides devoted paragraphs to praising the type, largely because their readers would never know the misery of living in one. She'd seen her share of them around Little Farnleigh. In winter, they were freezing; in spring, full of mice; in summer, flies. In all four seasons, they smelled of turnips and threatened to collapse on the inhabitants in a strong wind.

Like her cottage, Nanny was a bit of a specimen. Her dark wool gown was topped with a striped pinafore apron and her hair was covered with what the Scots called a kertch, a linen scarf tied behind the neck. *Seventy years*, said her wrinkled face, but her sparrow-brown eyes gave off a lively spark.

Knees crackling, she curtsied to Min. The obeisance was enough to send Min bolting from the cottage then and there. But Nanny was excited by the visit and Morag's glances were admonishing, so she smiled the countess smile she was perfecting to go along with the countess nod and allowed herself to be pointed toward the best chair. A fat tabby vacated it following some terse Gaelic phrases from both Scotswomen. Good dame MacDonald sat on a stool and Morag stood.

Chipped cups were filled with scalding black tea from a kettle on the hob. For a minute or two, they all sipped in silence. The tea was so bitter that the portion of her lips left after the first flesh-searing sip curled inward. No sugar on offer, nor milk, but perhaps local custom forbade them. Like purists decried the watering of wine.

I will not think of wine. Nor grapes nor France nor almond soap nor... so many things.

Some gentle prompting from Morag included the word 'MacDonald'. At that, the old woman launched into a circuitous tale about the first earl, 'Langworth, from Northumberland. Queen Bess give 'im title. A rare thing, 'twere, for a Saxon to get an earldom in Scotland.'

An old title and a rare one, too. That explained at least some of Langworth's desperation over not begetting a male heir. To be known as the one who lost a venerable earldom or surrendered it to Scots custom and a woman... How the prospect of that must have galled.

'Aye, from *sassaunach* roots were sprung our Langworth, but wife, Isobel MacDonald, she were from Glengarry and a Scot through and through. A gentlewoman, too, as lived in a castle afore she marrit the earl. Her grandsire were Balgair...'

Tales of multiple MacDonalds and their exploits followed. Without saying it in so many words, Nanny made it clear that Isobel MacDonald had married beneath her. A recitation of goods and wealth the bride brought as her dowry went on and on. Cattle and chests, coaches and horses, gold and silver. A bride price from Langworth to Isobel's family was also mentioned, derisively. The long speech dissolved into coughing at the end.

Morag took a crockery jug from the smoke-blackened timber mantel and poured a healthy measure of something into Nanny's cup. After a swallow, Nanny capped her story with, 'Countess brought fam'ly wi' her when she cam fra Glengarry. An' servants as had been wi' her fam'ly fer years. All MacDonalds, mind.'

Min squirmed with embarrassment. Who was she, compared to such venerable antecedents? Nanny had brought the truth right up to her nose. There was far, far more to being a countess here than answering to 'my lady'. The meanest of Tyvallich's inhabitants probably knew more about Dunmara, its lineage, retainers, and ancestral history, than she would know if she devoted herself to bedside reading for a year.

What did she even know about Scotland, other than that the Queen of England kept a castle in Aberdeenshire called Balmoral, where she rode Highland ponies named Fyvie and Flora?

Just before her discomfort resolved into a dash for the street, Morag prompted Nanny to tell about the second marriage of Mary MacDonald, to Asa Hawkins. Min was instantly alert.

'Nay, nay, she was not marrit afore, our Mairi. Never till yon sour-faced Methody come with bride price in hand. Wanted a bonny young lass and got one. A hundred English sovereigns he give that graspin' auld cadger Iain, Mairi's da, fer the lass.'

The recitation paused while Nanny waved at the mantel. Morag took a small tin from it and filled a clay pipe with tobacco, then lit it with a twig from the fire. Once Nanny had her pipe and was filling the cottage with the smell of rough cut, she took up Mairi MacDonald's epic.

'Off she went to England, then, but Methody wouldna tak the bairn. "Mah bride'll come wi' me," he told Iain, "but her bastard stays in Scotland where she was got and whelped."' The old woman winked at Morag. 'And so you did, *a thasgaidh*, mah wee darlin'.'

The bairn? Her bastard? Min squinted suspiciously into her cup. Could there be whisky in it?

'Are you saying...' The rest of the question dug its heels into her voice box, refusing to budge. Morag and Nanny waited, expectant smiles on their faces. She dragged the words out, kicking and screaming.

'Are you saying that she...' She looked into so-startling, so-familiar blue eyes. 'Morag, are you... Mary Hawkins' *daughter*?'

'Aye.' She took Min's cup, since it was about to fall to the floor. 'Got on Mairi by th' wicked ways of young earl, tho' he was but viscount, then, as old earl yet breathed.' She filled the cup from the kettle and handed it back. Min took it, glad of the warmth. Her hands had gone icy cold.

'Lady Dunmara didna hold it agin me, bein' a natural child. She tuk me as her maid when I were but thirteen. I were by her side fer year upon year. Was wi' her when the earl locked her away in madhouse, not knowin' she carried ye. Nor carin' a whit, havin' tuk a new wife.

'Wi' her, I was, when she bore ye, in the hour just after midnight. She believed ye wouldna survive, nae more than th'others.' Her face crinkled in a wry smile. 'Ye were a pale snip of a thing, wi' yer nose an' fingers and toes all blue as whelks. An' ye didna cheep nor greet. Grave as a wee judge, ye were.'

'"She willna last the night," my lady said. "But I wouldna have her die wi'out a name. I shall call her Minerva, for strength, and Eilish, for my mother."'

'But God willed that ye lived till morn, an' we spirited ye away as neat as fairy folk.' She poured more of the hellish tea into Nanny's cup. ''Twere another warder at madhouse, then, not so evil as Cawsey. Tabbit were his name. My lady had been allowed some of her jewells, and she give him a ruby ring to get ye to Mairi Hawkins in Little Farnleigh.'

'He were promised a pair of emerald earrins if he brought back a note from Mairi sayin' ye'd arrived still breathin'.

'Mairi writ the note in the Gaeilige, mind, so we'd know 'twas her.'

Min was in a state so far beyond bemusement it had no name. Part of her disquiet was the sheer volume of words Morag had used to get the story to this point. It was as though she'd held them inside for years, waiting for this place and this moment. Waiting, perhaps, for her.

Nanny waved a claw-like hand at the mantel. 'Show it her, Morag. It be whole, it be of a piece! I take a keck on Bride's Day every year.' She beamed at Min. 'Day o' yer birth, my lady.'

February first, St. Brigid's Day.

Morag reached for a small pottery jar on the mantel. The cork stopper resisted her efforts for a few seconds. When she got it open, she shook an inch-wide coil of paper into her palm and held it out to Min.

She would have accepted a loaded pistol with less trepidation. She screwed up her courage and took the coil, then gently unrolled it, one-handed, on her knee. It was greatly yellowed and the handwriting faded. Because they were Gaelic, she didn't understand the words at all, but the letters were well-formed. Morag spoke the three sentences aloud from memory.

'Bairn safe. I will raise her as my own, since my husband canna give me one and they wouldna let me keep the other. Blessed Bride be wi' her ladyship.'

The answer would change a thousand things, but they would

only come to pass if Min asked the question. 'Who is your father, Morag?'

'Och, th' same as yers, my lady. His Lordship Edgar Sterling Halpern Langworth, Earl Dunmara.' She smiled shyly. 'We're sisters.'

She did drop the cup, then. It splashed black tea on the floor and broke into a dozen pieces.

Chapter Thirty-Eight

Tramp, tramp, tramp.

It was his third day hiking through or around half the benighted settlements on Ireland's east coast. The way was as unpleasant as he had suspected it would be. One foot after the other, mile upon mile, he came to an intimate knowledge of each pebble in each rutted lane through the thinning soles of his old boots. His shoulders, too, proved disagreeable companions. It was necessary to shift his pack very often, one shoulder to the other. In the one, he had strained a muscle heaving bales of fur over the rail of the *Siobhan*. The other was diligent in its reminders of an old bullet wound.

This programme of small but soul-wearing vexations was not lightened by thinking. Indeed, he should have preferred not to think at all. But unless he developed a profound interest in hedgerows, there was nothing to occupy his mind except reflection. What he reflected most upon was that when his life went wrong, it always seemed to go wrong expansively.

Getting Min to Scotland should have been a simple proposition. But like that other simple proposition – ridding her of a blackmailer – it had developed many and varied complications.

He should have expected them. Nothing about Minerva Hawkins had ever been simple. At the very moment two years ago, when he first lost himself in those guileless hazel eyes, a long road of complications began to unfurl. He had wasted no time trotting down it like the donkey he was.

Tramp, tramp, tramp.

He ate what he found, slept where he could, and grew more worn and ragged with every day. Under sun and clouds and rain, he kept moving south. The roads, when they existed, were the type one expected to find in Mongolia or the Russian steppes. Bad as they were, they might be used by bandits or officials. He skirted them. In most hamlets where he stopped for food and water, he was treated to the same scorn he supposed the locals handed to Gypsies, English landowners, and the district RM. In the countryside, dogs were needlessly proprietorial about their sheep, even though he demonstrated no interest, culinary or carnal, in a single ewe. More than once, a farmwife looking over her gate had recoiled at the sight of him. Two had crossed themselves.

He had to get back to France before he was burned at the stake.

Tramp, tramp, tramp.

It might be time to admit he was getting too old for this sort of thing. He missed Les Pinsons. He missed the vines in their neat rows, the voluptuous little breasts of the grapes rolling between his fingers. He missed his kitchen and his coffee pot. He even missed Remy cursing him and Balthasar from the same lexicon of insults.

And even though he was where he was because of her, he missed Minerva Hawkins. Constantly, painfully. He was not comforted by the warning he had issued himself about the inevitability of pain. *You will hurt. It will pass.*

Passing was not yet the issue. Surviving until then had become a matter of some concern.

At the same time, missing Min came with a sweetness that

made it almost worth the pain. Every thought of her sparked pleasure in his loins. The phantom taste of her filled his mouth like wine.

She was the bottle of *Château d'Yquem* he had saved in his cellar for a special occasion. Sweet, strong, complex. He should have opened it when they were together at Les Pinsons. If he had, they might have gotten drunk enough to make love for the first time in his bed and not in The Eel's Pocket.

It was one of an infinite number of possibilities that would never now arrive.

Tramp, tramp, tramp.

He put his troublesome brain to the task of remembering old contacts in Dublin. The Irish gangs were unwelcome in London, though occasionally their members ventured, in ones and twos, to the capital. For serious business, they went to Liverpool or Manchester and pestered the Italians. But to sneakily observe and learn from the justifiably famous Jacks... Ewan Exeter was vain enough that he tolerated their envy.

Once, an Irishman in London had run headlong into what Ewan, in the voice he used to mock the toffs, called 'a spot of bother'. The Jacks had made the bother go away, and the Dubliner was effusively grateful.

Or lying through his teeth; with his sort one could never be sure. But he had sworn on *'the head o' me sainted muther'* that he would repay the Jacks, each and any one, if they should ever need a favour in return.

What was the man's name? Beatty? Bolan?

Byrne, that was it. Tommy Byrne. A grinning, free-swearing thug with a brogue as thick as a millstone. Not a foot soldier, Tommy. He had been well up in the Dublin gang ranks, with forty bully boys at his back.

Tramp, tramp, tramp.

At the top of a short stone bridge, Étienne finally came across a mile marker. He put down his pack, scrubbed his hands through his hair, and squinted. It was one of the old granite markers, the carving nearly erased by time and weather. *Malahide, 1 M. Dublin, 9 M.* Those would be Irish miles, longer than English ones. He did not remember the ratio.

Sammy said Malahide had a coastguard station. He would avoid awkward encounters by going far, far around the village on the land side. It would mean more tramping through fields, more dodging of bulls, and the unsatisfying discussion of rights of way with sheep dogs. He shifted his pack to a fresh shoulder, grunted, and plodded onward.

'Let us discover,' he told his left shoe, whose sole had procured an Act of Parliament against the upper and was celebrating divorce by flapping with each step, 'how long is the memory of Monsieur Byrne.'

CHAPTER THIRTY-NINE

She was a countess. She had a sister. In a jerky and splintered fashion, Min began to reconcile her life when she wasn't and didn't with her life when she was and did. She couldn't say her new attributes felt natural, like the colour of her hair (still reddish-brown, though she was sure the past month had given her a few grey strands) or her hazel eyes. Morag said the eyes were the earl's, which made her queasy.

She'd been queasy enough before, trying to get from dawn to dusk each day without thinking of Étienne. Her tiny ember of hope stayed alight, barely. She breathed memory on the spark and concocted plans that she rejected, one by one, as impractical or impossible. The interval of planning was restricted to the half-hour she lay in bed between waking and rising. Afterward, she applied an iron self-discipline she grudgingly admitted she'd learned from Asa Hawkins to get through the rest of the day.

In every hour, she staggered under the weight of Nanny MacDonald's disclosures. Those multiplied exponentially because Morag could not seem to stop talking. She was like a tongue-tied child whose power of speech had been restored by surgery. Day after day, while the two of them mopped floors and washed windows and cleaned hearths, the late Lady Dunmara's maid cheerily rattled on about the previously blank portion of Min's life, starting from the moment she'd been born at Raeburn House that February night.

'*Là Fhèill Brìghde.*' She used the Gaelic name for St Brigid's Day. 'Caud as an iron nail.' She spat on the rag she was using to wipe the glass in the kitchen window. Min had tried to discourage the spitting in favour of a basin of vinegar water, but she had to admit the spit gave a good shine.

'We wrap't ye up best we could. Countess were verra weak from the birthin', but she made me tie th' moon round yer neck.'

Min reflexively touched the double pendant, tucked under her dress collar. It gave her the oddest feeling to know her mother had worn it against her skin, had held it with her hands. Pure fantasy to think some essence of the woman had gone into the two farthing-sized discs, but no more fantastic than the rest of her story.

'Raeburn writ up th' record of yer birth, my lady, wi' me as midwife. What he done wi' it, I canna say.'

Min could. He'd submitted it to the Lunacy Commission as a stillbirth which, at the time, considering the countess's obstetrical history, he might have thought it was. He'd most certainly not been in the room when the baby was delivered. Morag and the countess told him it had died and he was relieved to know. An unwanted, inconvenient, female child. There was already a healthy male heir by then, born to the second countess.

Morag's disjointed but informative narrative also explained how Raeburn had known Min survived being 'stillborn'.

Tabbit, she said, had not been young when he'd been the warder at the asylum. While Min grew from babe to young woman in the Hawkins' household, Tabbit grew from middle age to dotard at Raeburn House, ending, finally as an inmate in the paupers' shed.

'Puir oul' Tabbit. Didna know his heid fra th' hearth, by then.'

He'd known and shared enough to be useful to Raeburn, though. Shiny buttons for a crow's nest.

Chapter Forty

It took two weeks of knuckle-skinning, shoulder-straining housework with Morag for Min to admit she'd have to attempt her first important task as a countess: hiring staff. She'd put it off as long as she could, but Dunmara Manor was simply too much for her and Morag to manage by themselves. They'd scrubbed and polished and laundered and – in Morag's case – spat on the windows with a will, but they simply couldn't cope with two storeys and eighteen rooms.

Hiring domestics wasn't something she'd done before. She'd seen Aunt Mary – Min couldn't keep calling her either Grandmother or Mary Hawkins – take on and let go day help for years. No mean feat in a village the size of Little Farnleigh. There weren't many candidates and rancour still lingered from sackings during the reign of Edward the Confessor.

Morag was invaluable. She slipped easily into a role that mingled sister, maid, and aide de camp without fully being any of them. A few days after she issued an informal Situations Offered among the locals, she stood sternly at Min's side, greeting a procession of people who'd come to the service door just after daybreak. Everyone in the queue was cheerful. Why not? Gentry were back in the manor house and wages would follow.

Gentry. That would be her, though she was no more inclined than ever to believe it was. Perhaps she'd plait into it, the way she did her hair every morning.

The interviews were surprising, confusing, and a godsend. Morag translated the applicants' speech into standard English when necessary. From her ease with the task, Min suspected she'd done it for the late countess – *the legitimate one, Amica Joan Langworth, Lady Dunmara* – before they'd both been shipped off to an asylum.

In addition to knowing the drill, Morag was thrifty, ever-alert to what Dunmara Manor should or shouldn't offer in wages. Between them, with Min always considering the accounts from Messrs Gordon and Blackford, they ended the interviews with a cook and two maids (one house, one scullery), a gardener, and the gardener's boy at half wages. The boy, at full wages, would double as a groom. If and when there were horses, a development Min did not plan to encourage. She tried not to blame the dapple grey and the Shire, but the horsing life just wasn't for her.

She wasn't sure Dunmara needed the gardener. Between the salt air and the Scots climate, it seemed unlikely there'd ever be lush gardens around the manor. It wouldn't hurt to make an effort, she supposed. And there were the peacocks, whom she'd named Bad and Worse, to Morag's delight. Having a strapping man about the place was probably a good idea, too. Poor Bodach looked to have been in the gatehouse to fend off Viking raiders in the ninth century.

She drew the line at a butler, footmen, and a lady's maid for herself. One of the housemaids could answer the door, she had no idea what footmen did, and she hadn't spent years making corsets to require help getting into and out of one.

Not that she wore a corset very often these days. Unless she went into Tayvallich on some business, she went blissfully stayless, as she was now. She ran a hand over her stomach, flat under lilac silk taffeta. Nothing like vigorous housework for keeping one fit. It was getting late in the summer for the frock, but it was a lovely day today and she wanted to wear it while she could.

She'd pulled the dress from the trunk Evie had sent. Morag had got hold of Callum MacDonald, who'd gone all the way to Oban, the nearest railway station, to fetch it. She wouldn't quibble about the usefulness of inheriting so many 'braw' kinsmen with the estate. She and Morag now had clothing enough for their roles in *The Unexpected Countess*, even if Min still had stage fright and frequently forgot her lines.

If the candidates for employment at Dunmara Manor were disappointed by her scanty hires, they hadn't shown it by noon, when the last of them left. Perhaps they were biding their time until she came to her senses and realised she was a genuine titled person who needed an entourage.

Morag went off to Nanny MacDonald's cottage and Min made herself lunch. A delivery of foodstuffs – grains, vegetables, eggs, a quarter of beef, various tins and jars – had arrived an hour after she'd taken on the first of her hires, the cook. It was frightening proof of the woman's efficiency and intent. Now would be Min's last chance to muck around in Dunmara's kitchen without Astrid Tweedle spearing her with a proprietary eye.

Sighing, she lowered herself into a chair at the big kitchen table and focused her own proprietary eye on a steaming pot of tea and a plate of cheese and pickle sandwiches.

After lunch, she'd be able to tackle the daily packet of post. Bodach dropped it on the front steps each morning after directing a heavily Scottish yell of '*Post!*' at the door.

There'd been almost none at first, but she'd noted more since word had gotten round about new occupants at Dunmara Manor. Representatives of various Glasgow firms offered to divest the house of moths or install one-piece ceramic flush toilets. She had

Aunt Mary's recipe for moth repellent, but she'd put the toilet offer aside for more study.

After her second cheese and pickle, she plucked today's top envelope from the packet. It bore Jillian and Kell's direction in Hackney and was postmarked three days ago. She tore it open.

As she unfolded the single sheet of paper, covered on both sides with close lines of handwriting, a cold thread of unease dragged across her fingertips.

Her body sensing disaster before the rest of her.

CHAPTER FORTY-ONE

20 August 1894
Dear and very much missed Minerva,
Étienne Sansecours is in Newgate Prison.

With a cry, she dropped the paper as though it was on fire. A tremor started in her feet and rose to the top of her head, while all the blood in her body seemed to flee in the opposite direction. Quaking and keening low in her throat, she snatched up the letter and read on.

The way Kell put it was 'Dague's banged up in the pitcher.' Apart from his explaining that 'pitcher' was 'stone pitcher', a name for the prison, I could not get much more from him. I did secure an incomplete version of events from Evie, who was disconcerted in greater measure (so we all thought, at first) than one would expect by the gaoling of a man she barely knows and has not seen in over two years.

What I can tell you is this. Some few weeks ago, Sansecours crossed from Dublin to Liverpool by ferry. Members of Her Majesty's Customs, the Dock Watch, the City of Liverpool

Police, and Scotland Yard (!) were waiting, with official papers, manacles, and leg chains (!!), to take him in charge.

We all have mixed opinions of Detective Inspector (soon to be Chief, rumour has it) Ewan Exeter, but I hasten to tell you that he had nothing to do with the arrest. He learned of it quickly, however, since most of the outstanding warrants for Mr Sansecours, however far they wandered, originated with the Metropolitan Police.

Evie had the news from Kell, who had it from Ewan Exeter. It seems Ada had it from the Detective Inspector even before Kell, but she said nothing to her brother nor to her sister Eileen. And Kell, in which decision I would not have concurred had I known about it at the time, informed Evie before me.

When I upbraided Kell about that, he confirmed that there are feelings between you and Mr Sansecours. He could not, in good conscience, withhold what he knew about the arrest from Evie, your particular friend, who would assuredly know where to reach you in the shortest time.

Kell believes you visited Mr Sansecours in France. Is that true? We all now know he came to London over a month ago to address some danger he believed you were in and intended to follow you to Devonshire. (Don't be angry with Evie for telling about the asylum. Mr Sansecours pressed her and you shouldn't have gone haring off alone the way you did.) I hardly know what to say, except to opine that this is a very complicated affair.

The upshot is that Evie is not speaking to Ada and Kell is not speaking to Ewan Exeter. Kell and I do not engage in the silent treatment, since we adore each other, but we will both admit to some terse words. Eileen and Ada are not speaking (though that is not uncommon), and Madame does not wish to hear about any of it.

If it is any comfort, we are all stunned and confused to find that Ada had enough contact with Exeter to learn from him about Mr Sansecours' capture and imprisonment before *anyone else. She is mum on that, just as she is on her reasons for not sharing the news with the rest of us. Since no one is speaking to her, we may never know. As to why Ada made no effort to find and inform you, I can only think it is because she was concerned for your welfare. She is chary of anything involving the Jacks and was alarmed from the outset (as was I, if you remember) by Mr Sansecours' attraction to you and yours to him. But that is only surmise. You shall ask her yourself, if you get back this way and think it worth the effort.*

Along with other recent shocks, we are all now aware that you are a Scottish countess. That revelation did not come from Evie. Some newspaperman ferreted it out and there was a small, vaguely worded, but sensational article in The London Illustrated News. 'Corsets to Countess', the article was titled, which is both euphonious and silly. For an obscure reason, the piece bore an image of Edinburgh Castle.

Your elevation will take some getting used to. Congratulations?

Despite the local epidemic of not speaking, I am still speaking to you, as this letter proves. In the interest of time, I did think of sending a wire, but there was no earthly way I could have explained all this in a telegram. Kell feels that Mr Sansecours is, for the moment, unlikely to be moved from 'the pitcher', as he awaits business with its neighbour, the Old Bailey.

If you come to London (and I am not certain you will want to or should), and if your old room is not available, you are most welcome to lodge at the East London Pugilists Academy in Poplar, since the flat at the top is vacant. Now that Andy is gamboling about and The Next Child is due soon, we spend all the hours we are not working at the Hackney house. It is better and roomier for children. And for Tige (our dog, if you remember) who likes the back garden.

I refuse to close this letter with Your Ladyship's obedient
servant.
    Affectionately,
    Jillian Kelly
    P.S. If you think to visit your Frenchman, Kell suggests you
do it sooner rather than later. Either he or Ewan Exeter will
accompany you. The prison is a very unsavoury place, and <u>you</u>
<u>must not go alone.</u>

Min had to press both hands on the table to rise. Once on her feet, she could not, at first, step away. If she quit the table, if she broke the connection of her hands and the solid surface, she and the world would collapse like a house of cards.

She had done this. Going to Les Pinsons with her daft plan for Étienne to save her had ultimately condemned him.

Because of her, he had left the shelter of France and travelled to England, where he'd defied the dangling noose of multiple arrest warrants. Not for himself but for her, he'd enacted a dangerous ruse to penetrate Raeburn House and rescue her from the entrapment of her own folly.

Because of her, he'd risked his life to guide her and Morag across Devon to Plymouth, thence to sea and to Scotland. Not to hide himself, not to escape back into protective anonymity. He'd done it to give her the title, the life of ease and privilege, that he'd only learned were hers a few weeks before.

Because of her, he'd become enmeshed in the smuggling world he'd left behind more than a decade earlier. That enmeshment had somehow, horribly, put him in the right place at the right time to be apprehended by the police.

He'd said, 'Go home, Minerva.' None of this would have happened if she'd listened.

But no, she hadn't. She'd thrust herself into a world of practised criminals where she would be as likely to survive as a moth in a bomb blast. She, not Étienne, should be the one blown to bits. She, not he, should be the one to suffer for her rash and thoughtless actions.

And she'd imagined she was saving him! All she'd done was grasp at some poetic tale in which she was a fairy monarch and he was an enchanted prince.

She must fix this. She *would* fix this.

She shouted for Morag twice before she remembered her sister was with Nanny. They'd be hours over cups of tea.

She made frantic little sprints, kitchen to hall and back again, and spotted her handbag on the table. Did she have enough inside to buy railway fare? She'd given Morag money to buy tobacco and tea from the village shop for Nanny, along with writing paper and ink for the manor. Even if she had the funds, how would she reach the train for London? The nearest station was Oban, twelve miles distant, and Dunmara had no horses.

Bodach. The old man was stronger than he looked. His English was sketchy, but she'd learned a few Gaelic phrases from Morag and thought she could instruct him to walk to Tayvallich, secure some sort of transport, and come back with it. No one in the village would ask to be paid on the spot for the hire; she was the countess. For the first time, she was thankful to be one.

She ran again from the kitchen to the front hall and wrenched open the door.

'Bodach! Bodach! *Trobhad!* Come–'

Cold steel touched the side of her head at the same time she heard the odiously familiar voice a few yards away.

'Watch yourself, she bites.' Fitzsimmons strode across the lawn to smirk at her.

'She won't bite this.' Raeburn pressed the pistol harder into her temple. 'Will you, darling?'

Chapter Forty-Two

Fitzsimmon's storky legs carried him onto the drive, where his boots crunched gravel.

'Nice little estate.' He spread his arms, taking in the house and grounds. 'You were right, Raeburn. Why settle for monthly dribbles when marrying our newly-minted countess,' he gave her a mocking bow, 'will turn the fountain on full.'

Raeburn leaned in close, and Min's jaw tightened. She spoke through clenched teeth. 'I will *never* marry you.'

'Yes, you will.' His bright assurance was worse than if he'd struck her. 'I've made a career of getting women to do what I require.' Not shifting the pistol an inch, he used his free hand to lift her braid and bring it to his nose. 'What I *want*.

'Bring the carriage around, Fitz,' he barked at the chief constable. 'We've a drunk parson waiting a mile from the railway station. With luck, he'll tie the knot before he's sober and my bride and I can still make the five-fifteen to London.'

His voice became a smooth slither, an asp. 'A few months at the Savoy, the opera, the best restaurants, and society will change all this ugliness to gold.' He clutched her elbow and dragged her down the manor steps to the drive. 'It will be a...' He punctuated each word with a tap of the gun barrel against her temple. 'Beautiful. Love. Story. We might visit Italy, before we return to the manor.' Raeburn's tongue swiped her cheek and she jerked in revulsion. '*Our* manor.'

There was a jangle of harness and the scrape of coach wheels on the drive. A black brougham, drawn by a muscular bay, pulled up at the bottom of the steps. Fitzsimmons, in the high seat at the front, had the reins in one fist, a carriage whip in the other. A crooked copper, pretending to be a coachman in a long coat and a John Bull hat. Waggling the whip, he spoke around a cigar in his mouth. 'Need a hand getting her in?'

'Not at all,' Raeburn said. 'She'll be a perfect kitten.' Gripping her arm more fiercely, he pushed her forward, the pistol never leaving the side of her head. 'Or I'll let the Webley have its way with her.'

'If you shoot me,' Min rasped, 'I'll be a dead kitten. That'll spoil your plans a bit.'

His laughter was the barking of a wild dog, too near, too loud.

He'd let her precede him into the carriage. For that, he'd have to release her arm. It would be her best chance. Putting one foot on the iron step, she dove head first into the compartment, kicking back with both feet. She'd hoped for the groin but from his cry and curse she'd caught him in the gut. Scrabbling to her knees, she lunged for the other door, but it was latched fast.

Before she could wrestle open the lock, Raeburn grabbed the back of her skirt and hauled her back to him.

The coach seats were smooth leather. Facedown and scrabbling, she couldn't get a handhold anywhere on them. Straining against his pull, Min kicked backwards again, but her skirt and petticoat were caught under and around her and she couldn't gain leverage. Only because Raeburn was working one-handed, the other gripping his pistol, did she have any chance at all.

Writhing, shrieking, and thrashing from side to side to distract him, she got her fingers under the top button of her bodice and tugged at the thin ribbon holding her pendant. She'd never got round to replacing it and the silk might come untied or even break, if she pulled hard enough. One tug, another, and the freed ribbon was in her hand. The open window was just above her head.

With a painful wrench of her back, she rolled over and drove her boots into Raeburn's face. Useless. The entanglement of her skirts kept her from landing a solid blow. If he tried to climb atop her, she might be able to ram a knee between his legs. Still kicking, she used hands and feet to scramble backwards until she was crouched against the locked door. She brought her hands overhead to grasp the top of the window frame. Braced, she might land a two-footed kick at his head.

Raeburn got his free hand around one of her ankles. Trying to dislodge him, she lashed out with her other foot and caught him a glancing blow on the side of his head. It barely counted as a distraction, but at the same time she screamed like a cat and flung her pendant backwards, out the window. *Please land on the drive. Please don't hang up on a wheel or the coach body.*

Raeburn shouted something to Fitzsimmons and hurtled into the compartment as the brougham started moving. She had a split second of elation. There was no sign of the pistol. Raeburn's hands were empty.

But formed into fists. They drove forward, his full weight behind them.

Guncotton exploded in her middle. Some faraway observer noted she was clutching herself and gagging. *Hurts, hurts.* The interior of the brougham was too small to contain such agony. It would explode, *she* would explode. Parts of her would fly out the windows like bomb fragments.

Must. Breathe. But her lungs didn't work. Her vision was a blurred field, black at the edges. Her ears rang like ten bell towers, all going at once. *Can't. Breathe.* Breathless and in pain, she would die in this cramped compartment. Mouth open, gasping like a fish in a creel.

Raeburn snarled through his own panting. 'Stop being dramatic, you tiresome slut. Start breathing or I'll punch you again. Harder, next time.'

He bent forward and clutched a handful of her bodice, lifting her out of her seat by it and shaking her violently. The action shocked her diaphragm back to work and she clawed in a breath. Another, a third, each one a searing rattle through her throat and mouth. He opened his hand and dropped her back on the seat.

It took three more struggling breaths before her vision cleared. Raeburn had folded down one of the corner seats opposite. He perched there, blond-grey hair dishevelled, legs crossed at the knee, face like thunder.

The Webley was back in his hand.

For a taut interval, there was only the squeak and clatter of the moving carriage, the bay's hooves clacking on the road, and her ragged breathing. Those, and Raeburn's boot, tapping irritably on the floor.

She wouldn't, couldn't look at him. Instead, she mordantly detailed the brougham's interior as for a builder's catalogue. The seats, black as the exterior, substantial leather and beautifully dressed. Mahogany woodwork, burnished to a mirror shine. Metalwork, entirely of bright brass. Silk tassels, alternating gold and black, dangling from the window curtains.

The details of her predicament formed a separate catalogue, every page bordered in fear. She was trapped with two men whose joint profession was extortion and whose moral compasses were non-existent. One was a ranking policeman. He could get them through any barrier and his say-so would not be questioned. The other had as good as killed her mother and locked her sister in a filthy shed for years. No one knew where she was.

Raeburn broke the laden silence with false sympathy. 'Ah, poor little countess. How hard it must be to surrender to the inevitable.

But,' he turned a hand palm up and shrugged, 'your large French accomplice is not here to stand between me and what is mine.' Another of his jackal laughs. 'Viscount de Vaux, indeed. What *is* his actual name? Jacques? Pierre?

'Do you know – true story, now; I have many and can be very entertaining – I had a woman at my asylum for a while who'd owned a poodle named Pierre. How she'd mourned him after being shut away!' Raeburn's voice took on a wobbly falsetto. "Oh, Pierre! My precious, my baby! Who will care for you, now?"

'So very aggravating. Took quite a lot of treatment to stop her muling.'

He settled back on the seat and uncrossed and recrossed his legs, propping the heel of the pistol grip on one knee. His hair wasn't the pomaded perfection of their last meeting. Strands fell over his sweaty forehead. He'd popped some buttons from the bottom of his waistcoat getting her into the coach. The striped silk gawped over his stomach.

'I think I shall call your accomplice Pierre. I'll give him this, he is quite the actor. Had me going for a bit with his Sigmund Freud and Thomas Bond. Where did you pick him up? Drury Lane?' More laughter from his corner, and a mocking yelp of '*Oui, oui!* Bow wow!'

Raeburn was the dog, and rabid, to boot. How had she not noticed the coarse underlayment of his speech before? The practised vowels were part of a role as false as the trumpery credentials and the fine consulting room. All meticulously crafted to hide the pure evil beneath.

She must not let him see how terrified she was; it would give him more control than he already had. She locked her gaze on the view from the window next to her shoulder, wondering if she could get the door unlatched before he shot her. She might be able to jump. Less likely she'd survive it.

The road to Oban skirted the coast, close to the cliff edge. The westward sky was a glowering mess of thick, dirty-white clouds that skimmed the horizon. *Clabberin'*, Morag would call it, since it resembled clotted cream before it was quite set. Wind bore the smell of the sea through the window, and her heart clenched painfully. Étienne had been out there, on the *Siobhan*, surviving seaborne danger only to encounter catastrophe on land. Trapped behind stone and steel in Newgate, was he thinking of her, believing her safe? *Oh, my love, I'm not safe, not safe at all.*

By now, Morag might be back at Dunmara. She might find the pendant. *I might turn into a gull and fly out the carriage window and across the Jura Sound.*

And poor Bodach, who'd not answered her call. What had happened to him? If Raeburn and Fitzsimmons had harmed the old man, she'd–

She jerked at a heavy touch on her leg. Raeburn was bent toward her. Gun still pointed, businesslike, at her middle, his fingers diverted themselves on her thigh. A drag, a slide, a possessive finger walk along her skirt. She cringed against the seat back, but he gripped her knee, squeezing and releasing, squeezing and releasing. The crackle of the taffeta, the lumbering of the carriage on the rough road, her fear and disgust... Any second, cheese and pickle would decorate his suit.

Raeburn crooned silkily. 'He's had you, hasn't he? Not an accomplice, then. A paramour. Pity. I'd hoped for the pleasure of being your first. No matter. You'll give me years of enjoyment in the sheets. And marrying you is an act of patriotism! Can't let a pretty English ewe go to a lusting French ram, can I?'

If I use one hand to peel his fingers off my leg, I can use the nails of the other to gouge out his eyes. Jam them into his mouth and watch him choke. She wanted to do it more than she wanted another breath. But his steady hold on the firearm reminded her that any move might be her last. *It's worth it. I'd rather die here and now than let that monster touch the body that belongs to Étienne.*

Self-preservation was abandoning the rampart between thought and deed when Raeburn withdrew his groping paw and sat back in his seat. 'Did you know?' he drawled casually, as though he'd not just been mauling a woman at gunpoint. 'Electrical current, judiciously applied, can produce the most convulsive sensations during sexual congress?

'We'll explore the horizons of that, you and I. After a year with me, *Countess*, you won't remember the French ram's name.' His words were the ugliest she'd ever heard, until his next ones.

'Or your own.'

CHAPTER FORTY-THREE

The greatest part of a fear-stretched hour passed. Afraid to turn her gaze away from Raeburn in case he sent a predatory hand to her knee again, she used most of it to stare through the small glass partition between the compartment and the driver's box. Fighting the opium-like effects of shock, she thought, at first, that she was hallucinating a low, heavy pounding outside the brougham. Or, given the ominous sky, that the threatening storm had broken.

But the pounding increased in volume and proximity. It was a visceral rumble, a rolling, nearing thunder from the slopes that rose northward from the road to the mountains of Morvern and Ardmour. With the sound came a palpable vibration, as though a herd of American bison were stampeding across western Scotland to the coast.

Other noises coalesced above the thunder. The whinnies of horses, the shouts of men, a blood-chilling ululation like the cry of a Viking berserker. Through the glass partition, she heard Fitzsimmons, cursing blue and harrying the horse. His whip cracked once, twice, three times.

The brougham sped up on the uneven road, rocking alarmingly. The whirring of its wheels and the clatter of the horse's hooves added to the din. Min and Raeburn both clung to the straps in the coach, she with both hands, he with one. He still pointed the Webley at her with lethal steadiness.

Clamour crowded the brougham from behind, but she saw nothing from her side except the sea. And the cliff edge along which the road ran. Frighteningly, it was only a dozen yards away. Raeburn had positioned himself so she couldn't see out the window on his side, just flashes of light and rocky landscape.

The vehicle slewed from side to side. Surely, any second it would go over the cliff. With a final, sickening lurch and some particularly foul language from Fitzsimmons, it lumbered to a halt, nearly throwing its occupants onto the floor of the compartment.

For an anticlimactic few seconds, the only sounds came from outside. Snorting and stamping horses, the jangle and squeak of tack.

Then, there was scuffling and thumping and garbled speech from the front of the brougham, which juddered on its springs. The bay squealed and someone shouted gutturally, 'Stand, cuddie! Stand!' Fitzsimmons yelled unintelligibly, his voice eclipsed by dragging noises, like the ones she and Morag made moving furniture from room to room at Dunmara.

She craned to see out Raeburn's window, but he kept it blocked with his body. Damn the man, he managed to keep his gun on her the while, just taking in whatever was outside with quick sidelong snaps of his head.

Abruptly, he plunged across the compartment and seized her arm. 'You'll step down first,' he snarled, so close a spray of spittle hit her face. He got behind her and shoved her ahead of him to the door. As he reached around to turn the latch, he hissed, 'I will be directly behind you. Remember...' The barrel of the Webley clarified his point against her backbone. 'You will still be a countess if I put a bullet in your spine. Just a countess without the use of her legs.'

Her hand quavered so violently she could barely manage it, but she got the door open and looked down, trying to locate the narrow step. It was a near thing, but she made the step without tripping over her skirt hem. Raeburn was pressed so close at her rear that she heard and felt the wool of his coat brushing her dress. His hot breath grazed the top of her head.

They both touched earth. Too frightened to do more than stare at her feet, Min shook like a sapling in a high wind. Without moving the gun from her back, Raeburn wound her braid around his free hand, jerking it painfully against the nape of her neck. She stifled a cry of pain. He pulled again, hard, forcing her to look up.

She'd alighted from the brougham to a Jacobite uprising.

Ahead of her were arrayed at least a dozen mounted men. Scots – no, Highlanders. MacDonalds, from the smattering of red-and-green kilts and the plaids thrown over shoulders or across horses' withers. To a man, they were lavishly armed. Pistols in gnarled hands, dirks in muscular fists. One man carried what appeared to be a claymore. And one had a bow, arrow nocked at the ready.

Incoming mist from Loch Sween swirled and rose around the horses' legs, reinforcing the impression of warriors out of time. *Or,* she pleaded, *just in time.*

The man at the front of the assemblage was Callum MacDonald, dressed in ordinary clothing. With one exception. His shock of ginger hair was mostly hidden under a bright blue woollen bonnet.

Three horses were riderless. They stood with the other mounts, waiting in a mannerly fashion while the men who'd left their backs conducted unmannerly affairs to one side with Chief Constable Fitzsimmons.

Fitzsimmons was on his knees in the dirt, flanked by two standing MacDonalds, a third behind. The one behind had his fingers in Fitzsimmons' hair, gripping it so brutally that the policeman's head was drawn back and his throat exposed, a pale swath of skin over his collar. The cords of his neck bulged and his eyes darted wildly.

She would have said it was a poor posture from which to convey authority, but that didn't stop Fitzsimmons from trying. 'See here, you sodding rebels.' The words were forced, half strangled by the angle of his head. 'I am the Chief Constable of Great Torrington, and–'

The rest of his comment was lost in a gale of laughter and rude noises from the Highlanders. One stocky redhead among them called out, '*Grrr*eat To*rr*ington, is it? Aye, that's guid to know. We'll wish to send condolences ta yer widow.'

A second burst of hoots and laughter nearly drowned Fitzsimmons' bellow. 'I am a duly appointed servant of the Crown! I'll see every man jack of you brought in on charge! You'll swing for this, you rabble of unwashed, dog-eating–'

'Haud yer wheesht.' Callum MacDonald punctuated his order with a nod to one of the Highlanders flanking the policeman. A dirk was drawn in a flash of steel, the point placed at Fitzsimmons' throat.

A wise man watching would have kept still. But at her back, Raeburn chose to be loudly confrontational. 'What's the meaning of this outrage? We will not be waylaid in this manner!'

The Highlanders assumed bland and uncomprehending expressions. They might have been attending a lecture in Urdu.

Raeburn raised his voice another notch, and Min was gratified to hear it quaver. From rage, perhaps. From fear, surely. 'Do you understand *English*? Move on, you Scottish barbarians, we've a train to meet.'

Several of the men smiled faintly, one picked his nose.

Raeburn scaled his volume up still more, lading it with the umbrage of a thwarted Englishman. '*Make way*, I said. My fiancée is *the Countess of Dunmara!*'

The eruption of mirth among the MacDonalds was loud and long. As it diminished, Callum MacDonald shook his head. 'Nay, nay, English. She's nae mair yer fiancée than aul' Jamie there.' He jerked his chin toward a bearded rider, who waggled his fingers at Raeburn and smacked his lips in a kiss.

'Ye're right aboot one thing. She is the Countess Dunmara, and we are the men of Dunmara, cam to tak her back. So step awa' an'–'

'If you think I'll let you deprive me of my property, you're sadly mistaken.' Raeburn whipped the gun from her spine to the side of her head, pressing it into the same sore place he'd pressed it before. Min stopped breathing.

Callum's voice was deadly ice to Raeburn's boiling froth. 'Step awa', English. Or harm'll cam to ye.'

'Is that what you think?'

She heard the click of the Webley's hammer and bit her cheek not to sob.

'Think again!' Raeburn roared, out of control. 'So help me God, I'll spatter her brains and yours on this godforsaken spot if you don't let – us – go!' He snatched the pistol from her head and pointed it at Callum.

Whirrrr-thunk. It was so close and loud she was sure Raeburn had shot her. For a stunned instant, she waited to die. It didn't hurt. Shouldn't it hurt?

It was only when her braid flopped down and she felt cool air on her neck that she looked for the source of the sound.

The superintendent lay at her feet, a crumpled heap in a fine suit. Half an arrow protruded from his eye, the feathered fletch vibrating merrily in the breeze. There wasn't much blood. The parts of her that weren't preparing to vomit found that interesting.

An enormous peal of thunder made the ground shake and all the horses squeal. The sky released a torrent of rain.

It might have been the driving rain that made the next half hour seem like a stage play with particularly good effects. With frightening dispatch, one of Callum's men took the cheekpiece of the bay horse's bridle and coaxed it gently forward a score of feet, putting the brougham's far wheels right at the edge of the cliff. With equal gentleness, the same man unhitched the horse and led it out of the shafts.

Two men picked up Raeburn's body and heaved it onto the coachman's seat. Propped there, he looked appallingly like a driver who'd fallen asleep in his perch. The arrow was gone from his eye. She couldn't bear to look at the clotted black mess of the socket.

The largest of the men, almost Étienne's size, kicked at the spokes of one wheel of the brougham until half a dozen shattered. Three other men held the carriage in place on its remaining wheels, so it wouldn't collapse on that side.

She was utterly confused by the performance until she saw half the MacDonalds brace themselves on the land side of the coach and begin to push it. With a rhythmic chant – counting in Gaelic, she guessed – they rocked it back and forth, back and forth. Raeburn's body rocked along, a sight to give her a year of nightmares.

On the sixth count, the fine black brougham, silk tassels, brass fittings, and all, gave a loud crack and a scream of splintering undercarriage. It teetered for a breath on the edge of the cliff, then went over with a sort of fatal majesty.

The sounds it made falling and the heavy crash when it hit the bottom... She would expect to meet them in her dreams, too.

Fitzsimmons, still on his knees, had a seat in the stalls for the entire spectacle. As she watched, audience and actors changed places. A crescent of MacDonalds formed before Fitzsimmons, all but one. A young man she'd heard the others call Rabbie unwound his plaid from his shoulders and draped it over hers. She smiled wetly up at him. The wool wasn't much drier than her now-soaked dress, but it helped suppress her shivers.

'Weel, now,' Callum began, facing Fitzsimmons. 'We've a few

questions to put ta ye, an' I'm sure ye'll answer like a gentleman, won't ye?'

Fitzsimmons said nothing. The man behind him, still holding his hair, bobbed the policeman's head down and up twice.

After the general laughter died, Callum began. 'Did ye obsairve how we deal wi' those who cam inta oor midst an' mak off wi' oor kin?'

'I did.'

'If ye're asked, ye'll say naught but that ye barely escaped a most grievous coach accident. If ye mak any other report ta any magistrate, ta any agent of the law, ta a wee wren in a bush, aboot th' rest... Weel, do ye have any doubt we'll hunt ye doon?'

'I don't.'

'Do ye have any doubt we'll kill ye?'

'I don't.'

'Do ye have any doubt we'll kill anyone ye've ever loved, yer kin, yer horse, yer dog, anyone ye've ever shared a dram wi'?'

'None whatsoever.'

'Let th' man rise.'

The Highlanders stepped away and Fitzsimmons lurched to his feet. His trousers were sopping with rain and stained with mud to mid-thigh.

'Ye've a fine stretch o' road from here ta Oban. Six mile, I make it. If ye shift yerself, ye can be there by dark. Awa' wi' ye.' Callum made a shooing motion, and Fitzsimmon walked jerkily up the road, not looking back.

The Highlanders, all but Callum, collected plaids and weapons and mounted their horses. One of them had the bay from the brougham on a lead behind his own horse. Min wondered where the carriage horse had come from. Not from Raeburn's stable at the asylum, or Étienne would have taken him along with the Shire. She supposed sooner or later someone would miss him, but it was long odds they'd find him.

Callum led over his horse, a big, dun-coloured beast with

shaggy fetlocks. 'Ye maun ride wi' me, my lady,' he said. 'I hope ye won't take it amiss that ye'll have ta sit astride and hold on ta me.'

Her hair dripped water down her face and off her chin, and her lips were quivering so violently she almost couldn't manage speech. 'I-I don't mind. I've ridden astride b-before.' Best part of week, but the less said of that, the better.

Callum mounted and pulled her up behind him. Before she wrapped her arms around his waist, she pulled Rabbie's drenched plaid over her head.

'Morag?' she asked over his shoulder. 'And Bodach?'

'Och, they're braw, Countess. Bodach's a wily old badger. Old'un smelled trouble on th' *sassaunachs* before they ever made th' drive at Dunmara. He legged it fer Morag at Nanny's hoose. 'Twas Morag found yer wee jewell on th' grass and fetched me and th' lads.'

'Mr MacDonald, I'm deeply grateful.'

She really should say something more. More about the rescue, the boldness and risk and horror of it, but reaction and cold made her stupid. And what could she say? Countess or not, she was a nuisance and a danger to these people. And nothing that had happened had gotten her closer to London and Newgate. To Étienne.

'I should,' she went on hastily, before the rain and a moving horse made speech impossible. 'That is, I must go on to Oban and the train. It's imperative I reach London as soon as possible.'

Callum, bless him, didn't ask why, just shook his head. Droplets flew off his bonnet. 'Ye canna travel in a stoatin' rain, my lady. An' ye'll no be goin' wi'oot an escort. The morrow'll be guid enough. Cam hame fer th' night.'

Hame, indeed.

Chapter Forty-Four

'You wouldn't be here, you French muttonhead, if you'd listened to me.'

Étienne didn't need anyone to point out Dublin had been a trap. The kind that walked on two feet and had a cheerful Irish brogue. Now, he was in what Newgate called the Visiting Box, a cage at the prison end of the front courtyard. He strove for patience while Ewan Exeter belaboured the obvious.

His fingers were hooked into a wall of steel mesh. There were two such walls separating prisoners from visitors, a yard-wide space between them to prevent the transfer of contraband goods. Exeter had bribed large to get him into the space between, so the policeman was just on the other side of the mesh, leaning casually against it.

The discretion of the warder at the prison end of the cage was no doubt due to an additional bribe. He stood, legs braced, whistling softly. Paying close attention to his fingernails and none to the exchange between prisoner and visitor. The furnace of Newgate put out impressive heat from the fuel of pound notes.

'Always, I have listened to you, Ewan.'

'Bollocks. None of the Jacks listened to a single order I gave.'

Only two feet apart, they kept their voices low. No state secrets were being passed back and forth, but even the bricks in Newgate had ears.

'I made the assumption that our system of governance was parliamentary.'

'Right. A parliament of owls.'

'If so, you were the prime minister of owls.'

'I was a flea on one wing, ignored by all and sundry.'

Their discourse halted while they watched a rat, fat and greasy, waddle along the seam where the outer steel barrier met the paving stones. The rat stopped to dig at something between two stones. It excavated a bone, small and ivory, darkly stained. Might have come from a chicken. Or a finger.

'Bother you much?' Exeter said, nocking his chin toward the rat.

'Not at all. I am grateful that the prison management enlarges our diet with meat. Sundays, we have *fricassée de raton*. On Wednesdays, *corbeau farci*.'

Exeter sucked his teeth meditatively. 'Never had stuffed crow. How is it?'

Étienne gave a very Gallic shrug, solely because Exeter would hate it. 'The cook is not *sympathique*. Spices elude him.'

'Don't whinge. You've only been inside for a fortnight.'

'Eighteen days. It seems longer.'

'Yeah.' Exeter turned a bleak look on the courtyard's perimeter wall. Twice the height of a man, topped with lethal steel chevrons, it was – discouraging. 'Always seems so.'

Exeter would know. Before he discarded his birth name and became Scraper, king of London's most notorious gang, he had whiled away nearly three years in Borstal. He had been sixteen at the start.

'Ewan.' Étienne touched the notched collar of his charcoal grey wool waistcoat. 'Thank you for the clothing.' A bit subdued for his tastes, but he had come to Newgate in little more than rags. The waistcoat, trousers, and uncollared shirt restored a particle of his dignity.

'Don't mention it. Your unnaturally large size was the only real challenge. Luckily, my tailor had some tents left over from a commission by the Army.'

'I will take great care not to spill anything on them at the weekly tea dance.'

'See that you do.' Exeter waved a lanky, well-tended hand at Étienne's face. 'I see the prison barber's earning his bribe.'

He fingered his chin. 'Adequately, at best. To his face, my praise is more liberal. I am told he was gaoled for a particularly gruesome murder.'

'Reduced to manslaughter. In gaol or out, one should always be pleasant to a man with a razor in his hand.' Five seconds ticked by. 'Too bad about the gold, Dague.'

'Tommy Byrne should enjoy it while he can.'

'He thinks you won't get out.'

'He is wrong.' Was he? He would not allow himself to think Byrne had put him away for life.

Exeter shifted a few inches closer, putting his mouth against the wire. 'Listen. I know a District Inspector in the RIC. He can paint "Fenian bomber" on Byrne in letters a foot high.'

'No. When I am freed, I will see to it.'

'As you like.'

A rustle brought their attention back to the rat. It was scuttling off, bony prize in its jaws. Étienne watched it dispassionately. Even disgust became boring after a while.

Boredom changed to needle-sharp attention when Exeter said, 'I have news from Scotland.'

Attentive or not, he had learned long ago to give Ewan Exeter the smallest window possible into his emotions. 'Is that so? A work stoppage of cattle? Revolt among the makers of bagpipes?'

'Hah bloody hah.'

The jest earned him petty punishment from his old chief. He

counted off a minute for the taking of the fine cigar from the coat. Another minute for the hunting in pockets for the silver vesta box. A third for the lighting of the cigar.

Only after Exeter had savoured a few draws did he add, 'It's too late to feign disinterest, mate.'

'I am not disinterested, only annoyed. The holes in this grate are too small to permit me to reach through and strangle you for withholding news. *Minerva. Hawkins.*' He snarled the name, just to be sure Exeter knew he only allowed liberties with his patience because they were separated by steel wire. And, perhaps, because it was a game they played. They had been deadly, once, even toward each other. Now, it was habit. Perhaps it kept them young.

Exeter picked a particle of tobacco from his lower lip and flicked it away. 'Your countess.'

'She is not mine.'

'Fine. *Some* countess was tossed into a carriage by an alienist and a bent copper from Great Tuckabump.'

Through the red sheet of fury that sprang up before his eyes, he spat, 'C. Augustus Raeburn and Chief Constable Fitzsimmons.'

A curt nod, seen through smoke. 'They were spiriting her away to an anvil wedding.'

Étienne's fingers tightened in the grate until his knuckles whitened. 'She is–'

'Safe.'

He was suddenly glad of the wire and the grip of his fingers in it. His legs had gone feeble as jackstraws. 'What happened?'

'According to the sixth-hand report I got, she was rescued by a heavily armed force of Highlanders–'

'Highlanders. Do you mean kilts and–?'

'Stop interrupting. A heavily armed force of Highlanders who made sure...' Exeter gave him a meaningful glance. 'That she would never be troubled by either pesky villain again.'

'In what way do you mean – sure?'

'Both dead as Billingsgate mackerels. Alienist went off a cliff in a carriage wreck.' Exeter's glance included a lift of both eyebrows. 'The chief constable took a long walk in a cold rain. After which, he contracted lightning pneumonia and coughed up his lungs.'

'And Min?'

'Her Highland retinue put her on a train for London.'

He put his head against the grate and cursed. *Incroyable.* The story itself, but equally incredible that the woman simply would *not* stay put. After all he had done to get her to the lands and manor that were hers, to insure she would have the life she deserved, a fine life, a safe life...

A life undarkened by the kind of man whose past had hunted him down, bagged him, and was now preparing to age the meat for a few dozen years in prison.

'She belongs in Scotland.'

'Too right. I'd tell her that, except I know what happened to the alienist and the copper from Great Thingummy. Or...' Exeter removed his hat and stood aside, vacating his place at the wire for a visitor entering the courtyard. A visitor with a long brown braid pinned under a jaunty little hat and a slender body skimmed by a walking dress in dark blue silk. 'You can tell her yourself.'

CHAPTER FORTY-FIVE

'Hello, Étienne.'

'*Minerve.*'

That was all, at first. Two words from her, one from him. Still too many, when all she wanted to do was press her mouth to his through a gap in the steel mesh. She did it with her gaze. He did it back.

Exeter, a yard away, cleared his throat and said cheerfully, 'Oh, no, please! Thanks are unnecessary. All I did was spread threats and quid like heavy snow to get her in here when it's not Visiting Day. A few more to get yon turnkey to whistle up a cab for her when the two of you are done breathing on each other.'

'Go away, Scraper.'

Exeter's grin startled all three of them. 'Toodle-pip, old chap.' He popped on his hat and tapped the brim. 'Countess.' With that, he strode toward Newgate Street, whistling.

She curled her fingers through the grate. Étienne curled his around hers. Even with gloves, her hands were cold from nerves and the damp, oppressive air in the prison courtyard. The warmth of his naked skin was breath in her lungs, blood in her veins.

'Please don't be angry with me.'

'I am not angry.'

He said it, '*hang-ry*,' and her heart turned over. 'I'm going to get you out of here.'

'Min.'

He was going to say something she wouldn't like, so she didn't let him. 'I've found a defence solicitor. He's very famous, so I'm told. I'm confident that–'

'Minerva.'

It was never a good sign when he said her name in English. She didn't want to hear it, anyway. She only wanted to hear '*Minerve*.' The way he rumbled it, the way he whispered it from the next pillow, the way he begged her with it when they made love.

His voice was already low. He lowered it more, letting it fill with the anger he said he wasn't feeling. 'Tell me about the incident in Scotland.'

'It's over.'

'Over is not what I need to hear. Are you hurt? Did Raeburn and Fitzsimmons hurt you in the least, smallest way?'

'No. Not really. It was– I was a little scared.'

Maybe she should just have told him they flogged her with a cat o' nine tails. The black rage that crossed his face was certainly up to hearing that.

'Scared.'

'Yes, you know. *Zézayer.*

'That means "to lisp". The word you want is *effrayée*. The men frightened you.' He turned his head to one side and swore in French. At least, it sounded like swearing. From his tone, he wasn't wishing anyone well.

'I'm fine, really. Toward the end it was a little... One of the MacDonalds – they're my kinsmen, actually, though that's rather a long tale. Anyway, one of them had a bow. You know, like Robin Hood. I think his name was Jamie, but it might have been Fion. There were so many of them, you see, Angus and Rabbie and Callum and... Did I tell you Morag is my sister? Half-sister. She's a

MacDonald on her mother's – that is, my grandmother's side, though I must call her Aunt Mary, now. And that's not why so many MacDonalds are around Dunmara. They're – well, it's not important to know that. The MacDonald who had the bow, whatever his name is, aimed it at Raeburn, who had a pistol–'

'A pistol.'

'Yes. A Webley. That's a very good gun, I'm given to understand, by the MacDonalds. So, Raeburn had the Webley, and it was pressed against my head.' She tugged one hand away from Étienne's and made a gun shape from it, touching her index finger to her temple. 'Which was very *effrayant*. But then he pointed it at Callum. And the MacDonald who had the bow... It was terribly fast, and the arrow went into his... into his...'

She slid the tip of her finger under the lens of her spectacles to rest in the crease of her eyelid, just under the bone. The touch took her back to the moment, and for a horrible few seconds she was there, on that rain-lashed clifftop, hearing the sound the arrow made when it streaked through the air and buried itself deep, deep into human flesh.

Her mouth opened. Nothing emerged. The silence, the expectant, awful silence, stretched on and on. She knew the word she wanted was 'eye' but couldn't get it out. She just stood there, finger still in place.

No conscious thought drove her to press her body against the cage. But tremors, waves and waves of them, worked their way up from her feet, or maybe down from her head, growing more violent with each wave. In a few seconds, she was a rattling mess of unquiet flesh that needed propping up before she fell. Étienne was her first choice, but he was on the other side of the wire. She let herself sag against it.

With frustrated need apparent in every line of his big body, he pressed against her from the other side. She took her hand away from her eye and thrust as many fingers as she could through a gap. He took them and held them tight. If there hadn't been steel gridwork between them, she would have laid her head against his chest. He would have rested his chin on her hair. The want of that howled in her heart.

They clung that way for a while, grateful for the spaces between the wires. In those hundred small apertures, they were together.

'I'm going to get you out of here,' she repeated, soft as a sigh.

He rubbed her fingers. His face was lowered; she could feel his breath on her forehead. 'Min, I am not a schoolboy who has pulled a prank upon the headmaster. The charges against me are serious. Much effort has been expended to bring me here.'

At that, she raised her head. She needed him to look into her eyes, to see the resolve there. 'I don't care if they brought you here in a howdah on the back of an Indian elephant.' Because part of her plan was to ignore his objections.

She unhooked one hand from the cage and ferreted under the collar of her dress until she was able to tug out a slender, plaited wool necklace. Morag had made it to replace it the black silk ribbon, the one whose tendency to come untied had saved her life. Both her pendant and his gold signet ring now dangled from it. She held up the ring. 'There's something engraved inside. What does it say?'

'I don't need to see it to tell you. But of what importance is—'

'Just tell me, Étienne.'

He treated her to one of his long-suffering French sighs. '*Audi, vide, tace*. In English—'

'Hear, see, and be silent.'

'If you know, Minerva, why did you ask?'

She stuffed the necklace back into her dress. 'Just confirming something.'

'*Minerve...*'

'You can take that tone all you want with me, Étienne Sansecours, and it's water off a duck's back.' She kissed his knuckles, right, left. 'I must be off, now. But I'll be back soon.'

'Min, you–'

She took a few steps. Turned and retraced them. 'Yes, me. Me and you, you and me. Together. Don't think you can change that.' She waggled her fingers at his scowl. '*À tout à l'heure,* Pierre.' She marched away.

'*Qui est–*' He raised his voice. 'Who the bloody hell is Pierre?'

She'd already gestured to the turnkey to open the gate and didn't answer.

CHAPTER FORTY-SIX

'Hear, see, and be silent,' the motto of the Grand Masonic Lodge of England. Asa Hawkins had been a Freemason; it was the only reason Min knew it. The rest of the Latin original was 'if you wish to live in peace,' but there'd be no peace for her until she got her man free.

Her plan had taken two days and a night to enact. In the end, she wasn't unhappy with the results, especially since the idea was audacious in the extreme. At nearly dusk on the second day, she sat on a wooden chair in the courtyard at Newgate Prison and watched it unfold.

She'd been reared an unenthusiastic Methodist, so she had no idea what Catholic confession looked like. She imagined it could not be too different from the way Lord Chief Justice Rufus Melman Fenton Stoddard, Baron Stoddard, GCB, PC, leaned in close to the inner steel mesh wall of the Visiting Box, exchanging low words with Étienne. They'd also swapped a furtive handshake, somewhat awkwardly due to the wire. Since it was furtive, she probably wasn't meant to see it.

They'd been at the talking for quite a long time. Ewan Exeter had accompanied her to the prison and secured her a chair. He stood. The two of them waited on the other side of the courtyard. Exeter, hat under his arm, hummed 'Putting the Penny in the Slot' under his breath.

Min couldn't have hummed to save herself from walking the plank on a pirate ship. She could barely swallow. Breathing was an effort.

She'd attribute some of her breathlessness to her corset. Scotland being, well, Scotland, she'd allowed herself to go native for a time. No corset. The least prepossessing dresses from her trunk. Hair unpinned, loosely trapped in a braid. Battered and stained boots, the ones in which she'd trekked from Meeth to Plymouth and then sailed to Scotland on the *Siobhan*.

Today, she was wearing the same smart rose-coloured dress and hat she'd worn to visit Baron Stoddard's townhouse earlier in the day. Ensnaring the judicial lion in his den had begun yesterday morning, by lifting the direction from Madame's client list. One never knew when the list might be useful. Min had always made it her business to remember the names. One was Lady Olivia Stoddard, the baron's young second wife. She had the most extraordinary violet eyes and wore a Number Four corset. Her waist was the circumference of a dessert plate.

Had she lied to Lady Stoddard? Well, yes, she had. And she'd flung around her new title a bit. Quite a useful thing, the title, especially since it was decidedly higher than her target's.

She'd sent a note (on the loveliest cream paper; she'd bought it in Regent Street just for the occasion). In it, she made a fulsome apology for the direct approach. She'd been at her estate in remote Scotland for some time, she wrote, and had become *quite barbaric* as a result. She then revealed she'd been mistakenly delivered an *exquisite and novel* corset that was, from the enclosed card, Lady Stoddard's. Having unboxed the item, however, she was *utterly entranced* and wondered if Her Ladyship would care to meet for tea and share how and where she'd commissioned such a *magnificent* creation. The design was clearly French, the dyeing and hand-painted fabric... *absolumente délicieux*! A one-of-a-kind artist's creation, impossible to duplicate. She must know more!

She'd suggested they meet the following day, at Claridge's. Her Ladyship replied forthwith, suggesting Lady Dunmara take luncheon at the Grosvenor Square home where she resided with His Lordship the baron. Min responded on the instant, signing, *Minerva Eilish Langworth, Countess Dunmara.*

She and Evie had stayed awake all the night, making the corset. The work continued into today, from dawn to noon. Madame was so elated at the notion that 'our own little Minerva, now a countess, would you believe it?' was rubbing shoulders with London elites that she swept aside the workroom's other projects and put all the corset girls, including Jillian, who'd got wind of the project from Kell through Eileen, onto the task.

Ada was the only *corsetière* missing. Madame had sent her on a series of errands that ensured she was out for the whole day. Might have been coincidence. Might have been Madame being shrewd.

When the sewing was done, they all stood around the worktable, giving the corset the silent reverence it deserved.

It was blue silk, the colour of twilight. Up one side and across the half-cups supporting the bosom, Evie had painted purple irises so lifelike they all but fluttered in the breeze. Tiny brilliants winked in each golden centre. Pomona green leaves arched gracefully from behind the blooms. The edge binding along the bustline and the bottom of the corset was half purple, half blue moiré silk. It had demanded the most delicate touch to join the narrow bias strips together before they were lapped over the edges and fixed with virtually invisible stitches.

Outlining the whole corset, tiny pale blue silk organza ruffles flirted impudently. The corset was laced both front and back with hand-rolled round laces, dyed by Evie to a shade that exactly matched the flowers. Every brass eyelet through which the lacing passed was over-sewn in purple silk thread; not a speck of metal showed. A silk, inch-wide Pomona ribbon tied the top of the busk in a coquettish bow. Even the lining was exceptional. A light blue Chinese silk brocade in a design of exotic birds.

Never mind they'd made it themselves; they'd give a year's wages to own it.

Min, red-eyed and groggy, had wrapped the corset carefully in layers of tissue and placed it (to Madame's delight) in a Salon Sirena box lavishly tied with the salon's signature mauve ribbon. She'd given herself just enough time to return to her borrowed flat above the East London Pugilists Academy and turn herself into a person who lunched with a baroness.

And what an interesting luncheon it had been. She'd liked the young baroness and the feeling seemed mutual. They'd talked at length, frankly, during the meal and after, when they took coffee in the drawing room. When Lady Stoddard tapped at the door of her husband's study and begged him to meet her guest in the drawing room, Min almost collapsed from relief.

Now, she fought the urge to rub her eyes, still scratchy and tired from sixteen hours of sewing. She was quite wobbly inside and appreciated being able to sit, even though she'd been sitting for most of the time it took to bring *Le Jardin Divin* – The Divine Garden, Madame's name for the corset – to life.

She appreciated that coin had almost certainly changed hands to get her the chair. More than just wobbliness made it advisable for her to sit. If she stood, she would pace. She was sure pacing wasn't something countesses did in public.

Working down the fingers of her brown mousquetaire kid gloves, she clasped her hands together to keep from rubbing her tired eyes. Another not-done thing. Countesses did not screw their fists into their eye sockets like sleepy children.

The Lord Chief Justice and Étienne seemed to be ending their secretive chat. She rose, resting one hand on the chair back to mask the wobble. *Steady. Don't dash over there. Let the baron come to you. Repeat after me: I'm a countess, I'm a countess, I'm a countess.*

When he reached her, Baron Stoddard began without

preamble. 'There will be some clucking and squawking among my fellow justices. But as soon as my wife showed me this,' he handed her Étienne's gold ring, 'there was only one possible action I could take. We cannot have the last living descendant of Templar Master Robert de Lille, and a Master himself, treated like a common footpad. That signet, the coat of arms...' He slowly shook his sleek grey head, a man in the grip of wonder. 'I never thought to see it in this life.'

Wonder over, his attention snapped to Exeter. 'Detective Inspector, I'll leave it to you to sort the policing end of things.'

Exeter made a short, deferential bow. 'My lord Justice Stoddard.'

'One thing, Countess.' The Justice ran a gimlet eye over Min. 'Nothing I have done to secure your husband's release will stand should he remain in England even one more day. He is, for all intents, on licence, and can put not one foot wrong. Without fail, he must be on the train from Victoria Station tomorrow morning. I will not say he can never return here. Neither will I say he can, or when. But...' At that he smiled, a glimpse of warmth under the cool judicial mien. 'I am married long enough to know ladies arrange these things and men, if they are wise, simply go where they're told. I will count upon you to see him safe, and quickly, across the Channel.'

She caught herself an instant before she curtsied. 'You have my assurance, Baron. My gratitude knows no bounds.' Out came the countess smile, followed by a particularly elegant incline of the countess head.

At a gesture from the Chief Justice, a loitering turnkey rushed to supply hat and cane, then sprinted for the gate to open it. Just before the baron passed through, he wheeled about and hailed Min.

'Lady Dunmara!'

Dread took a knife to her heart. *He won't change his mind, he can't.* Min risked a demure trot to the baron's side.

He bent conspiratorially toward her. 'My wife tells me you managed the return of a valuable item of hers that had gone astray. I don't know what it was, but she was most insistent I address your husband's predicament before the day elapsed. More than that, she would not explain. But she told me I would understand this evening, when we retired.'

Chapter Forty-Seven

'I told her not to come.' People milled about Victoria Station, porters dodging them with laden trolleys. Exeter pulled out his hunter and flipped it open, then snapped it shut and dropped it back in his watch pocket. 'She doesn't listen to me any more than you do. Fifteen minutes, Dague.' He strolled languidly in the direction of a pillar, where he propped his long body against it, crossed one leg over the other, and looked supremely bored.

Étienne watched Min cross the platform to stand before him. She wore the mouse-grey traveling suit she had been wearing when she came to Les Pinsons. Then, she had an overlarge handbag clutched to her breast and a preposterous request on her lips. The handbag was missing, now, but at her feet she'd placed a leather valise like the one he carried. A hat bearing a stuffed bird rode precariously on her neatly coiled braid. The bird's glass eyes seemed to drill Étienne hatefully. Perhaps Justine had eaten one of its ancestors.

She should not be here. Yesterday, at Newgate, he had recited to her the many reasons why. And yet, here she was. His heart and his cock, both stupid beyond belief, took immediate notice.

Her eyes, limpid as woodland pools, and her voice reproached. 'You were going to leave without me.'

'I *am* going to leave without you.' *Mère de Dieu*, it would have been easier to stab himself in the heart than see what those words did to her. But they must be said, again and again, until she accepted them, though they were both bleeding from the dozen wounds the words had made being said and heard before.

'*Écoute, Minerve*. I was born into a midden, a refuse heap of violence and low morals. At sixteen, when I escaped, I had a chance. I could have made something good of myself, something clean. What did I do? I became a thief, a smuggler, a pair of fists and a set of knives in the employ of London's worst gang.

'You have done the impossible. You have given me a second chance. This time, I will do the right thing. This time, I choose honour over self-interest. Let me do it, *mon coeur*. Let me do it for you.'

'What about what *I* want to do, Étienne? If you just let me do what I want, you won't have to make any more choices about honour and morals and all that. You won't have to do a thing. Just let me love you. Easy as sleeping or waking. Just... let me love you.'

'Such a choice is possible in Paradise, perhaps. This is the world, where I am still, despite a brief interval of freedom for me to board this train, a man behind bars.

'Go home, Min.'

'Home is... home...' She struggled with the word, with the next words. He could not help her, however much he wanted to. He dropped his valise – another gift from Exeter, another debt to repay – and put both hands on her shoulders. Their fragility was always a shock. How could such a delicate creature have, as she did, the strength of nations? He must remind her of that.

'With titles come persons who depend upon them. You have now a sister, yes? Are there not others in your household, on your lands?' A shadow crossed her eyes to say he was right.

'The MacDonalds of which you told me. They are your kinsmen and women. They are of your blood. Surely, they suffered when the estate was in disarray. They wait, they hope, for affairs to improve.

'You have also the chance, *Minerve*. Do not remain a maker of corsets all your life. Do not throw in your lot with a farmer from Bordeaux.'

As though her body could not resist a last effort to hold him in place, she put her hands on top of his and clasped them. They stood that way for long moments, the monstrous flame of hurt consuming them both. He must douse it, once and for all.

'*Àdieu, ma chère.*' He bent and brushed a kiss across her lips. Anything more and they would both be lost. One short nod to Exeter, to confirm she would be escorted away from the station. Exeter nodded back.

He pulled his hands from her, picked up his valise, and boarded the train.

She didn't expect him to look back. But the brute machinery of hope whirred away in her, even though events gave it no coal.

There was no backward glance. He took hold of the handrail alongside the train carriage door and swung inside. One strong, lithe movement, ignoring the steps. She would never shed her amazement that such a large man moved so gracefully. Everything he did, buttering bread, hoisting a sail on *Siobhan*, lifting her hips so he could drive into her... all done with perfect economy and art.

I'm your wife! She wanted to shout it after him. But she wasn't, despite the ring he'd insisted she put back on the cord around her neck. It had never been a wedding band, she reminded herself. Just a prop in the little play they'd performed at a hotel in Plymouth and in the courtyard of Newgate Prison. *A Marriage of Convenience*, with a cast of two.

Some last-minute passengers clambered aboard. Railway

guards waved and shouted and blew whistles. Clouds of steam billowed and lashings of grit swept the platform as the train began rolling ponderously forward. *Away, away. Taking him away.*

Her face spasmed briefly with grief. She silently cursed it and dashed her gloved hand across her wet eyes.

In bed at The Eel's Pocket, he'd said *'our life'*. Even had he not said the words, his whole being had expressed them a hundred ways. The touches of his hands, the light in his eyes when he saw her. His murmured praise of her lips, her breasts. His shuddering release, and the way he enfolded her possessively afterward.

Upon every mile of that hellish trek through Devonshire, with every league of that journey on the sea, in every hour he'd languished in Newgate Prison... It was all for 'our life'.

He might now be suffering from transient amnesia, but her memory was in perfect working order.

'Back to the East London Pugilists?' Ewan Exeter held her valise. His arm was bent for her and so she took it.

'Yes.' The word came out thickly. After a moment to get her voice sorted, she added, 'Thank you for everything, detective inspector.'

'Not at all. It's what family does.'

Her startled glance hooked a wry smile from him. 'How're you at keeping secrets, Countess?'

Her life was nothing *but* secrets. 'Just Minerva. And I keep them very well.'

'Here's one only four people know. You'll be the fifth.' He inclined toward her and lowered his voice, even though it would've required celestial intervention to separate their conversation from the surrounding din.

'Before I was Ewan Exeter, I was Ewan MacBride. Clan MacBride is a sept of the MacDonalds.'

A sept. Her mind skipped back to Dunmara Manor and her bedside table there. To *A History of the Highlands and of the*

Highland Clans, the little book that bored her to sleep. A sept was a part of a larger clan, its members bearing a different surname.

Exeter patted her hand. 'Cam along, wee cousin, let's get ye hame.'

He guided her carefully, carefully through the throng, as though she was a porcelain cup with a crack in it. She kept her eyes ahead and squared her shoulders. If her new cousin was waiting for her to shatter, he'd wait a very long time. For however long she was a countess, she would not display hysteria in a railway station.

And besides, all would be well. She had another plan.

CHAPTER FORTY-EIGHT

'Why am I not surprised, 'Tien? You return without the woman.'
The remark had the rushing-forth quality of champagne that had
been very tightly corked and could not wait to get out.

'I am impressed, Remy. For such an old man, your eyesight is
still acute.'

Remy had perhaps expected to see Minerva Hawkins tucked
under his arm, like a goose he bought at market. With rare
wisdom, his foreman did not enlarge upon his disappointment.
Nor did he launch an interrogation about what had happened to
the scion of the House of Sansecours whilst he was in England.
Hauling a much-folded paper from his trouser pocket, he began
reading a long list of things for the scion to do.

Étienne displayed his own wisdom and did not editorialise on
the list. He silently set to work.

The *cuvée Sansecours* would save him, as it had saved him once
before. Keeping memory at bay would be easier when his hands
were busy pruning the vines and his arms were taxed with lifting
barrels and scrubbing vats. More tasks than wine demanded
attention. Chickens must be fed. The henhouse had developed a

leak and must be roofed anew. The steel rims on both wheels of the donkey cart had rusted through and must be replaced.

Working his way through Remy's list reminded him that, above all, he was a *proprietaire viticulteur*. He had been gone for weeks at the height of the maturing season for the grapes. The *vendange* loomed. All that was right and healthy for him to do was give himself to the work. The days would bleed together, an aquatint sketch someone tried to make with too much water on the brush. Blurred, but better than the painful clarity of his mind when he left London.

He worked feverishly the first day. Worked as though his father was still alive, beating him with a leather strap. Beating him whether he'd done right, done wrong, or, more usually, no matter what he did.

He had always balled his fists by his side and taken it. It was either that or know his father would take the rage out on his wife, using her perversely in the night.

In the room they shared, Achille and Leo, his half-brothers, laughed when they heard the carrying on. They were amused and aroused, too, by the thought of what their father did to their mother – their stepmother, not that that should have made it any less disgusting. But to the sons of the first wife, it was just another jibe at the son of the second.

'Givin' to your maman pretty good, tonight, eh, *porcelet*?' Piglet. His step-brothers' favourite name for him. After the slur, Leo would snort like a hog, kicking up his pelvis in mimicry of what he imagined his father was doing.

Their father. Brutally assaulting his wife as though she had no more to say about it than a whore. Worse than a whore. He would have been thrown out of a whorehouse if he handled one of the women like that.

All the while, his brothers laughed and laughed. And Étienne lay in bed imagining in colourful detail the ways he could kill his father without getting killed himself.

It had all changed when he turned sixteen. That's when his father's six-foot, two-inch, fifteen-stone son had taken the strap from the monster's hand and beaten him senseless with it.

He wiped the sweat from his face with the tail of his shirt. Roughly, trying to wipe away the painful past along with the painful present. He was done with the repair to the wheel rims and the light was departing. He had no choice but to enter the house.

The fifty yards from the stable to the house felt like a mile. Once in the door, he dropped his shoes and soiled shirt on the floor, then stood looking around with no plan other than to get through the next hour. The next ten minutes.

The house was cold, or perhaps he brought the cold with him. It certainly defined empty in new and unpleasant ways, the worst of which was the insufficiency of everything he had once thought comforting and his. The chair at the kitchen table. The simple cups and saucers. The brown teapot.

The bed.

Thankfully, he had a few hours before he must converse with the bed on the topic of ownership. For now, he crossed to the kitchen table and stared at the flat box that had, for years, contained his knives. It was open, just as he had left it when he rushed after Min, following her to London. To ecstasy and devastation.

The knives, of course, were gone. They had been in his pack and the pack had been thieved by Tommy Byrne, along with Étienne's freedom.

What would Byrne do with *poignards* like those? Nothing that merited their excellence. He was tempted to rage over the thought of them in someone else's hands, but what would rage avail? He had retired the knives years ago. If he had not been a fool and brought them back to their trade, they would not now be pressed into some low service in Dublin.

No matter. Byrne, because he could not throw the knives, would stick one into the back of a mark who, with luck, would be someone important. The cur would swing, then, knives or not. One of his gang could use them to cut him down from the gallows and take his body back to his sainted mother.

He moved aimlessly through the kitchen. Taking a pan off its hook, putting it back. Counting logs in the basket by the hearth, making no effort to start a fire.

He should eat. It had been a long day of work with no sustenance since coffee at dawn. But want of food was a stranger to his body, the desire to cook an impulse he could not imagine ever feeling.

People spoke of the hollowness of loss. But he was filled entirely by the huge animal of Min's absence. It devoured his heart while it still beat.

Chapter Forty-Nine

The Judge's Tavern was its usual comfortably neglected self. Archibald Fowlkes propped his elbows on the bar and stared out the grimy front window into the street. He displayed little expectation and no regret that patrons weren't queuing to enter. The detective inspector and a boxer, both former members of London's worst gang, were the only bodies at a table. It was sufficient custom, apparently, that Archie's composure was unruffled.

'Stone me. She asked for a *forger*?' Kell needed to hear Exeter's answer again; it was that unbelievable.

'She did.'

'Did she say why she needed one?'

'Not to me. However, I have it from Ada who had it from Eileen who had it from Evie that she needed a forged certificate of marriage.'

'For her and Dague?'

'No. For some couple who've been dead for some years.'

'Go away.'

'Solemn truth.'

A thoughtful pause ensued. Both men applied themselves to

their pints, nothing being better for sudden shock than drink. After Kell wiped his mouth on the back of his hand, he picked up where they'd left off.

'I'm guessin' you gave her Simon Kaan's direction?'

'I did.'

'Should we tell Dague? We could post a letter. Or a wire. He said there's an office in Baguette-sur-la-Mer, or whatever's the name of his village.'

'No.' Exeter took a long, long draught of his ale. The Judge's Tavern, compensating for its murk, supplied an excellent bitter. 'I think we'll just let it play out.'

CHAPTER FIFTY

The *vendange* came and went.

The harvesting required the most labourers and made for the longest days. Beginning each morning when there was barely enough light to see, a hired force went row to row in the vines. Most of the workers were experienced. Locals who did not have vines of their own. Itinerants who swarmed the region from July to October. Gypsies who brought wives, babies slung on their backs, and children, all but the babies picking.

Experienced or not, Étienne followed them closely. The vines were his. He did not give them lightly into the hands of others.

After the harvesting, the pickers took their pay and moved on to other fields, other *vendanges*. Every year, Étienne and Remy picked a handful of men to stay behind, to help with the sorting, crushing, and removal of the stems. Only the best grapes were preserved. The sorting gained raucous musical accompaniment when they tossed the discarded grapes into the shed yard, where flocks of birds descended and fought noisily over them.

Balthasar was sequestered in his stall throughout, since grapes gave him appalling flatulence and he could not be endured for days. He brayed his indignation for the duration. Apart from the donkey's digestive vice, animals, with their pissing and shitting and hair-shedding, did not belong in the sheds during any part of viniculture. The exception was Justine, since even less welcome than cat hair were rats.

After mashing in large tubs, the select mixture, the *must*, went into vats for fermentation. At that point, everyone sat for a while on two long trestle tables in the yard, where Étienne put out food and a dozen bottles from his cellar. Not his rarest bottles, to be sure, but the helpers were happy with *vin ordinaire* as long as they could get soused while stuffing themselves on bread and cheese and sausages. They were then sent away, pockets fat with pay, a large smile on each face. By design, he and his foreman were left alone.

Remy, even more than he, demanded no witnesses to fermentation. Each vat, with its specific grape varieties, had its own formula, and Remy lived in deep fear of spies. Étienne held the opinion that everything about winemaking had been discovered by the time the Romans trudged across France, but he also understood his foreman must be appeased in all things. The shed doors were shut fast, and they worked in seclusion. Since they had neither women nor families to distract them, their resemblance to Benedictine monks required only brown cloaks and prayer.

At each phase of the *vendange*, he told himself, as he did every year, 'This is the worst part.' The truth was that every part was the worst. Altogether, a harrowing and exhilarating experience, like piloting a canoe through rapids or scaling a mountain without ropes.

This *vendange*, he also told himself he was over Minerva Hawkins. *La vie continue*, life goes on. He had survived much; he would survive this.

There was always a lull after fermentation was set in motion in all the vats, the *vigneron*'s intervention being suspended for some weeks. At that point, it was in the hands of God or Bacchus or the thousand things that could go wrong. Remy, however, did not acknowledge any higher agent in the process than himself. He spent those weeks living in the shed instead of his squat stone cottage a hundred yards away.

Étienne had either a lower opinion of himself or a higher opinion of his bed. He gathered his things to return to the farmhouse. He was thinking of *une omelette gratinée aux champignons*. One of the grateful workers on the *must* had brought him a basket of mushrooms, *cèpes* and *chantarelles*. It was a kind gesture. Also, the man angled to be taken on the year round, since he was barely scratching a living from a smallholding between Les Pinsons and the village. It was a possibility. If Les Pinsons wished to increase its production, it needed more hands than Remy's and his own.

Pondering that, he made it almost out the shed doors when Remy reeled him back in.

'It is not as though the bootblack chases the queen. You are stinking rich. Or do you think I do not know about that?'

He would not turn around. He would stay where he was, make one quelling remark over his shoulder, and then be on his way.

'I am certain there are depositors in the *Credit Suisse* of Zurich whose balances are known to you. My account poses no challenge. Now, if you have no more financial advice, I–'

Remy addressed the cat, languidly observing from her customary perch atop a barrel. 'You are my witness, Justine. The bugger made me do this.' Complicit in accusation, the cat fixed yellow, unblinking eyes on Étienne.

No help for it. He would have to face the music. He turned.

Remy had the look of a man settling down to a long lecture, though he was on his feet. He had a clean rag in his hand and was meticulously polishing a wine corker. While chairs were prohibited in the shed during the *vendange*, Remy had moved in a straight-backed wooden one to furnish his temporary lodging. Étienne took it, turned it round so he straddled the seat, and crossed his arms across the back.

'You know,' Remy began ponderously, 'to look at me now, you might not believe it.'

'Trust me when I say I would believe anything of you, Remy.'

'But it is only truth that I was once in love. Yes, I, *le misanthrope*. It was long ago. I had hair. Her name was Iseult. She was to me as the lambent moon is to a beetle in the dirt. I worshipped her, as a beetle should.

'*Hélas,* she was the youngest daughter of the Duque d'Auverne. The story grows dark, as it must when aristos enter.'

Remy was a devoted Jacobin. A reader of Montesquieu and Rousseau, a tireless campaigner for the common man. His politics were frustrated by the guillotine going out of style. Étienne shifted in his chair. Where was his foreman heading with this and how long would it take?

'I met her at– not important. She loved me, I loved her. She played the piano. She quoted Molière and Voltaire and de Fontanelle. She could dance and speak Italian and German.

'And me? I was in the grip of a false chivalry that denied her the desires of a real woman. I had perhaps read too many fables. On the other hand, I was too much in touch with reality, the most glaring aspect of which was that I was an ignorant peasant who did not see ten francs in a week and whose mother might or might not have been married to his father.'

Remy scowled at the wine corker in his hand, as though it deserved a share of the blame for his failure at *l'amour*. Since, even piqued, he would never abuse a vintner's tool, he wrapped his rag quickly twice round the corker before he dropped it on the barrel top next to Justine, who hissed.

'I told her... *non*. I *bullied* her into returning to her family. All our romance came to was a few hours in a wood near her father's chateau.

'She made a good marriage.' He nodded several times, resignedly. 'It was expected of her, and I pray she was happy in it. There were children, I believe. But,' he waved at the vats, 'look around, *mon ami*. Do you see *my* wife? Do you see *my* children? *My* happy future?

'You see twenty barrels of wine. Among them, an old man and a stupid young one. As stupid as I was at the age he is now. Too stupid, just like me, to give a woman what she wants because he is determined to give her what she needs.'

Étienne stood, turned the chair around, and placed it carefully to one side. 'Are you finished?'

Remy did not answer, just picked up the rag-wrapped wine corker and went back to polishing it. The cat's yellow gaze remained fixed. He felt both man and cat watching him as he walked away.

The basket of mushrooms on the kitchen table was no longer appealing. What appealed was his knives. Three months ago, he had dismissed their loss without a second thought, but now he craved them back with an intensity bordering on mania.

He needed blades he could drive deep somewhere. Over and over and over.

Fists clenched, head lowered like a bull, he stood in the kitchen and glared at old, familiar furnishings that didn't deserve what he thought of doing to them. He had to hit something. He had to–

He snatched up the basket and hurled it at the wall. Mushrooms flew into the air, bouncing with squashy little thuds as they fell on the floor, the chairs, the table. One bounced onto on his foot and lay there, laughing at him. What sort of man unleashes anger on a heap of fungi?

...a stupid young one. As stupid as I was at the age he is now. Too stupid, just like me, to give a woman what she wants because he is determined to give her what she needs.

As usual, Remy had seen it when he had not. His insistence

that he was over his attachment to Minerva Hawkins was the twittering of a deluded mind.

He took up a colander and began retrieving mushrooms. Most were only slightly damaged. He would give them a good wash and then put them to simmer with garlic and butter.

The sort of mental derangement that had ended with him launching mushrooms in his kitchen was the very thing he had tried to avoid. He thought he had succeeded. Had he not begun sleeping again? He had. Sometimes. He had stopped losing weight. He no longer twitched with irrational hope when a noise from the drive made him think a cart was bringing her to his door.

And yet, here he was, longing for his *poignards* and abusing mushrooms because a few pages from Remy's autobiography had swatted the animal under his skin, the one that had been chewing his heart all along. Rage lit him like a torch.

'*Putain de bordel de merde!*' He tossed the colander in the sink with a clatter and stamped out the door to the fermentation shed.

Without a doubt, Remy knew all along he would come. He was in the chair, which he had moved into a pool of light under a hanging lantern. Feet propped on an overturned pail, he was reading a French translation of *Moby Dick*. The very pattern of insouciance, his foreman, as if he had not, a quarter hour earlier, lobbed grenades of provocation. He casually licked a fingertip and turned a page before he acknowledged Étienne's presence, and then only to the cat.

'Look, Justine. 'Tien has come to apologise for his rudeness toward the story of my life.'

'No.'

'Have you come to invite me to dine?'

'No.'

'Why, then, are you blocking the light with your too-large body so that I cannot read this excellent novel about *pride going before a fall*?'

'I cannot go to Scotland to get her.'

'This is not news.'

The war between the next few words and Étienne's pride was violent but short. 'I don't know what to do,' he mumbled.

'Speak up. I am an old man, as you point out every three minutes, and my hearing is poor.'

'I don't know what to do!'

Another touch of a finger to Remy's tongue, another turn of a page. 'Some forty-two years ago, a cable was laid across *La Manche*. The English Channel.'

'The telegraph.'

Remy looked up. His smile was broad. His dim-witted student had finally got something right. 'Unless I am much mistaken, the apparatus still operates.'

CHAPTER FIFTY-ONE

Public opinion was that trains were getting speedier and more reliable, but the one that was taking her across France had clearly been exempted from the improvement scheme. It stopped working four times before Tours. Finally, partway between Tours and Poitiers, it halted for nearly three hours for repairs.

It might be her last chance to enjoy life as a countess, so she'd simply locked herself in her first-class compartment, unhooked her spectacles, shut her eyes, and tried to doze.

Sleep refused to come. Even sitting still was a challenge. She was so excited she thought if she left the train, she could probably run the rest of the way to Bordeaux. It was hard to believe she was on the same train, albeit traveling in the opposite direction, she'd taken after Étienne sent her packing from Les Pinsons.

She clutched the telegram in her hand the entire way from Dunmara. It had, in fact, been out of her grip or off her person only for washing and dressing in the past seven days. Three words. That's all he had written, the best three words ever sent from man to woman.

Come home, Minerva.

Just because she could, she put her eyeglasses back on, unfolded the telegram, and read it again. There was magic in it, a spell that rendered it so much more than a slip of greyish blue paper, thin as a leaf. All of Étienne was in it. The voice in which he'd thought the words before he wrote them. The hand he'd used to hold the pen. The tigerish eyes he'd lifted to the clock to mark the time the message was sent, and to calculate the time the messenger would arrive at Dunmara with the envelope in hand.

She folded the paper again and tucked it into the pocket of her dark blue silk dress, the one she'd worn when she'd visited Étienne in Newgate Prison the first time. If she'd not been able to get him out, she'd have burned the damn thing. Maybe thrown herself on the pyre, like widows in India did. It hadn't come to that, thankfully. For him and her, but also for the dress. She smoothed the skirt.

Noises outside made her peer through the window, open from the top a few inches for air. Normally, nothing bored so thoroughly as an unmoving landscape. But even with the train stalled in the middle of rural France, a surprising amount of activity was taking place. A great many passengers had stepped off. Some stood around waving their arms and saying what sounded like uncomplimentary things about the locomotive. Others made the best of it, chatting loudly, laughing even more loudly. Because it was France, shrugging was plentiful. With hands turned up, arms crossed, one-shouldered, two-shouldered. With and without rolled eyes.

An enterprising vendor made the rounds with toys to keep the children occupied. Several ran gleefully in circles, waving paper whirligigs on sticks. A few had whistles, adding to the general din. A stout woman in a suit with a thick fur collar walked a fluffy dog on a lead. The dog bore an uncanny resemblance to the collar. Min amused herself by imagining the woman saying, '*Ah, oui, poor Lala, ma pauvre. When she died, I could not bear the parting. I told my furrier to immortalise her, et voila!*'

Don't be unkind, she reminded herself and sank back into the seat. Behind the dog and the stout woman and the laughter and whirligigs, there might be a hundred stories of suffering and redemption, absence and reunion.

The terrible day of their parting at Victoria Station, Étienne had been right when he told her, '*Surely, they suffered when the estate was in disarray.*' The 'they' was the people of Dunmara. Once she'd dragged her heartbroken self back to the estate from London, she understood just how deep into disarray it had fallen.

She should have seen it from the start. Would have, if she hadn't been so fixed on not taking up the title. The indifferently tended grounds. The fine furniture mouldering away under dust covers. The empty outbuildings. The hedges uncoppiced, the walls unpatched, the tenants at loose ends. What had the late earl and his son been doing before they'd gotten themselves killed in a carriage accident? Not managing the estate, evidently.

And all around the disarray, MacDonalds, MacDonalds, and MacDonalds. Waiting to be told what to do.

Politicians and philosophers could rant until the moon turned purple. The new order, self-determination, the end of the ruling class. But at Dunmara, the old way – the Scots way – prevailed. She wasn't just their countess.

She was their laird.

She acknowledged her role and moved to fulfil it. At the same time, she began the laborious process of escaping it.

The first instrument in that process arrived just a week after she returned to Dunmara. In a stack that included post from Gordon and Blackford and a letter from Agnes Broadripple, was a slim parcel from Simon Kaan.

Kaan's forgery of marriage lines between the young not-then-an-earl Edgar Sterling Halpern Langworth and Mairi MacDonald was, in the forger's one-word assessment included with the document, 'Incomparable!' If believed, Kaan's forgery would present the marriage as the only genuine one of Langworth's three.

It made both Min and Langworth's son bastards. The son was dead; bastardy meant nothing to him. Nor to her. What mattered to her was that it bolstered Morag's claim, as Mairi's child, to Dunmara's title.

Would the College of Arms accept it? Her explanation, if she ever had to give one, was tenuous but not unbelievable. She'd say her grandmother had told her that because the marriage was of the anvil variety, the lines had gone to the bride and were not recorded in a parish register. They'd only recently been found when Min sifted through her late grandmother's effects. Kaan was perfectly confident the forgery would pass muster. Min was... hopeful.

The second instrument of succession was in the envelope from Gordon and Blackford. The solicitors wrote that Earl Dunmara had instructed them to post the enclosed statement to his heir within six months of his death. They'd cut it fine. The parcel arrived on the hundred seventy-ninth day after the earl and his son had met their ends. The statement, in the earl's hand, attested:

I have a child, sired in my reckless youth on one Mairi MacDonald, then fifteen, of the village of Tayvallich. I know not if the child be male or female, but I do hereby claim and acknowledge it as mine own. I do therefore command my heir to discharge a debt of honour and give the child (or its children, if it lives not but has issue), the sum of one thousand pounds. With that sum, go the apology and regret of a very poor father.

Even though the earl was careful not to mention wedding the child's mother, the statement declared Morag as his. When shown the letter and cheque, she collapsed into a chair and began weeping.

It was done. As done as it could be, until the Heralds at the College either did or didn't accept the reassignment of the title to Morag. As Gordon and Blackford had assured her months ago, there were no limitations on the title's succession and Morag was the earl's first-born child – the most rightful heir of all.

Min jumped at the piercing shriek of the train's whistle. The passengers milling outside screamed in a sort of chorus. Everyone ran for the train, the fur-collared woman at the rear, furry dog bouncing in her arms. There was a second ear-rending blast from the train and it started forward with a violent lurch, almost unseating Min. She rescued her hat and handbag from the floor and looked at her watch, pinned to her bodice. When she'd left Calais, she'd set it for what she thought was Paris Mean Time but wasn't sure she she'd got it right. She could never remember if it was ahead or behind Greenwich by ten minutes.

Another two hours till journey's end. Till life's start. Checking the corridor through the half-glass of the compartment door to be sure it was empty, she did a little dance in place on her seat.

Lawn bowling bishops, as Ada would say if they were speaking. It was good not to be a countess.

After she'd done what she could to shrug off the title and give it to Morag, it had remained only to convince her. For that, Min enlisted Nanny and Callum MacGregor. Between the three of them, they urged, advised, badgered, and begged her half-sister until she threw up her hands.

'Haud yer wheesht! Th' Heralds 'ave nae mair sense than toads ta say I'm a countess, but I'll do it ta shut yer gobs.'

It had taken a month more to hand over, project by project, the estate and its workings. The entire time, Min waited to feel some twinge of regret that she was hurling a coronet into the sea. It never came.

The last post Bodach flung onto the porch of Dunmara arrived almost simultaneously with Étienne's telegram. Just one item, a charming and spectacularly misspelled letter from Agnes Broadripple. Sent from Plymouth, the letter began with assurances that she and her sister Sal were well. They had decent lodgings in the town. Agnes had found a position in a millinery shop and Sal was keeping house for them both, as well as undergoing treatment for her '*unfortoonit condishun.*'

Agnes went on to write that she'd alerted the '*the Loonasy Comishun*' about Raeburn House's predicament before departing for her and Sal's new life on the coast. Inspectors had descended en masse, been appalled, and assigned the asylum a new superintendent. Agnes considered him to be making '*a proper job*' of his post.

In an act of petty larceny both sly and prudent, Agnes had rifled Raeburn's office before the inspectors arrived. Nothing she'd found interested her except one document. The former wardress had enclosed it with her letter.

'*This eer's from ol Tom, I rekkon,*' Agnes wrote. '*Whar 'ee keppit yers and yers, none kin say, but by end Raeburn got fist on it.*'

As soon as she'd seen the coarse, speckled paper, Min knew it was from Asa and Mary Hawkins' cottage. Never a poor man, Asa had nonetheless pinched pennies in so many ways. Cheap paper. Oil rather than paraffin for lamps. A tight budget for food, so Mary was taxed to make poor cuts of meat palatable and they rarely had sweets except for berries from hedgerows, which cost nothing.

She'd unfolded the age-brittle document carefully. More than the paper was familiar. The writing was Mary Hawkins': neat and spare, identical to the Gaelic note Nanny MacDonald kept in a jar on her mantel, but in English. Dated *1 February 1870*, the handful of lines shone light into the last dark corner of her life.

On this night a newly-born girl child, delivered of Amica Joan Langworth, inmate of Raeburn House Asylum, was given into my care. She comes only with a name, Minerva Eilish, and a broken pendant on a string around her neck.

Mary MacDonald (Mrs) Hawkins

Aunt Mary's signature, the letters strong and crisp, and beneath it, '*Witnessed by these who make their mark.*'

Two names followed, the first in the careful block letters of the marginally literate, *Tobias Tabbit*. The second signature was bold script, backward-slanting, *Asa Bernard Hawkins*.

It stole Min's breath. In the hundreds of times she'd pictured the hour she'd been left at the Little Farnleigh house, she'd never once put Asa in the scene. She should have. A stranger fetching up at the cottage in the middle of a winter night. Dismounting his horse and asking to see Mary. It would have been Asa who answered the pounding on the door. Asa who'd seen the babe taken in, its cold wrappings exchanged for warm shawls. Asa who would have paid for a wet nurse, for clothing, for books and tutors, for years of care.

He might not have done it with a father's love, but he had done it. Why? To assuage guilt over refusing his Scots bride her own bastard child? For love of Mary? For Christian duty? Because he could not bring himself to sacrifice an innocent?

There'd been a lot of sacrifice that night. All of it, at heart, to give Min the chance at the truth of her life she'd finally found. However long it had taken.

And Raeburn, for years, sat on Mary Hawkins' testament like a dragon on its hoard. Waiting for the earl and his son to die and for the flimsy piece of paper to turn to gold.

A bone-deep shudder ran through her. From what she'd read in a back issue of *The Times*, the carriage wreck that had killed the earl and his son was pure mischance. But what if the earl had started balking at the staggering 'maintenance' he paid to Raeburn? What if he'd said he wanted to see his captive countess, the one whose death Raeburn had been concealing for years? Or Raeburn might have had grounds to fear the heir would not keep up the payments when he came into the title.

Any one of those could have pushed Raeburn and Fitzsimmons to stage a carriage accident. A few months ago, the very idea would have seemed mad, the stuff from which lurid novels were made.

Now, after she'd been at the two men's mercy, the plausibility of them murdering for gain seemed perfectly, horribly sane.

It was suddenly too close in the compartment. She stood and pushed the window down another few inches. She braced her hands on the frame against the sway and jostle of the train and took deep, cleansing breaths. Even the air in France smelled different. Different in some ineffable way from Devon's or Scotland's or London's. It would be her air, from now on, her skies, her land.

She returned to her seat. Mary Hawkins' testament was in her traveling handbag. She hadn't determined whether to keep it. She'd opened the compartment window, and so she might tear the letter into bits and feed them to the wind. As the air was different, so was she. It was the perfect time and place to reinvent herself.

Agnes's letter had ended with the news that the marble gravestone Min had ordered for Lady Dunmara had arrived and been installed in a pleasant spot on the asylum grounds. '*Rare luvly, 'tis,*' Agnes wrote of the stone.

Perhaps Lady Dunmara's tormented spirit could fly away on the wind, now, too.

Two wires had raced across the Channel in the last days before she'd left Dunmara. One to Étienne to say she was coming, and when. One from him to say he and Balthasar would meet her at the stop in his village.

The donkey cart wasn't really necessary. She didn't mind walking and had no luggage apart from her handbag. Her trunk had been shipped from Scotland, but she'd rather waited until the last minute. For a week or so, she might have only the clothes on her back, but a shortage of wardrobe didn't worry her in the least.

It might be some time before she needed any clothes at all.

CHAPTER FIFTY-TWO

Heavy and soft with repletion, she lay atop him. He would never again require a blanket if she would only, for the rest of his life, drape the satiny heat of her body across his.

Her hand was exploring the skin of his shoulder. A ship was tattooed on that one, and her forefinger outlined the sail. Perhaps she wondered if it was the *Siobhan*, but the ink had gone in long before he knew Samath Rao. It must be strange for her to see his unclothed body in daylight. Until this day, when they had gone directly from the train stop in the village to Les Pinsons and bed, she had seen him naked only in dimly-lit rooms. It must be, for her, like knowing someone for years, only to discover they had the ability to turn into a zebra.

He bent his head to inhale the scent of her hair. Chamomile and Min. With her, he was the first man, taking his first breath, on the first day of the earth. 'Is it certain, this change of the title?'

He felt her shoulders rise and drop. They were becoming very French, those shoulders.

'Taken together, what I sent the College of Arms is convincing. Simon Kaan does excellent work, as you know,' she pinched his arm, '*Herr Doktor Habsburg*.'

'Ah, Simon praised his own work.'

'You'd turn over a lot of bushels before you found the one he's hiding his light under.' She wriggled, making herself comfortable, making him aroused. Again.

'Even if the Heralds rule against Morag, it will take years to unsnarl that ball of yarn. In the meantime, she'll do all the countessing there is to do at Dunmara.'

'She's so much better suited to it than I am, Étienne. She's competent and kind, well-known and well-loved in the area. She's a native speaker of Scots Gaelic and knows the stories of every local, great or small. And she has plenty of help. All those MacDonalds.'

Should she tell him that Ewan Exeter was a cousin to all those MacDonalds and, thereby, to her? *Ummn, no.* Perhaps later. Three or four years later.

'But you are also a MacDonald, yes?'

'No. I'm just Minerva Hawkins of Little Farnleigh, Devonshire. A London staymaker.'

'A woman of singular intelligence. A warrior of rare courage.' He brushed his lips across her hair. '*Ma femme.*'

She lifted her head and the glow of dawn through the bedroom window caught the green-brown sheen of her eyes. Their colour was the wings of the moon moth, *Actias isabellae*, that fluttered in the high hills of the Pyrenees. The sight unmanned him, but no more than her whisper.

'Your wife?'

'*Jusqu'à la fin des temps.*' He slid his hands to her hips, moving her against him. 'To the end of time.'

They did that thing, and another, and some others. Finally, she rolled to the side. They lay face to face in the warm chaos of the bed sheets, her hand resting on his chest. She had made a friend of the beast within, so that it no longer gnawed at his heart. It was quiet, now. Protective, loyal. Hers.

She turned her face up to him. 'What shall we do with the rest of today?'

'Exactly what we are doing now.'

'And tomorrow?'

'Tomorrow, I have some little affairs to conduct regarding the grapes. You may do whatever you wish. Order furniture from a catalogue. Visit Justine in the wine shed, she has new kittens. Write letters. I will have Remy harness Balthasar to the cart and you may drive to *la bôite aux lettres*, the postbox, in the village. While you are there, choose a building you wish me to buy for a corset shop, if that interests you. If you prefer to spend the day with me, I can show you how one makes–' he lifted his chin toward the half-empty bottle of *Château d'Yquem* on the bedside table, 'a wine like that.

'Whatever we do, when we are done, I will make dinner. *Le magret de canard grillé*, I think. Grilled slices of duck with mushrooms and potatoes. With it, a Merlot, very rich and red.'

She let her hand drift south and his body rose to meet it. '*That* is an excellent plan.'

ALSO BY ANNIE R MCEWEN

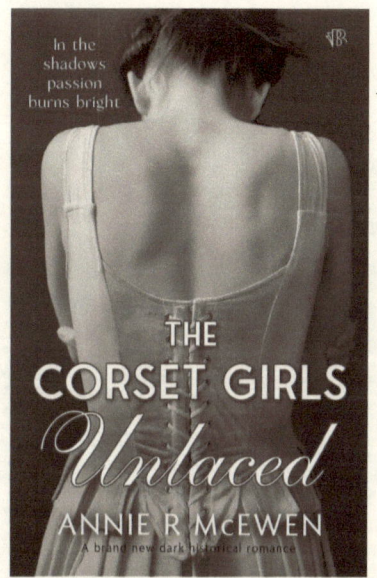

The Corset Girls Unlaced

In the shadows of Victorian London, passion burns bright...

In a world where love is the most dangerous game of all, will they find redemption, or will the darkness claim them both?

BUY NOW

ACKNOWLEDGEMENTS

With deep gratitude, the author acknowledges the expertise, diligence, and unflagging good humour of the team at Bloodhound Books.

About the Author

A career historian, Annie R McEwen has lived in six countries and under every roof from a canvas tent to a Georgian Era manor house. Winner of a 2022 Page Turners Writing Award (Romance Category), Annie garnered both a First and Second Place 2022 RTTA (Romance Through the Ages Award), the 2023 MAGGIE Award, and the 2023 Daphne du Maurier Award. Her short fiction appears in numerous anthologies.

When she's not in her 1920s bungalow in Florida, Annie lives, writes, and explores castles in Wales. Find her online at: www.anniermcewen.com

A NOTE FROM THE PUBLISHER

Thank you for reading this book. If you enjoyed it please do consider leaving a review on Amazon to help others find it too.

We hate typos. All of our books have been rigorously edited and proofread, but sometimes mistakes do slip through. If you have spotted a typo, please do let us know and we can get it amended within hours.

info@bloodhoundbooks.com